KNIGHTFALL

THE INFINITE DEEP

D0958007

HISTORY.

KNIGHTFALL

THE INFINITE DEEP

DAVID B. COE

KNIGHTFALL: The Infinite Deep
Print edition ISBN: 9781785659096
E-book edition ISBN: 9781785659102

Published by Titan Books
A division of Titan Publishing Group Ltd
144 Southwark St, London SE1 0UP

Visit our website: www.titanbooks.com

First edition: March 2019
10 9 8 7 6 5 4 3 2 1

A CIP catalogue record for this title is available from the
British Library.

Printed and bound in the United States.

For Nancy

CHAPTER 1

MAY 18, 1291, MEDITERRANEAN SEA, NEAR ACRE

At this distance, beyond the death cries of the soldiers who still fought, beyond the clash of swords and the snap of crossbows, far removed from the screams of hunted women and children, Acre appeared deceptively peaceful. Smoke rose from the lost city, a shifting gray cloud against the pale blue of the western sky. Their small vessel, the *Gray Tern*, bobbed on the gentle swells of the Mediterranean. Landry could almost convince himself that he and his brother Templars had chosen to take to the water; that they hadn't been driven from their stronghold by Khalil's Mamluks.

Almost.

Dried blood tightened the skin on his brow and cheek, and stained his surcoat and mantle. He saw his own wounds mirrored on Godfrey's face. Tancrede's also. Gawain sat near the ship's stern with eyes closed, his back against the hull, his injured leg stretched out before him. Pain etched lines in his youthful face, and sweat dampened his dark hair. Blood oozed from

7

where the bolt had struck, darkening the mail of his chausses. The Jew, Simon, lay nearby, his leg in an even worse state than that of the knight. His young daughter was curled beside him, her begrimed face streaked by tears long since dried.

Landry turned away once more to lean on the rails and squint against the glare. The sun's reflection on the surface of the sea fractured and scattered like soldiers in retreat, only to coalesce again a moment later.

God, let this not be the end. Let us return to reclaim all that we've lost this day.

The magnitude of their failure overwhelmed him, stole his breath, roiled his gut. Everything. They had lost everything. The city itself, their last stronghold in the Holy Land, was now in the hands of the Saracens, who had proven themselves more than a match for the finest soldiers of Christendom.

So many had died in their vain attempt to hold Acre; not only Templars, men he had considered brothers, but also too many innocents to count. And, of course, the Grail, that most sacred of treasures, the object of all for which they fought – it, too, was gone, perhaps destroyed. On the dock in Acre, he had spoken bravely of journeying back with a new army, of retaking the city and all the Holy Land. But they had still possessed the Grail when those brash words crossed his lips.

Was that my punishment, Lord? Did my arrogance convince you to deprive us of the Grail?

Like so many of his brothers, Landry had thought the city unassailable, their forces too mighty to be defeated. He hadn't counted on the Saracens battling them with such relentless courage. He hadn't thought the armies of the enemy could defend their homeland and face down yet another wave of Christian soldiers with such unflinching determination. He hadn't credited that Khalil's men might be just as canny, just as strong, just as skilled as the Templars. None of them had.

Yes, arrogance. And now all lay in ruin.

He clenched his teeth against the bile rising in his throat.

"Landry."

He straightened at the sound of his name and marked Godfrey's approach. A faint breeze stirred the commander's wheaten hair, and sunlight gave his pale eyes a ghostly look. He was tall, bearded, his face lined from years of combat and journeying. Tancrede followed a pace behind, an angry gash on his cheek making him appear even more gaunt than usual. The sun's glow lent a reddish tinge to his closely shorn hair and beard. He wasn't as tall as the commander, nor as brawny as Landry himself, but he possessed a keen wit and the bravery of ten men.

"Brother Draper has made inventory of our provisions," Godfrey said, halting before him. "We have enough for a few days, perhaps a week if fortune smiles on us."

"That would be a change," Tancrede muttered.

Godfrey cast a disapproving glance his way. "Brother Tancrede wishes to make land somewhere to the north. Perhaps Sidon."

"We can replenish our stores," Tancrede said, sunlight in his blue eyes. His gesture indicated the others on the ship, those who weren't Templars. Blood stained his fingers. "Maybe we can see some of these people to safety. And we must find a healer for Gawain. He might never walk again if we don't."

Landry considered them both. "Do we have gold? Silver? Anything we can trade for food?"

Godfrey and Tancrede shared a look.

"We have our weapons," Godfrey said. "And our armor. The rest was lost with… with the other ship."

With the Grail.

Guilt flickered in Godfrey's expression. He would be blaming himself, just as Landry did, as all their fellow Templars did. Brothers in defeat, as in victory.

Landry forced his thoughts past Acre. Stopping at Sidon struck him as extraordinarily dangerous, but he kept his expression neutral. "What do you think of Tancrede's suggestion?" he asked Godfrey.

"I fear for us all if we don't find a safe harbor within a few days, but I do not believe Sidon is that place."

"It has the virtue of proximity," Tancrede said. "Small communities of Christians remain there. We can sail in under cover of night, gather provisions, and be on our way."

"The danger is too great, and there are too few of us," Godfrey said, exasperation in his tone. Landry sensed that this wasn't the first time he had made this argument. "We would be putting the others at risk."

"Gawain—"

"Gawain is a Templar," Godfrey said, his voice rising. "His faith in the Lord is strong. By His grace, he will endure."

"God's grace will not be enough without a healer's care."

Godfrey faced Landry again. "I would know your thoughts on the matter. Tancrede has made his clear. If you agree, I'll heed his counsel, and we'll make for Sidon."

"Where would you have us go?"

"There is a Hospitaller fortress at Kolossi on Cyprus."

Tancrede's eyes widened. "Cyprus? That will take us days—"

Godfrey silenced him with a raised hand. "It lies near the southern shores of the isle. Naturally, I would prefer to find Templars, but given our plight, I believe we can convince the Hospitallers to shelter us. We'll secure more food, maybe even reinforcements." He looked at Tancrede again. "They'll have healers."

"It's too far."

Godfrey turned away from him. "What say you, Landry?"

Landry took a steadying breath and regarded both men, unsure of how to answer. Considering their meager provisions and Gawain's wound, Cyprus *did* strike him as too far. Just as a landing at Sidon struck him as too perilous for such a small contingent of knights. They were caught between bad choices. But for more than half his life, Godfrey had been his guardian and mentor. Over the years, Landry had learned to trust his judgment, even in the most dire of circumstances.

"Forgive me, Tancrede," he said at last, "but I must agree with Godfrey. Sidon will not be safe for us. Not compared to Kolossi. The Hospitallers may not be our allies, but they are Christians. Despite our differences, we are united in our devotion to God. They'll offer us aid, and they'll minister to Gawain. Yes, Cyprus is far, but with a favorable wind we can be there within the week."

"A week might be too long. You saw his wound."

"A landing at Sidon could kill us all!"

"Enough," Godfrey said. "We make for Cyprus."

He wheeled and strode away, leaving Tancrede and Landry staring at each other.

"I knew he would listen to you," Tancrede said, a sad smile touching his lips and then vanishing. "Just as I knew what you would say."

"Tancrede—"

"One of my uncles was a sailor. My mother's brother. Did you know that?"

Landry shook his head.

"These waters can be as dangerous and canny as an army of Mamluks. Not always, of course. But it's a long way to Cyprus. God help us if the winds aren't at our backs."

"By His grace, they will be."

"Yes. By His grace."

Tancrede walked away from him, his bloodied hand resting on the hilt of his sword.

Landry started to turn back to the sea. As he did, though, he saw that Gawain sat straighter, pale eyes watching him, his lips set in a hard, thin line.

For what remained of that day, a light wind carried them to the north and east. By dusk, as the sun, huge and orange, sat balanced on the western horizon, Acre had receded to little more than a smudge of smoke on the pale mass of the Holy Land.

Draper did what he could for Gawain's wound, bathing it with salt water – which drew howls from the knight – and bandaging it with strips of cloth cut from Gawain's own mantle. He could do less for

Simon, though he managed to splint the man's leg.

With the last light of this endless day silvering the sea, Landry joined the others for a meal almost too meager to be worthy of the name. Stale bread, a bit of goat's cheese, a fig or two. He understood that they needed to ration their stores, but even after they finished eating, as the sky darkened and stars began to emerge in the velvet blue, he remained famished. He still feared a landing at Sidon, but he wondered if Tancrede was right about the distance to Cyprus.

Matters grew far worse as the night deepened. With the appearance of the gibbous moon in the east, blood red, its glow shimmering on the satin surface of the sea, the last of their wind dropped away. The single sail slackened and the vessel slowed.

Landry hoped the lull would prove temporary. But as the moon rose higher, its color leaching from blood to bone, the wind did not rise again.

"Find oars," Godfrey said. "We will row to Cyprus if we must."

Landry and Tancrede searched for sweeps, looking first in a chest that sat under the warped rails on the port side of the ship. It contained two wine flasks, one empty and one full, and a pair of rusted swords. There were no oars. They walked the length and breadth of the ship. Landry used the hatch near the ship's stern to descend into a small, musty hold beneath the deck. Oar holes dotted the hull here, beside worn benches for those who would man them. But the sweeps themselves were nowhere to be found.

He climbed to the deck, where Tancrede enlisted Brice, Nathaniel, and Victor, the youngest of the Templars, to help them in their search. Together, the five of them scoured the vessel a second time, and a third. Nothing.

They informed Godfrey, who didn't believe them at first. He led them on yet another search of the vessel, which proved no more successful. They halted at the ship's stern, not far from Gawain, who regarded them with concern and, Landry thought, a hint of disapproval. Landry glanced at the sky, at the glory of a million stars. In all the time he had spent at sea, never had he been more displeased by the prospect of a clear night.

"Ill-fortune at every turn," Godfrey muttered. "What kind of ship carries no sweeps?"

Tancrede lifted a shoulder. "We took it in haste, with the city falling and battles raging all around us. We never thought to check."

Godfrey nodded, grim in the moonlight.

None of the passengers spoke. There were twelve of them in all: men, women, and the one child. They watched the Templars, apprehension in their gazes. All of them seemed to be holding their breath, like the world itself.

"Our breeze will freshen with daylight," Godfrey said eventually, straightening to his full height and pitching his voice to carry. He sounded more confident than he appeared. "It grows late. Try to sleep. We'll make up the lost time come morning."

Murmurs met this. Simon's daughter stared up at Landry, her dark eyes wide and luminous. Landry saw fear in their depths, and a silent plea for a comforting word.

"Come, Adelina," her father said, beckoning her to his side.

Landry nodded to her, but couldn't bring himself to offer assurances. Instead, he looked to Tancrede, who was watching him. Their eyes met, but neither of them spoke. At last, Landry turned away.

He found a place to bed down near the ship's prow, knelt before his sword to whisper a prayer, and tried to make himself comfortable. He remained awake for a long time. Usually, he did not mind the gentle to-and-fro of a vessel at sea, but on this night he heard ominous portents in the quiet creak of the deck, and the soft slap of swells on the hull.

His slumber, when it came, was fitful. He woke eventually to a golden sunrise and air as still as death.

He sat up, his muscles aching from the previous day's battle, his head fogged with fatigue and hunger. Peering over the rails, he saw nothing but water in every direction. No smoke from Acre by which to orient himself, no hint of land. And no evidence of wind.

Godfrey and Tancrede still slept, as did most of the others. But Gawain regarded him from across the ship, looking pale and haggard. Landry stood and approached him.

Squatting beside his fellow knight, he untied the bandage on Gawain's leg and considered the wound beneath. He allowed himself no outward reaction, but inside he cringed. It was a gruesome injury to begin with, and the skin around it had grown livid and swollen.

"How does it feel?"

"How do you think?" Gawain said, his voice flat.

"With all that happened yesterday… I said this once, but should have done so again. Thank you. You saved my life."

Gawain held his gaze for only a moment before looking away. But he nodded once. "Can you do the same for my leg?"

"You will not lose your leg," Landry said. "I won't allow it."

"God may intend otherwise."

"By His grace, you are a Templar Knight." Landry forced a note of surety into his assurances. "He will see to it that I keep my oath."

The dark-haired knight shifted, wincing as he did. "And what of our wind? Do you have the power to raise that as well?"

He glanced up at the cloudless sky. "It cannot remain still forever. We'll have our wind before long."

"Perhaps if we had voyaged westward, as Tancrede wished, we would have it now."

"Perhaps. Or perhaps we would have been captured by the Saracens. Maybe our throats would have been slit by now."

A third voice said, "We can't know either way."

They both turned. Godfrey had propped himself on one elbow, his hair wild with sleep, but his eyes clear.

"How is his leg?" the commander asked.

Landry faltered.

"It grows fevered," Gawain said. "I need a healer."

"You will have one."

"When?"

"When God wills it. Until then we will rely on Draper's talents, and your strength."

Godfrey stood, and as the others roused themselves, he distributed the morning's rations.

The hours crawled by. The sun climbed higher, blazing bright, burning like Greek fire in the stagnant air. It didn't take Landry long to understand that starvation was the least of their worries. The heat and the lack of fresh water were far more likely to prove fatal, in particular to Simon, his daughter, and Gawain. For the entire complement of passengers aboard the ship they had but a single flask of wine, and no way to water it.

The currents of the Mediterranean carried them westward for a time, and then northward, but not far in either direction, and at a speed that was barely perceptible. By the end of the day, all of them were parched and famished, frightened and discouraged to the point of despair. The sail, dingy and patched in several places, marked with a red cross, hung slack.

That night, Draper gathered all the Templars' armor, and spread it across the deck, positioning each helm and each bracer just so.

"What is the point of this?" Landry asked, as the man worked.

Draper smiled, his dark eyes dancing, long black and silver hair framing a face round and open. "You'll see come morning."

Landry stared at him, waiting.

At last the Turcopole paused in his labors, and indicated the nearest of the helms with a thick hand. "The metal will cool with the night air, and when it does it will gather dew. By morning, we should have fresh water to drink. Not much, but some."

"Ingenious."

Draper shrugged. "A trick I learned from my father. Genius would be summoning a wind."

"I believe that would be sorcery."

"I'd be happy for it just the same." He glanced about, sidled closer to Landry. "Gawain's leg grows worse by the hour," he whispered. "The other man, Simon, he is in great pain. I can only do so much for them. We need to find a port. We need to move."

"I'm no more a sorcerer than you are, brother," Landry said, dropping his voice as well. "I can pray, but beyond that, I'm helpless. Not a comfortable feeling for a knight."

Draper regarded him, his mien grim, before turning his attention back to the positioning of the pieces of armor.

The following morning, they had water to drink, but the *Gray Tern* remained adrift, at the mercy of the sea's fickle currents.

So it went for days. Their supplies dwindled. The air warmed and cooled with the rise and fall of the sun, but the Templars and their fellow passengers encountered nothing more than the faintest breath of a breeze, not nearly enough to fill their sail.

Simon's leg, splinted and bound, began to heal. Gawain's wound proved more stubborn. Fever took him. The flesh at the site of the injury grew hot to the touch. With little water and less food, his strength flagged.

By the ninth day, they were all suffering. Adelina, the little Jewish girl, spear-thin when they fled the Holy Land, was now wasting away before Landry's eyes.

Godfrey stood at the prow of the ship, staring out across the sea, as if he might will a wind to rise or land to appear. Brice and Nathaniel, one dark-haired, the other fair, spent much of their time practicing their swordsmanship, their blades ringing like chimes when they met. They sweated under the sun, their youthful faces flushed, but their exertions served as a welcome distraction for the others.

Landry would have liked to join them, or at least take some pleasure in their display, but Acre haunted him, as did Gawain's continued suffering. He prowled the ship like a restless panther. On occasion he forced himself to stop, to sit and converse, or watch the swordplay. But always he found himself in motion again, scanning the horizon, avoiding Gawain's accusatory stare.

This may have been why he was the first to discern the pale landmass to their north.

He thought it a mirage, an illusion born of too much sun, too little food, too many days lost at sea. He blinked, rubbed his eyes with his thumb and forefinger, and yet it remained.

"Land," he whispered. And then louder, "Land!" He pointed.

The others rushed to his side, their weight threatening to overbalance the ship. They pointed, faces alight. One woman wept. "Land," they repeated again and again. "We've found land."

"It doesn't matter."

They fell silent, all of them facing Gawain, who remained as he had been, propped against the hull, his leg extended.

"There's no wind," he said, speaking to them as he would to a child. "We can't reach it. What is the use of sighting land, if we have no hope of getting there?"

"You answer your own question, brother," Godfrey said. "Hope. Land lies to our north. If I had to guess, I would say that is Cyprus, where stands the Hospitaller fortress. Wind will come, and it will carry us to the isle's shores. Our salvation is at hand. Hope. Faith. These will see us through until we reach those shores." He faced Landry. "Mark well the position of that land. The currents may carry us beyond sight of it again. When a wind rises, I want to know where to point this ship."

"Of course," Landry said.

He crossed to the ship's dry compass and used it to note the precise line toward the isle. Heartened though he was by their sighting, Gawain's words had sobered him. They'd had that effect on everyone. The others wandered back to where they had been sitting or standing, although they all continued to glance northward, perhaps to assure themselves that the pale mass hadn't vanished.

By the next morning, the currents had dragged them beyond sight of the isle, further dampening the mood aboard the vessel. But Godfrey drew their attention to the western horizon, where a different source of hope had appeared during the night.

"Clouds," he said, voice ringing. "A change in our weather, sure to bring wind. By God's mercy, we shall be delivered from this ordeal."

Delivered they were. Near to midday, large white clouds began to crowd the sky above, bringing with them a steady westerly breeze. The ship's sail billowed, and – a miracle, it seemed – the vessel crept forward, slowly at first, its speed building with the wind. Tancrede took the helm and, with Landry pointing the way, piloted them on a tacking course northward.

Within hours, they spotted the isle again. By morning it loomed large before them. Even Gawain's spirits rose.

Certain now that they had found Cyprus, they navigated toward the bay at Limassol, confident that their trial was at an end, and that the gleaming stone structures and arid hills would provide them with all they sought: food, water, shelter, healers. The bay was broad and gently curved. Small buildings lined the shoreline, and a few larger ones loomed beyond them, including one with a lofty spire. More structures, modest but solid looking, dotted the hillside above the settlement. It was more a village than a city, but under the circumstances, Landry thought it the finest town he had ever seen.

Again, many of the passengers wept tears of joy. Landry, Draper, and Tancrede were not immune. Godfrey merely smiled. One might have thought he had known all along that they would be all right, and maybe he had.

Tancrede steered the ship to a strand near the city docks, and allowed her to glide up onto the white sand. Before the vessel had come to a complete halt, several of the passengers leapt onto the shore and dropped to their knees.

Godfrey and the other Templars followed, Landry and Draper supporting Gawain between them.

"Find a healer," Godfrey told them. "Kolossi lies a couple of miles inland. I want his leg treated and bandaged before we attempt the journey. Tancrede and I will look for food. I believe we deserve a meal before we go much farther. Wouldn't you agree?"

Landry grinned, as did Gawain.

"Indeed," Landry said.

"Commander." Something in Draper's voice stopped them all. Every Templar looked his way.

He pointed to the ridge looming over the shoreline.

At first Landry saw nothing unusual.

"What is it?" Gawain asked.

"On the road," Draper said, still pointing. "Heading in our direction."

An instant later, Landry spotted them. He bit back a most unchristian oath. Warriors marched on the path Draper had indicated, bearing spears, swords, bows. Above them, rising and falling in the same wind that had been the Templars' salvation, hung a green banner bearing the crescent moon of the Saracens.

CHAPTER 2

Seeing that green flag, the sickle moon, its edges as sharp as a Mamluk blade, Godfrey was overcome with memories of the final battle at Acre, of blood, of death cries, of gleaming blades blurring in the desert sun, and of the shining ferocity and resolve of Khalil's soldiers. There was a reason why, after nearly two centuries of warfare, the Holy Land remained in Saracen hands. This was not an enemy he wished to engage again. They were too quick, too clever, too precise and deadly. He had lost enough men at Acre. He had no intention of losing more here.

As far as he could tell, the Saracens had yet to spot them. That wouldn't last, but it offered them some chance of escape.

"Food and drink, Tancrede," he said, his voice tight. "And whatever healing supplies you can find. As quickly as possible. We haven't much time."

Tancrede nodded once, eyed the Saracens again, and hurried toward the village.

Godfrey led Landry, Draper, Gawain, and the other Templars off the strand to a spot sheltered by a small copse of trees. Many of the passengers followed, including Simon and his daughter.

Once they were hidden from view, Godfrey faced Gawain and drew a long breath. "I'm sorry, brother. I would have preferred to find a healer for you. But we'll have to—"

Gawain cut him off with a jerk of his arm. He shrugged off Landry's support, and Draper's, to stand before Godfrey. He favored his wounded leg, of course, but his hand was steady as he drew his sword.

"I'm ready to fight," he said.

Godfrey gripped the knight's shoulder. "Good lad. Let's hope it doesn't come to that."

He stepped past Gawain to stand beside Landry at the edge of the copse. They watched the Saracens through gaps in the leaves, marking their progress as they continued down the road. Godfrey had hoped the warriors might turn off the path toward some other destination before reaching the strand. They hadn't altered their course yet.

"We need to return to the ship," Landry said. "I should go after Tancrede."

Godfrey laid a hand on his shoulder. "Not yet," he said. "The moment they see you – your mantle, your mail – they'll attack. We will give them a bit more time. They might still take another path."

"And if they don't?"

Godfrey glanced his way. "Let's hope it doesn't come to that, either."

Landry quirked an eyebrow and gave a quick grin. Godfrey answered in kind. They shifted their attention back to the Saracens, waiting to see where they would go.

Gawain hobbled to Godfrey's side. Draper followed, silent, grim.

"Can you tell how many there are?" Gawain asked.

"At least twenty. Too many for us to fight. And they have bows. They might kill us all without ever drawing a blade. I meant what I said: we'll be better off if this doesn't come to a fight."

Gawain looked like he might argue. So did Landry, but both men held their tongues.

Grateful as he was for this, Godfrey knew what they wanted to say. *We might not have that choice.* He understood this as well, and a part of him itched to strike at these Saracens, despite the danger, despite all he had learned of their prowess in combat. Spilling blood here could not atone in any way for their failure at Acre, but it might bring some small consolation to the knights he commanded. The risk, though, was too great. Godfrey was responsible not only for the lives of the other Templars, but also for those of the twelve innocents who sailed with them. He could not afford to be lured by his desire for vengeance.

"God be praised," Draper whispered, his accent thickening the words.

Godfrey saw it as well. A miracle. Or, at the very least, a change in their fortunes. The Saracens had veered off the road leading to the strand and followed instead a spur to the west. Godfrey didn't know where it would take them, but just then he didn't care.

He turned to address the men and women who had sailed with the Templars from Acre.

"It may be that some of you can make a new life for yourselves here. I don't know what awaits us on the sea, but I am certain it won't be an easy journey." He indicated with an open hand towards his tabard, with its bold red cross. "For obvious reasons, my brothers and I cannot remain on this isle, not if it is patrolled by Saracens. But perhaps you can. If not in this village, then in another. None of us will begrudge you this choice."

Several of the passengers traded looks. Simon never took his eyes off Godfrey.

"Adelina and I will find no life here. With your permission, we'll come with you."

"So will we," said another man. The rest nodded their agreement.

Godfrey felt a fullness in his chest that left him speechless and overwhelmed. He could see that the other Templars were moved as well. Before their last crazed morning in Acre, most of these people had been strangers to them. In the days they had spent drifting on the waters of the Mediterranean, Godfrey had not taken as much time as he should have to learn their names, their stories. A mistake, he now realized. They were courageous and loyal beyond measure. They deserved more than his indifference, however benign.

"Thank you," he said. "We'll be glad to have you with us." He lifted his chin in the direction of their ship. "Be ready now. We go on my word."

Gawain held up a hand. "Wait." He still stared out from the copse in the direction of the ridge from which the warriors had descended.

"What is it?" Landry asked.

"Tancrede."

"What about him?"

"That's where the Saracens are headed. To the village, where Tancrede is."

26

"Are you certain?" Godfrey asked.

By way of answer, Gawain pointed. Not at the road, but west of there, to another stretch of lane. Dust rose from that part of the slope, obscuring details. But through the brown cloud hanging over the road, Godfrey could make out the dull gleam of armor and spearheads.

He exhaled through gritted teeth. With reluctance, he pulled his sword from its sheath. "Come on then," he said to the Templars. "The rest of you get back to the ship as soon as you can."

Without another word, he stepped past his fellow knights. Landry, Gawain, and the others gripped their weapons and followed.

A sword hung from his belt. He wore mail and armor. He bore a cross on his chest. It would have been a vast understatement to say that Tancrede felt somewhat conspicuous. He might as well have written in blood across his brow, *I am a Templar and Crusader.*

As he neared the village, he passed a dilapidated stable. Three horses stood within, a gelding and two mares, all of them old and too thin. The horses swished their tails and twitched their ears. A blanket covered one of the mares.

Tancrede hesitated, glanced about, and stole into the stable. The air inside was overwarm and thick with the buzz of flies. It stank of manure.

"Forgive me," Tancrede said to the mare as he removed the blanket from her back. "A loan, I promise."

It was tattered, moth-eaten, and it smelled strongly of horse, which he had expected. But draped over his shoulders and tucked in at his belt, it made him slightly less noticeable. Slightly. If one didn't count the stink. He took care to keep his sword accessible. He had the sense that his "disguise" wouldn't fool many.

He left the horses and made his way into the center of the village, taking stock as he walked of what he might trade for food and healing herbs. He hadn't much by way of coin: only a few silvers from Acre. He carried a dagger, also sheathed on his belt, though he was reluctant to part with it, especially with Saracens on the road above the village. He wore a ring on a chain around his neck, a gift from his father. A Knight of the Temple wasn't supposed to cling to such adornments, but this he had been loath to give up. Still, under the circumstances, if the silvers weren't enough, he could part with it.

And the dagger, too, if need be.

Finding food proved easy. Fruits, cheeses, dried meats, bread. He could point, nod, hold the silvers in his palm and ask the question with his eyes: *How much?*

Before long, he had some food, a flask of light wine, and a container that he filled with fresh water from the town well.

But when it came to finding herbs for a poultice, he had more difficulty. None of the men or women he met spoke French, and while Draper had taught him a few phrases in Turkish, his knowledge of the language was too limited for this quest. He strode through the market, listening to conversations, hoping to hear a word of his native tongue. He had just started his second orbit, when he spotted the company of Saracens.

They had taken a different road and were approaching the village from above rather than from the strand. Had he not seen the billow of dust they kicked up, he might not have spotted them until their arrival made escape impossible.

As it was, he couldn't keep himself from ducking back into the shadows, and pressing himself to the side of a wooden booth in the agora.

"You smell terrible."

The voice of an old woman. Speaking a language he understood. It took him a breath to grasp this second point.

"You speak French!"

"How observant you are," she said, her tone as dry as desert sand.

Tancrede marked the position of the Saracens before slipping into her small booth. The woman was petite, white-haired, with a wizened, leathery face and thin, delicate hands. She wore a simple shift, and a shawl draped over her shoulders, though it was warm in the marketplace. She sat behind a broad table laden with bowls of spices and teas, watching him with unconcealed mistrust, onyx eyes bright in the shadows.

"I need healing herbs. Do you sell any?"

She shook her head, gestured at the table. "What you see. Nothing more."

"Does anyone here sell them?"

"Maybe. Who are you?" She motioned with her hand again, this time toward the lane, the Saracens. "Why are you so afraid of them?"

He faltered, unsure of how she would respond to the truth. "I just... I need herbs. A friend of mine is hurt."

The woman's gaze raked over him, head to toe, pausing fractionally at his belt. Belatedly, Tancrede shifted the old blanket to conceal his sword.

Her lips quirked with amusement. "Do you bear a cross over your chest?"

"We didn't come here looking for a battle."

"How refreshing."

He peered out toward the road again. If he tarried here much longer, he wouldn't be able to get away. "Never mind," he said. "I'm sorry to have disturbed you." He started away.

"I have borage," she said, stopping him, her voice low. "Betony, too. You might find madder root four booths down." She pointed to the right. "The three together should help an open wound."

"How much?"

"Do you bear a cross over your chest?" she asked again.

Tancrede turned slowly, and after the briefest pause, pulled the blanket away, exposing his tabard.

The woman stared at it. She started to reach for it, but then brought her hand to her lips.

"Where were you?" she asked in a breathy whisper.

"Acre."

She raised her eyes to his. "Acre has fallen?"

Tancrede swallowed past a thickness in his throat. "Yes."

"We've heard nothing of this."

"It happened not so long ago. Not even a month." It felt like longer, and also like yesterday. He cast a look over his shoulder. The Saracens were closer. "You say you have borage?" he asked, afraid to linger much longer. "Betony?"

"Were you... were you also at Tripoli?"

"No. You knew someone there?"

Her gaze dropped back to the red cross on his

tabard. But she didn't answer. After a few seconds, she roused herself with a start that ran through her entire form. "It doesn't matter." She stood, walked to a basket at the rear of her booth, and dug out two small leather pouches. She shuffled back to her table and held them out to Tancrede. They were fragrant, one cool and sweet, the other more pungent, biting.

He took them from her. "How much do I owe you?" he asked.

She shook her head. "Go. They'll be here soon. They patrol in small units – twenty men or so. But there are at least a hundred of them in an encampment above the village. You don't want them finding you."

"Thank you. God keep you."

"And you, Templar."

Tancrede tied the pouches to his belt, covered himself with the blanket once more, and stepped out of the booth. He walked swiftly now, while trying to seem unhurried. The fourth booth was one he had looked at before. This time, though, he noticed what he had missed previously: a small array of herbs at the far end of a table crowded with olives, roots, and greens.

He held up the last of his silvers, catching the man's attention.

"Madder," he said.

Puzzlement.

"I need madder," he said again.

The man opened his hands and shook his head.

He didn't have time for this.

A footfall behind him made him spin and reach for his sword. But it was the old woman. She said something to the man that Tancrede didn't understand, turned on her heel, and walked away.

The old man smiled and bobbed his head. He stepped to the herbs, sorted through them, and crossed back to Tancrede bearing a gnarled tuber. He held out his hand for the silver, which Tancrede gave him in exchange for the root. The man produced a worn purse and picked through it, apparently seeking to make change.

A cry from beyond the marketplace made Tancrede whirl again. He heard shouting and the clash of swords.

"Keep it!" he said to the man. He shoved the root into the bundle of food he'd bought and bolted from the booth, the provisions gripped in one hand, his sword in the other.

People streamed past him, fleeing the battle, fear in their faces. Tancrede fought through them, his blade held high to avoid inflicting injury. He shrugged off the encumbering blanket, chastising himself as he did. He hadn't meant to steal, or deprive either horse or owner of the cloth. But this wasn't the time for scruples.

Ahead of him, men fought in the lane. Saracens and his fellow Templars. The air around them was hazed with dust. Naked blades flashed and clanged. Bowmen stood nearby, arrows nocked, but useless in the bedlam.

One of the archers spotted him and shouted to his companions. All of them took aim, no doubt pleased to have a target. Tancrede ducked into a byway just as the bows twanged. A dozen arrows rained down on the street. A few stuck in the ground or thudded into building walls. A woman screamed, clutching at the back of her leg. A boy fell at the mouth of the narrow lane, an arrow in his back, and an old man collapsed near the lad, his neck pierced, blood staining his tunic.

Tancrede chanced a peek out at the street. The bowmen were already nocking new arrows to their bowstrings and running toward him. He slipped down the alley, away from the larger street. He needed to rejoin his fellow knights, but first he had to throw off the pursuit of these archers.

He hadn't gone far along the byway, when he happened upon a shed filled with goats. He heard the bowmen behind him, but they had yet to enter the alley.

Clutching the food and his weapon, Tancrede dove into the shed and hastily covered himself with hay.

Seconds later the first of the archers sped past, shouting back at his companions in the Saracens' tongue. More men ran by. Still, Tancrede remained hidden, until the slap of their feet on dirt had receded.

Only then did he climb out of the shed, brush off the hay, and sprint back to the mouth of the alley. Rounding the corner, he nearly ran headlong into two bowmen, apparently left there to watch for him.

The men stared at him for an instant, as if too shocked by his appearance to do more. Before they could call for aid, Tancrede dropped his parcel, grabbed the first man's shoulder, and ran him through with his blade. The second man let fall his bow and grappled for his sword. Tancrede pulled his blade free of the dead man, and hacked at this second warrior. His first blow bit deep into the man's neck. Blood fountained from the wound. A second stroke severed the Saracen's head.

Tancrede didn't even stop to wipe his blade. Blood dripping from the steel, he ran on to fight beside his brothers.

* * *

Gawain kept his back pressed to the white stone wall, his sword a gleaming blur of silver and crimson in the bright sun. He didn't know what building he had chosen. A shop? A home? A temple? It didn't matter. The wall protected his back and helped him stand upright. Beyond that... Well, it could have been a mausoleum for all he cared.

Pain radiated from his knee, shooting down to his heel and up into his groin. Every twist, every thrust and parry, every blow he blocked with his sword, made his body shudder and brought a new wave of agony.

And still he fought.

What choice did he have? Surrender meant death. His death would endanger the lives of his fellow Templars. This was unacceptable.

Already, two Saracens lay dead at his feet. Even hobbled, forced to fight on one leg, he remained a match for these warriors. Had he not been sweating like an overworked horse, he might have taken some satisfaction in that.

But this man – the third – was different. Bigger, stronger, older. That last might prove decisive. Gawain bled from gashes on his cheek, his neck, and his hand, all inflicted by this warrior. The first two had charged, heedless of his injured leg and the limitations it forced upon him. This one was canny. It had taken him mere seconds to see what the others had missed. He danced forward, struck, danced away again, beyond the reach of Gawain's blade.

He wore a mocking grin, cruel mischief in his dark eyes. Now and again, he spoke. Gawain understood not a word of what he said. But he could guess at the man's meaning. He cursed his own infirmity, his weakness.

The Saracen glided in again, hammered a blow at Gawain's side. Gawain parried, ground his teeth together as anguish knifed through him. He aimed a strike of his own at the man, but already he had backed away. Gawain's sword whistled through dry air.

Landry, Godfrey, and Nathaniel fought on one side of him; Thomas, Victor, Draper, and Brice on the other. All of them had wanted to keep him from this battle, but he had insisted that he be allowed to fight. Outnumbered as they were, the others could not argue for long. He propped himself against this building, and raised his sword, inviting attack. Now the wall was splattered with blood, like his tabard and his mantle.

He didn't think any of his friends had fallen. Not yet. Likely he would be first to go down. The wall held him up, but it hindered his movements, limited what he could do with his blade arm, and kept him from backing away. It appalled him that he should be reduced to this, unable to advance or attack, waiting for mistakes from a foe who seemed unlikely to make any.

The Saracen leapt forward again, sword raised to chop at Gawain's neck. Gawain lifted his weapon to block the attack. But at the last moment, the Saracen shifted his blade to his other hand, and aimed a strike at Gawain's bad leg.

Gawain wrenched to the side, reached across himself to meet the blow. The effort tore a snarl from his throat. He dropped to one knee. The warrior loomed over him, sword held high again. A killing blow. There was nothing Gawain could do.

But before the Saracen could strike, a blade burst through his chest from behind. Blood frothed at the man's mouth. And Tancrede appeared at the Saracen's shoulder, his teeth bared, blood from a wound over his eye making him look like a ghoul.

He pulled his blade free, allowed the Saracen to topple to the side. Then he held out a hand for Gawain and helped him up.

"Thank you," Gawain said.

"You're—"

"Behind you!"

Tancrede spun, deflected an assault from another Saracen. This man was joined by two others. Tancrede backed away, coming up against Gawain's wall after two steps.

"I don't recommend this as a tactic," Gawain said.

Tancrede's gaze flicked from one warrior to the next. "No, I don't imagine."

"They know I can't fight them, that I can't even step away from this wall."

"Can't you?" Tancrede asked.

Their eyes met for the span of a heartbeat, no more. But that was enough. Roaring with rage and the anticipation of anguish, Gawain lifted his sword and lurched at the man on the right. The Saracen fell back, eyes wide. He tried to counter Gawain's blows, but clearly he had thought he battled a man crippled by his wounds. He wasn't prepared for Templar skill, or the speed of a Templar blade. Gawain staggered after the man as he backed away, every step bringing torment. But it was the Saracen who tripped and fell, crashing onto his back. Before he could regain his feet or roll away, Gawain pounced. Grasping his sword with both hands, he drove the tip through the man's chest, into the dirt beneath him. The warrior's back arched and he screamed his last breath before his body sagged.

Gawain yanked his sword from the man, and turned on his one good leg, intending to help Tancrede. Instead, he watched his friend dispatch the second Saracen. One stroke hacked off the man's arm. A thrust through the throat killed him. Gawain dropped to his good knee again, keeping his wounded leg straight.

Landry, Godfrey, Draper, and the others had prevailed in their battles as well. More than a dozen dead Saracen warriors littered the street, but the Templars were bloodied and exhausted.

Landry pointed toward the road leading up the ridge. "More are coming," he said, panting the words.

"There are a hundred of them up there," Tancrede said, retrieving several parcels from the ground near where Gawain and he had fought. "Perhaps more."

At a questioning look from Godfrey, he added, "I talked to someone in the market. My point is, we can't fight them all, which means we can't stay."

"Very well," Godfrey said. "Back to the ship."

Tancrede and Draper helped Gawain up, and supported him as they hurried toward the strand.

They hadn't gone more than a hundred paces when the first arrow took Landry in the shoulder. He gasped, and fell. Barbs rained down on the knights, forcing them to scatter off the lane and seek whatever shelter they could find.

Gawain, Tancrede, and Draper ducked into a small recess at the front of another building. It offered scant protection.

"Do you see them?" Tancrede asked.

Draper scanned the street. "No. They could be anywhere."

Gawain also searched, but the Saracens had hidden themselves too well. From behind him and above, he heard the footfalls of many men. They hadn't much time.

"If we remain here, we're dead."

"And if we step out in the open, they'll kill us," Tancrede said. "Not the best of choices."

Before any of them could say more, a new sound reached them. Shouts from the marketplace.

"What now?" Draper muttered.

Tancrede laid a hand on his arm. "Wait. Watch."

A crowd of people came into view. Men, women, children even, walking in a tight pack. Gawain thought there must be at least two hundred. At their fore strode the most unlikely of leaders: a diminutive, white-haired woman.

"What are they doing?" Draper asked.

"Saving us."

Gawain shook his head. "At what cost? They can't fight these men."

"I don't think they mean to," Tancrede said. "Be ready when they pass."

Seconds later, the throng reached them. They didn't stop, nor did they acknowledge the Templars in any way that would draw the attention of the Saracens.

But they opened a small gap in their ranks, revealing something Gawain had missed earlier. They appeared as a solid mass of people, but there was space at their center, room enough for the knights.

"Can you make it?" Tancrede asked him.

"I've no intention of remaining here."

"All right, then. Let's go."

With Draper and Tancrede helping him again, they rushed from their place of concealment to that gap in the crowd, and then into the center of the mass. Gawain would have liked to search for the archers, but he and his fellow knights kept their heads low so as not to be seen. He hoped the Saracens wouldn't loose their arrows into the throng indiscriminately. He hoped Godfrey, Landry, and the other Templars would know enough to join them in this human shelter.

The Saracens held their fire. The other knights scrambled in beside them. Landry gripped his shoulder, blood flowing between his fingers, the barb still embedded in his flesh.

Sooner than Gawain expected, the terrain underfoot changed from the compressed dirt of the road to loose sand. The smells of brine and fish suffused the air. Gulls cried overhead. They were on the strand.

At the same time, the horde began to shift, opening up ahead of the knights, closing ranks behind them. As they reached the front of the throng, Tancrede raised a hand, stopping his fellow knights and the men and women who accompanied them. He approached the white-haired woman.

"We owe you our lives."

"Yes," she said. "I suppose you do."

Despite everything, Tancrede grinned.

"Go," she said. "Get on your ship and sail from this place. Those bowmen will realize soon enough what we've done."

"There will be a price to pay. You know this."

She shrugged. "We would have paid a price for letting you die. A different sort, perhaps, but dear nevertheless." Her smile made Gawain's chest ache. "We chose with our eyes open, Templar. Now go. Don't waste what we've given you."

Tancrede knelt before her, before all the villagers who had saved them. The other Templars did the same. Even Landry, with an arrow in his shoulder. Even Gawain, for whom kneeling and standing were agony.

"God keep you safe," Tancrede said.

The woman motioned for them to rise. "Remember us."

The Templars stood. Draper and Tancrede supported Gawain once more. Godfrey put an arm out to steady Landry. The villagers made way for them, and the Templars strode over the firm, wet sand at the water's edge, into the shallow surf, and finally to the *Tern*. Already, Simon and several of the other passengers, men and women, had readied the ship for departure. Somehow they had secured oars – who knew from where? – and had set them in the holes below deck. Tancrede and Draper helped Gawain aboard. Nathaniel and Thomas did the same for Landry. The knights settled the two wounded Templars together on the deck, and went below to take up oars with the passengers. Godfrey and several of the villagers pushed the vessel beyond the shallows. Godfrey climbed in and the others began to row.

Gawain strained to see over the rail and keep his eyes on the strand. Once their ship was away, the villagers scattered in every direction. Except one.

The old woman remained where she was, facing the sea, eyes on their ship. Behind her, some two dozen Saracens streamed onto the strand and converged on where she stood.

She pulled something from within her shift, her movements deliberate, unhurried. Only when Gawain saw the flash of reflected sunlight at her hand did he realize what she had done, what she was doing. By then, it was too late to stop her.

He cried out, but they were so far away, and clearly the woman had long since made her choice. As he watched in horror, the woman plunged the blade into her own heart. By the time the warriors reached her, she had collapsed to the sand.

CHAPTER 3

Adelina stares back at the sandy shore, at the soldiers with their curved blades and bows. At the woman who lies at their feet. A few of the men have stepped to the edge of the water and loosed arrows at the ship. But by now the men and women below have rowed them beyond reach. The arrows slip into the water with a whisper and little splash. Two of the archers try again, but the rest retreat to where the woman lies.

Adelina believes the old woman must be dead.

"What happened to her?" she whispers. "Why did she…" The question dies on her lips as she looks up for her father. He isn't there. She remembers that he is one of those in the hold rowing their vessel away from the isle.

Two of the Templars gaze back at her, the two who saved their lives on the dock at Acre. One – Gawain – has a wounded leg. The other is Landry. Adelina has remembered his name since their first encounter. He's handsome – dark eyes, dark hair and beard, large, strong hands – and he has been kind to her and her father. Now he has an arrow in his shoulder. Blood glistens on his tabard and on the linked armor that covers his arm.

"Does it hurt?" she asks. A foolish question maybe, but it has often struck her that adults don't respond to pain as children do.

"Yes," he says, in a voice as deep as the sea. "Very much."

"I'm sorry."

A smile flits across his face and is gone. "Thank you."

She looks back at the strand again. The soldiers surround the woman now. Adelina can't see her anymore.

She points at them. "What happened to her?" she asks again. "The old woman."

"I'm afraid she's dead," Landry says.

"But how? I didn't see any of the soldiers do anything to her."

Landry drops his gaze, casts a glance at Gawain, who also refuses to look at her. Adelina turns from them back to the strand. Young as she is, she has seen a lot and heard even more. Since her mother's death, she has lived with her feet in two worlds, that of a child, and that of her merchant father. Following him has exposed her to much that other girls her age might not experience. As much as anything, this explains why she can make the leap she does. This, and the flash of steel she saw in the woman's hand before she fell.

"She killed herself, then. Self-murder." The phrase comes to her unbidden, from a memory she cannot quite summon.

Both Landry and Gawain appear surprised.

Shocked might be a better word. Their eyes widen and they look at each other again.

"Self-murder is a sin in the eyes of the Lord," Gawain says. "Our faith teaches this, and yours does as well, I believe."

"Then why did she do it?"

Landry shifts, winces, and reaches for his shoulder. "She did not wish to be captured by the Saracens."

"Would they have hurt her?"

"Probably, yes."

"Because she and her friends helped us."

"That's right. They might have forced her to tell them who else was there to aid our escape. And that would have gotten them in trouble as well. So rather than endanger the other villagers, she... she sacrificed herself."

Godfrey joins them at this end of the ship. He is tall and severe, and he bears bloody wounds from the Templars' fight on the island. Adelina is a little afraid of him.

"They aren't following," he says, eyeing the Saracens.

"No," Landry says. "They appear more concerned with what the villagers have done."

"I fear for them." Godfrey tears his gaze from the isle and kneels beside Landry. "Are you in much pain?"

"No." Landry winks at Adelina.

She grins.

"We'll unfurl the sails and get off sweeps. Once we've done that, Draper will see to your wound. And yours," Godfrey added, addressing Gawain. "Tancrede tells me he has purchased healing herbs. From the old woman, as it happens. We have food as well. I would have preferred to remain on the isle, but we're not as badly off as we were."

Adelina's mood lifts at this. She cannot remember the last time her belly was full. Her skin is stretched thin over her ribs now. The clothes she wears, the only ones she has left, no longer fit her as they did when they departed Acre. She is wasting away, as is her father. She has never seen him look so thin. In recent days, it has scared her. No more, though. *We have food...* In her mind, she pictures a feast.

Several men, her father among them, come onto the deck, unfold the sail, and hoist it into the bright sunlight. Adelina thinks the air feels still, and panic grips her. Hunger is one thing, but if they become becalmed again, she fears she might throw herself over the ship's rails. She can't imagine a repeat of that ordeal.

But as the men raise the sail the cloth billows, catching a wind she hasn't perceived. The ship carves away from the isle, rising and falling on the sea swells. She closes her eyes, relief washing over her.

Her father calls her away from the Templars, chastises her for bothering the men, then folds her into a tight embrace.

"Were you scared, Papa?"

"A little, yes. Were you?"

She nods. "That woman on the island murdered herself."

He frowns, inhales and exhales. "Yes, I've heard. You saw her do this?"

"Yes."

"I'm sorry for that."

"It's all right."

"No, I mean..." He trails off, shakes his head. "She

had her reasons for taking her own life, but it is not something God permits. I want you to remember that."

"Yes, Papa."

The knight Draper – her father calls him "the Turcopole" – approaches Landry. She likes Draper. He is not as tall as Godfrey and Gawain, and not as handsome as Landry. But he tells funny stories, and speaks with an accent that she finds intriguing, as if his very words might unlock the secrets of a new world. He holds pouches and strips of cloth. As Adelina watches, he speaks in a low voice to Landry. She cannot make out what he says. But a second later, he grips the arrow by the shaft, his fist close to Landry's shoulder, and says something else. Landry nods, closes his eyes. The muscles in his jaw tighten.

Adelina's father averts his eyes rather than watch. She doesn't. She wants to see, is fascinated by it all. Arrows, swords. Even blood. The act of healing fascinates her as well, the herbs, the poultices and bandages.

Draper pulls the arrow. He doesn't jerk it, but neither does he ease it out. The motion is both decisive and gentle.

Landry makes a sound deep in his throat, something between a moan and a growl. The sound builds into a wail, and then a violent gasp as the arrow comes free, dripping blood. Crimson blossoms at his shoulder, spreads over his chest.

Working with more urgency now, Draper, with help from Godfrey, strips off Landry's mail, his jerkin, and his shirt. Landry grimaces as they do this, hissing his breath through gritted teeth when the two Templars move his shoulder to take off the articles of clothing. The shirt and jerkin are stained with blood. His shoulder is a mess.

At the sight of the wound, Adelina does turn away, not because she is horrified, but rather because to stare seems a violation.

Before long, however, she faces the men again. By now, Draper has a poultice in place. Even at some distance, the fresh scent of crushed leaves reaches her. She wants to know the names of those plants, but doesn't dare ask. Instead, she walks to the men, and picks up the bloody shirt and jerkin. The latter is heavier than she expects, and she has to grip it with both hands.

"What are you doing?" Draper asks.

"These should be cleaned. I can use seawater. If... if you think that would be all right."

"That will be fine," the Turcopole says. "Thank you, child."

She carries the jerkin and shirt to the ship's stern, where she had been standing, and reaches for a bucket. Her father stops her, takes the bucket from her, and fills it himself. He hands it back to her and briefly cups her cheek in his hand. Adelina sees pride in his brown eyes. Her cheeks flush.

But she says nothing, and instead fixes her attention on the work she has offered to do. The stains prove stubborn, particularly at their center, where the blood has lingered longest.

She eyes the knights, wondering if they can see how she struggles with what should be a simple task. None of them watch her. Draper has set to work on Gawain's leg. She isn't yet certain what she thinks of the wounded knight. He almost never smiles and he rarely speaks to her. But neither does he seem cross or cruel. And he isn't as formidable as Godfrey.

Gawain regards the Turcopole as he works on the wound, but the men do not speak to each other. Adelina concentrates again on Landry's shirt and jerkin.

Though she scrubs the cloth until her hands are raw, and must ask her father for a second and then a third bucketful, she is unable to remove the blood entirely.

Still, when at last she surrenders, the shirt and jerkin both look better than they did. She wishes she had needle and thread to mend the holes in the material.

She takes them back to Landry, but the knight is sleeping, his breathing deep, late afternoon sun lighting his face. She sets the clothes beside him, spreading them so they will dry. Then she starts away, trying to keep her steps light.

"Thank you."

She halts, turns. "I didn't mean to wake you."

"You didn't."

"But—"

"I was resting, deep in prayer and contemplation." He tips his head in the direction of the clothes. "I'm grateful to you for cleaning these."

"It was my pleasure, sir. I'm sorry I couldn't do better with them."

"You did very well."

She looks away, to Gawain, who has his eyes closed. She wonders if he is asleep, or also in prayer.

"Where will we go now?" she asks.

Landry shakes his head. "I cannot say. But Godfrey will know what to do. He's very wise. He won't let any of you come to harm."

"You came to harm. So did Gawain."

"We are knights," Gawain says, his eyes still closed.

These Templars are difficult to judge. One can never even tell when they are sleeping and when they're awake. She thinks there might be a lesson there.

"We fight to keep others from harm," Gawain goes on. He opens his eyes, which are a cool blue, the color of the western sky. His hair is long, his face young and also handsome, though not as much so as Landry's. "But Landry is right. Godfrey will see you and your father and the rest to safety. All of us will."

"Thank you," she says, because that strikes her as the proper response.

Before any of them can say more, Tancrede approaches, a large bundle in his arms.

"Is anyone here hungry?" he asks, eyes on her.

Adelina struggles to contain herself. "Very!"

"I don't doubt it." He pulls from his bundle a small piece of rinded cheese, a hunk of bread, an apricot, and a morsel of smoked meat. He hands these to her. "There you go. For you and your father."

For several moments, she cannot move or speak. This is all? The fighting, the woman's death, Landry's blood? And this is all they get? Tancrede found food. That is what they have been told, and she had assumed this meant enough to make up for days of privation. But this... For both of them?

Her heart labors. She can barely swallow past her disappointment and rage. "Thank you," she whispers, blinking back tears.

Despite her frustration, she does not wish to seem ungrateful. Tancrede, though, is clever.

"We're all hungry, Adelina. But we need to make this last. If I could have gotten more – if there had been more time – I would have."

She is behaving like a small child, younger than her years. Pride makes her meet his gaze.

"I understand. Thank you."

"You're welcome," Tancrede says.

She starts to go, then stops, realizing her error. "We cannot have the meat and the cheese," she says. "Our faith—"

Tancrede's eyes widen slightly. "Of course. Forgive me." He hesitates before exchanging the morsel of meat for an extra bite of cheese. "Better?"

"Yes, thank you."

She hurries away from them all and back to her father. He greets her with a broad smile and generous words about the meal they are about to share. He says to her all the things she should have said to the Templar.

Her shame deepens as they eat, because she grows full so quickly. She has to force herself to choke down her half of the apricot. Notwithstanding her earlier ingratitude, she has been hungry too long. She can no longer gorge herself as once she did. She scans the ship's deck, searching for Tancrede. She should apologize. But she spots him sitting with the other Templars, deep in conversation with Landry, Gawain, and Draper. She leaves them alone, concentrates on trying to take pleasure in the sensation of not being hungry anymore.

The feeling, though, doesn't last long. As night falls, and Godfrey lights the torches mounted on the ship's mast, her hunger returns with a vengeance. Adelina finds it hard to believe she has eaten at all. She is certain she isn't the only one aboard the ship who feels this way.

* * *

The pain in Gawain's leg had not abated. He should have known better than to expect improvement so soon. A poultice of crushed leaves and root could not undo weeks of agony, not immediately. Faith and prayer and the mercy of God would bring healing. Draper's ministrations would help. But the Turcopole could not perform miracles; Gawain told himself as much, again and again.

And this served to make Landry's recovery all the more galling.

It had been mere hours. Not even a full night had passed. Yet already Gawain saw improvement in his fellow knight, who rested beside him. Landry breathed easier. He could move his arm, flex his shoulder. Not a lot, and not without apparent discomfort. But this limited progress outstripped what Gawain had achieved in all the days since the last battle at Acre. Where was the justice in that?

He had saved the man's life. Landry himself acknowledged as much. Did heroism and sacrifice count for nothing in the eyes of the Lord? Or was he being punished for some sin he had committed at Acre or before? He could think of no such crime against faith and grace. He attempted always to acquit himself with honor, with piety, to protect the weak and the innocent, to uphold the principles guiding Templar life.

What have I done, Lord? Tell me and I shall atone. But I beg you, grant me the strength I once had so that I might continue to serve you.

Draper approached the two of them, bearing fresh bandages and the pouches of herbs Tancrede had secured. "I would check your dressings once more before I retire," he said. "If I may."

"Of course," Landry answered. Even his voice sounded stronger.

Gawain merely nodded.

Draper knelt beside Landry and began to remove the poultice. "How does it feel?" he asked as he worked.

"Better. You work wonders, my friend."

The Turcopole returned Landry's smile. Once he had pulled the dressing away, he examined Landry's wound, squinting in the torchlight. He probed the skin around it with his fingers. For the most part, Landry offered little response, though at one point he did draw a sharp breath.

"I'm sorry," Draper said. "Is that the only place where it still pains you?"

"It all remains a bit tender, but that's the worst."

"Remarkable. You were fortunate."

That prompted another smile. "Perhaps. I still credit you."

Gawain looked away, his gaze straying to the crescent moon that hung low in the west. Draper worked in silence for a few minutes, no doubt placing a fresh poultice on Landry's wound.

When he finished, he stood, walked to where Gawain sat, and knelt again, this time next to Gawain's injured knee.

"How does your leg feel?"

Gawain glanced at Landry.

"Perhaps I'll stretch my legs," Landry said, climbing to his feet. His movements were stiff, but as he walked off he showed little effect from the day's battle.

Gawain ached everywhere. His back and shoulders, both legs, his neck. Disadvantaged as he was by his wound, every thrust of his sword had felt unnatural, every parry of a Saracen's blade had strained his muscles. He had been fighting himself as much as the enemy, and now he suffered for the struggle.

"Gawain?" Draper prompted. "Your leg?"

"It feels no different," he said, unable to keep the bitterness from his voice.

"I'm sorry for that."

"I don't blame you."

"I know that. What I meant—"

"I know what you meant, Draper." He eyed the moon again, blew out a breath. "I had hoped that Tancrede's herbs would prove as curative for my wound as they have for Landry's."

"They might still. We cannot judge their efficacy after only a few hours. You must give them time."

"Landry's wound is healing already."

"His wound was nothing compared to yours, and he sustained his today. If we'd had these herbs the day we sailed from Acre, if I had been able to treat you then as I've been able to treat Landry today..." His shrug was eloquent. "May I see the wound?"

"Of course."

He unfastened the bandage on Gawain's leg, his touch deft. He bent low to inspect the injury.

"It may not feel better," he said after some time, "but it looks much improved. The swelling has gone down, and with it the redness." He prodded the flesh above and below Gawain's knee, much as he had done with Landry's shoulder. Pain flared with every touch. Gawain clenched his jaw, resisting the need to give voice to his anguish.

"Forgive me," Draper said.

Gawain nodded, his eyes closed, waiting for the

agony to subside. When he opened his eyes again, Draper had already set a fresh poultice over the wound and was tying it in place.

"It will never heal, will it?" Gawain asked.

Draper kept his eyes on his task. "It is still too soon to say."

Gawain didn't respond. He watched the Turcopole, waiting until at last the man finished and sat back on his knees. Their eyes met.

"It's not going to heal," Gawain said again.

"It will heal, as nearly all wounds do if they don't kill."

"But?"

Draper frowned. He stared off to the side, his round face kind, even in profile. After a breath, he dragged his gaze back to Gawain's. "I fear you will always struggle with it. I no longer fear for the leg itself. You will keep it, and you will have use of it. But I believe you will walk with a limp for the rest of your days."

"You're saying I'm going to be a cripple."

Draper straightened. "You are going to be a Templar. But you will be burdened with this injury. Whether you are a cripple or a man with a limp…" He opened his hands. "That is entirely up to you. Rest well, Gawain."

Draper stood, and walked off.

"You, too," Gawain called after him.

He sat for a long time, Draper's words repeating themselves in his mind. At length, he fought to his feet and hobbled across the deck to the starboard rail. He leaned on the wood and tracked the moon's descent toward the horizon.

"You can't sleep?" Godfrey joined him, and leaned on the wood as well.

"Haven't really tried."

"Draper tells me your leg is improving."

He huffed a sharp breath, hands gripping the rail. "What else did he tell you?"

"Nothing that I haven't observed on my own."

"Am I that obvious, then?"

"It isn't a matter of being obvious. You're human, a man driven by pride and a fierce desire to serve God as one of His chosen knights. To be honest, I would be more concerned for you if you just blithely accepted your fate."

Gawain scowled at that and shot a quick glance at the commander. "My fate, is it?"

"Perhaps. That's for God to say, not me. And not you, either. Your leg will heal fully, or it won't. In the meantime, I need as many knights as possible. We are still a long way from home, and before we reach France again, I'm certain we'll have need of every sword on this ship. I need to know that I can count on yours."

Gawain stepped away from the rail to face Godfrey, setting both feet despite the renewed pain in his leg. "You can."

The commander continued to lean on the side of the ship, but he casually looked Gawain up and down. "Good."

"That's all?" Gawain asked. "Just 'good?'"

"You're a Templar. You expect me to bestow a medal upon you for standing straight?"

Gawain glared at him. But at a grin from Godfrey his pique sluiced away. Before he knew it, he was grinning as well, then laughing.

"The two of you are making a good deal of noise."

Landry walked to where they stood, holding his wounded arm to his chest.

"That they are." Tancrede emerged from the shadows to join them as well, Draper with him. Victor, Thomas, Nathaniel, and Brice followed. "I thought I heard Gawain laugh," Tancrede went on, "but I know that can't be right. A sea sprite, then?"

The others chuckled at this, though all of them watched Gawain, gauging his response. He allowed himself another grin, but he couldn't deny the truth behind Tancrede's jest. In the last days before Acre fell, all of them had been grim, and since his injury he had grown morose. But even before the siege began, when it seemed that the knights would hold Acre against whatever the Saracens threw at them, he had been so serious. He hadn't always been thus, and he couldn't say with any certainty what had changed him. He had no memory of the last time he had laughed, or taken simple pleasure in the company of friends. That bothered him.

"Where do we go from here?" Landry asked after a brief silence.

The others sobered at the question. Gawain looked to Godfrey, as did Draper and Tancrede.

"If we could sail all the way back to France, I would," the commander said. "But obviously, that's impossible. We have too many with us who aren't soldiers. We need to find a safe place to leave them. I thought we had found that in Cyprus."

"Do you think the Hospitallers have lost Kolossi?" Landry asked. "Is that why the Saracens were in that village?"

"I don't know. It's possible. I do know that there are few Templar strongholds left in this region.

Nevertheless, we once held a castle at Bagras, in the mountains of Cilician Armenia, and though that was lost some twenty years ago, Templars still hold passes in those mountains. If we can land at Rhosus, and make our way inland, we might join a larger force and improve our chances of eventually returning home."

"It could be several days before we can reach Rhosus," Tancrede said. "Depending on the winds, of course."

"I know. But thanks to you, we have food now, and healing herbs. As long as our provisions hold, we should be able to make it."

The lean knight lifted a shoulder. "Very well. Rhosus it is."

Godfrey considered each of them. "We've a long way to go. But I want you to know that there are no other knights I would rather have with me than the eight of you. We will get home. You have my word."

The knights exchanged looks. Gawain was reassured by what he saw in the faces of his brothers, and he allowed himself to believe Godfrey might be right.

"Off with you, then," the commander said. "Rest well. I'll take the first watch. Tancrede, I'll wake you in a few hours."

"Of course."

The Templars arranged themselves throughout the ship, keeping to the deck, where they could respond without delay to unexpected threats.

Gawain doubted he would find rest, but almost as soon as he lay down, he felt himself drifting toward sleep. His last clear thought was that Godfrey had been wrong: he *could* have a hand in determining his own fate. He resolved to become again the knight he had once been.

* * *

She wakes to darkness, to air that is sour and still and overly warm. Nearby, her father snores. Others do as well. But those are not the noises that have awakened her. She rolls over and surveys the small hold. Inconstant light pools on the floor beneath the hatch: the glow from the torches above.

A shadow shifts near that spot, wood squeaks and the shadow freezes. Adelina sits up, frightened now. She thinks about waking her father.

The shadow approaches her, takes form. Not a ghost or a pirate – she has imagined both – but rather Egan, another passenger, like her, like her father. He's round, soft. Or he was, early in their journey. Seeing him now in the dim light, she realizes that he has become lean over the past weeks. He has small, dark eyes, widely spaced in a round face. His light hair, which had been short, has grown unruly from neglect.

He holds a finger to his lips, says, "I didn't mean to wake you. I'm just…" He shakes his head, as if at something she has said. "You should go back to sleep."

She glances past him, then peers more closely at something he holds in his hand. He hides it behind his back, but by then it is too late. She knows what she has seen. Cheese, and a long strip of meat. Twice as much as Tancrede gave to her and her father that afternoon.

Egan's shoulders sag, and he darts his gaze around the hold before leaning closer to her.

"I'm just so hungry. You understand, don't you?"

She does, but she doesn't answer. She knows what he's doing, how wrong it is. But she says nothing, wakes no one.

"It can be our secret," he says, moving still closer. "You needn't tell anyone."

He rips the strip of meat in half. She can smell it. Smokey, salty. Her mouth waters.

Egan holds it out to her. "Here. Take it." He gives it a small shake. "It's yours. You have some, I have some. And no one else is the wiser." He smiles.

Adelina hesitates. *This is wrong*, she thinks. And then, *I'm so hungry*.

She stares at the food, caught between guilt and desire. Egan watches her. When he shakes the meat a second time, she reaches out and takes it from him, like a feral dog. He nods once, motions for her to lie down, which she does.

Egan creeps back into the shadows. Adelina is certain he will eat more than just the cheese and meat. Again, she thinks that she should tell someone. Instead, she takes a small bite of the meat, closes her eyes at the touch of salt and game on her tongue. She eats the strip in small bites, chewing slowly, savoring every morsel.

When at last it's gone, she longs for more. She thinks she can hear Egan still. She wonders how much he has eaten, what the knights will say come morning. Maybe they won't notice. She dismisses the thought as soon as it comes to her. They *will* notice. And there will be trouble. She will pay a price for those few bites of meat. All of them will. Her eyes well, and before she knows it, she is sobbing. She tries to stifle the sound, afraid to wake her father, terrified that he will smell smoked meat on her breath.

She hates Egan. She hates herself. She dreads the coming of dawn.

CHAPTER 4

Landry woke to a freshening wind and a cool gray sky. He sat up, hissed a breath at the lingering pain in his shoulder and back. The ship listed hard to port, a northerly wind filling her sails, driving them farther from Cyprus, but also from Cilician Armenia and their destination. Tancrede had taken the rudder and was trying to steer them to the east. Though Landry knew little of seafaring, he could tell that the ship and the wind fought him.

He stood, and nearly overbalanced. Stepping to the mast, he gripped the wood and gazed out over the Mediterranean. Her waters were roiled. White caps dotted the swells as far as the eye could see. The *Tern* rose and fell more violently than it had at any time since their departure from Acre. Several of the passengers leaned over the rails, vomiting the previous evening's meal into the seas.

Landry caught the scent of rain on the wind, and turning to the west saw a gray smudge in the distance.

He made his way to Tancrede.

"What can I do?" he asked.

"Not very much, I'm afraid. Unless you can control the wind."

"Are we in danger?"

Tancrede shook his head, a smile easing the taut lines of his face. "No. We're in for some discomfort is all. Rough seas and a good soaking. But I've come through worse storms than this in vessels that were less seaworthy."

Landry nodded. He locked his eyes on the horizon, hoping to calm his own stomach.

"You, too?" Tancrede asked.

"I'll be fine."

"Normally I would be distributing rations about now, but I doubt anyone will want them. You're welcome to try, though."

Landry returned his gaze to the horizon. "I believe I would rather skip that particular duty, thank you."

Tancrede threw back his head and laughed. Landry didn't share his friend's amusement.

Near the prow of the ship, Draper tended to Gawain's leg. Landry walked forward, knowing the Turcopole would want to change his poultice as well. If his brother knights were as uncomfortable as he with the ship's motion, they showed no sign of it.

"You look a bit green, Landry," Gawain said with too much relish.

"I'm pleased that my fellow knights find my discomfort so amusing."

"Were we better provisioned, there would be remedies I could offer," Draper said. "Ginger, for instance. Or even a sour fruit."

"There should still be fruit," Gawain added. "Apricots. Figs. I know Tancrede brought back both."

"Well, perhaps I'll try that then."

The thought of putting any food in his mouth grew increasingly distasteful with every rise and fall of the ship, but this he kept to himself. He remained by the rail, eyes on the horizon again, until Draper finished with Gawain's leg and beckoned to him.

Landry had taken no more than a step in the Turcopole's direction when Draper stopped him with a raised hand.

"Never mind," he said. "I will come to you. You truly do not look well. Your face is as white as our sail."

"I feel at home on calm seas. But this..."

"Forgive me, my friend, but this is nothing."

"Yes, so Tancrede has told me."

A wry grin lifted the corners of Draper's mouth. "I'm certain he did." He loosened Landry's bandages. "Stand still. Watch the horizon." He faltered. "And if you must be ill, please warn me first."

Despite himself, Landry managed a weak laugh.

It didn't take Draper long to change Landry's dressing, but in that short time, the weather worsened. Gusts of wind buffeted them, and fine drops of rain speckled the ship's deck. Landry felt sicker by the moment.

"Find some of that fruit," Draper said, when he had finished. "I understand that it seems impossible you could eat anything right now—"

"Or ever."

"Yes. But trust me. You will feel better in no time." He appeared to take note of the others bent over the ship's rails. "In fact, you should remain here. I will be back shortly."

Landry didn't argue. As Draper walked away, he leaned on the ship's side, willing himself not to be sick. Draper spoke briefly with Tancrede, then descended into the hold. He emerged again soon after, bearing several pieces of fruit. He cut them into small pieces, which he distributed among those suffering most from the vessel's motion. He came to Landry last, handed him a slice of fig, its rind bright green, the soft pulp within a rich purple.

Landry took a tentative bite. Flavor exploded in his mouth. It was sweeter than he had thought, but with a tang of citrus. He swallowed, his nausea receding with that first mouthful, as Draper had promised.

"That is remarkable."

"Eat the rest," Draper said, his accent rounding the words. "Slowly. When you need more, come and find me."

Landry nodded, took another bite. Many of those who had been ill – passenger and Templar alike – appeared to have improved with the arrival of the fruit. Landry finished the piece he'd been given and approached Tancrede.

"What do you need me to do?"

"You look better."

"I feel better. How can I help?"

"There really isn't much to be done," Tancrede said. He scanned the sea, staring into the weather bearing down on them and peering over his shoulder at the expanse they'd crossed thus far. "Stay dry, help anyone who's still suffering from the seas. I hope we'll be through this by the end of the day."

"Very well," Landry said, and left him to steer the vessel.

Conditions on the ship continued to deteriorate through much of the morning and into the afternoon. Rain lashed the ship, driven by a keening wind. As the vessel listed ever more, Tancrede called to his fellow Templars to shorten the sail, lest the storm wind tip the vessel too far.

"Should we go to sweeps?" Landry asked.

"I prefer not to," Tancrede shouted over the gale and the roar of rain and crashing swells. "We need to maintain enough speed to clear the swells." He frowned up at the sky, wind blasting rain into his face. "Yes, all right. Have them lower the sail. We go to oars."

Landry nodded. "Are you still certain we're in no danger?"

Tancrede didn't answer. He regarded Landry before setting his gaze on the sea again.

Draper and Simon tied ropes around their waists and scrambled up into the rigging to lower the sail. Godfrey led the other Templars and several of their passengers into the hold, where they took up oars and rowed. Gawain and Landry remained on the deck. Their injuries prevented them from climbing or rowing, but neither was willing to leave Tancrede for the safety of the hold. They positioned themselves at the hatch, and relayed instructions from Tancrede to those below.

At Tancrede's insistence, they secured themselves with ropes as well, and fastened them to the mast. Within the hour, they were thankful for the precaution. Waves surged over the rails, sweeping across the deck. One knocked both knights off their feet. Landry crashed into the leeward hull, and lay dazed for several seconds. Gawain crawled to his side and helped him up. Landry thought it likely that if not for the rope holding him to the deck, the wave would have carried him overboard.

Tancrede remained at the rudder, soaked by rain and brine, legs braced, back straight, like some hero from the ancient tales of mariners. He gripped the tiller with both hands, his knuckles white. Despite the raging storm, it appeared to Landry that his friend was enjoying himself.

After some time, Gawain limped below to check on those passengers who weren't rowing. He reemerged onto the deck minutes later, concern etched in his face.

"They're frightened," he said. "And sickened. I hope we're clear before nightfall."

Landry said nothing. For the life of him, he couldn't have hazarded a guess at the time. Already, this day had seemed endless. Were they an hour from dusk? Or three? Or five?

A huge wave doused the ship, staggering him like a blow. The vessel groaned. Another gust pulled at the furled sailcloth, bowing the mast until Landry thought it must break. The ship climbed a swell, dipped, and plunged into a trough. Landry and Gawain clung to the mast. Screams rose from the hold.

Landry whispered a prayer, something he should have done sometime before. The exigencies of the storm had banished thoughts of seasickness from his mind, but they had also caused him to neglect the exigencies of piety.

Beyond supplications to the Lord, however, he felt helpless. He remained near Tancrede, in case his friend required aid. Gawain stayed with him, and Draper joined them on the deck. All of them watched the sky, waiting for some sign of weakening in the storm, or, more ominously, the waning of daylight.

Neither was forthcoming. The storm raged on. Daylight lingered. It seemed to Landry that they were suspended in a timeless hell of wind and rain and vicious waves. Through it all, Tancrede remained steadfast and resolute. He must have been exhausted, chilled to his core. Landry was both, and he hadn't been steering the ship since early that morning. Yet Tancrede never wavered.

But neither could he protect the vessel from all the perils of the tempest.

Landry had never seen seas like these. Every wave towered over the *Tern*. Every redoubling of the wind threatened to tear her asunder. So perhaps it was inevitable that she should surrender under this onslaught. Another wave lifted the vessel and dropped her into a deep swale. At the same time, a fresh burst of wind slammed the ship. The hull shuddered. The mast screamed in protest. Still the wind built. The ship bucked, rose, and plummeted again.

Tancrede shouted a warning, his words swallowed by the storm, but his intent clear. Landry pivoted to face him, and heard behind him the rending of wood.

More cries, these from Draper and Gawain.

Someone crashed into Landry's back, knocking him to the brine-slicked wood. The impact jarred his shoulder. He cried out.

An instant later, the vessel rocked as if smote by a great fist. This elicited more screams from the hold. Tancrede called to them again. Landry had no idea what he said. He lifted his head, twisted to see what had happened. His shoulder burned in protest. Draper lay beside him, his long, dark hair soaked, each drawn breath sounding like a struggle. Beyond him, the top of the mast rested on the crushed leeward rail, having snapped in two. Cloth from the furled sail flapped in the wind, and a tangle of rope draped across the deck, like the web of a giant spider.

Gawain and Draper climbed to their feet on the far side of the mast. Landry did the same.

"I need the rest of you on sweeps!" Tancrede called. "And any below who can help. We need more speed to navigate these seas!"

The Templars started for the hatch. But Draper halted, forcing Landry to do the same.

"You cannot row!" he said over the rush of wind and water. "Not with your shoulder the way it is!"

"Yes, I can! You heard him! He needs all of us—"

"Listen to me, Landry! You cannot! What you can do is remain by the hatch and repeat his commands to those of us below. This is even more important now than it was before."

Landry hesitated. He would never have admitted this, but his shoulder ached, more now after his fall than at any time all day.

"We will need to know what Tancrede wants of us, and I fear bringing one of our passengers onto the deck. You must do this for us. I ask you as your friend, as well as your healer."

"Yes, all right."

Draper patted his good shoulder and followed the others into the hold. Landry checked the knot at his waist and positioned himself between Tancrede and the entrance to the hold. From here, he had a better view of the wreckage wrought by the fallen mast. It was remarkable none of them had been hurt. Beyond the damage to the rail, one end of the spar had pierced the deck, shattering at least two of the planks. Even if they survived the storm, they would be hard-pressed to sail the ship to any land, much less all the way to Turkey.

A wave pummeled the side of the *Tern*. She tipped and almost overturned. Landry hugged the jagged base of the mast.

"Tell them hard to port!" Tancrede said.

Right. First things first.

He repeated the instructions to those below, heard a woman's voice say it again. The ship began a slow turn. Another wall of water broke over them. They tottered, righted, continued to turn.

Eventually, the ship's motion took on a more normal cadence. Climb and descent. It was harrowing still – the swells were huge – but it was better than being assaulted by waves from the side.

"Straight now!" Tancrede said. "As much speed as they can give me."

Landry shouted the commands. The woman passed them on. The *Tern* crept forward.

On they went like this. Every few minutes, Tancrede called for a slight correction to their course, which Landry and the woman below repeated. Landry didn't believe they were making any progress, but as long as they remained oriented to the waves, they could endure. This, at least, is what he told himself.

After a time, he realized that the sky was darkening at last. His heart sank. How would they light torches in this weather?

Tancrede shouted to him again. He put a hand to his ear. His friend didn't bother to repeat himself.

Instead, he grinned and pointed.

Landry turned to follow the line he indicated. West. Dark clouds blanketed much of the sky, but far in the distance, just above the horizon, a thin strip of golden yellow sky brightened the sea.

He had never seen anything more welcome, or more beautiful.

Thank you, Lord.

"Tell them!" Tancrede said.

Landry nodded, leaned toward the hatch. "We see clear skies!" Several people below cheered this. He thought he heard the voice of the girl, Adelina. "We've some distance to go yet," he said. "But this storm will end, tonight, if not before dark."

The woman below shared these tidings with those rowing the ship. Her words were greeted with hoarse cries of joy.

Not long after, the rain let up, then ceased altogether. The wind shifted. It was still strong, but as it changed directions, blowing against the swells, it calmed the seas somewhat. Waves continued to batter the hull, but they no longer broke over the rails. The rocking of the ship grew less extreme.

As the sky darkened to charcoal, some of those who had been below peeked out from the hatch.

"It's all right," Tancrede said, waving them on. "You can come up now. We're safe."

Several of the women came up, and Adelina with them. Once they had a chance to survey the damage, their elation at the storm's passing gave way to renewed apprehension.

"What will we do?" asked the woman who had helped Landry with Tancrede's instructions. She was older, her chestnut hair touched with silver. He thought he remembered her name being Nila. "How can we go on?"

"We have the sweeps," Tancrede said. "Thanks to all of you who found them in Cyprus. We'll not be at the mercy of the sea, as when we were becalmed."

It was scant reassurance, but Landry knew it was all he could offer. The women seemed to accept it as such. Landry admired their courage.

Over the next hour, conditions improved further. This new wind died down, and the surface of the sea smoothed until the *Tern*'s motion felt no more extreme than it had before the storm. The sky lightened for a time, despite the late hour. Patches of blue appeared amid the dark gray, and the strip of golden sky to the west broadened and turned fiery with twilight.

Tancrede called for the men and women below to ship the oars and climb to the deck. All of them working together – passenger and Templar, men and women, even little Adelina – moved the broken mast off the rail and laid it along the length of the ship. Draper and Brice patched the hole in the deck as well as they could. Everyone remained above, watching stars appear in the clearing sky. None of them would want to go back below anytime soon. Landry couldn't blame them.

Tancrede stood by the rudder, though he had tied it in position for now.

"Are you all right?" Landry asked him.

"Fine."

Landry waited, offering no reply.

"I'm tired," the knight admitted, dropping his voice, his face more haggard than usual. "And despite what I said before, I'm not convinced we can get far without the mast."

"Can we repair it?"

"Of course we can, but only if we make land. And how can we do that without the mast? It's the worst sort of riddle."

Godfrey approached them. "How are you doing?" he asked Tancrede.

"Is every one of you going to ask me this? Shall I just announce to all that I'm well, and save myself the tedium of answering again and again?"

Godfrey raised an eyebrow, mischief in his mien.

"He seems a bit quick to anger," the commander said. "Don't you think? I believe a nap might be in order."

Landry laughed. Tancrede smiled as well.

"We should light torches," Godfrey went on. "And though I wouldn't have thought this possible a short while ago, I'm actually feeling hungry. I can't imagine I'm the only one."

"I'll get the food," Tancrede said.

He crossed to the hatch and went below. Landry, Draper, and Godfrey sought out the torches, their dwindling supply of oil, and a flint.

"I believe I owe you my life," Landry said to Draper as they worked. "My thanks."

The Turcopole shrugged. "You would have done the same." He paused in what they were doing to examine the base of the broken mast. "What does Tancrede have to say about this?"

"Nothing good."

He frowned, but nodded, appearing unsurprised by Landry's answer. They turned their attention back to the torches.

Tancrede stepped onto the deck again a minute later, his brow furrowed, a small parcel in his hands.

He beckoned Draper to him first, and the two of them spoke, their heads bent close together. Before long, Tancrede led the Turcopole back to Landry and Godfrey. Despite the failing light, Landry could see that both were troubled.

"What's happened?" Godfrey asked, as they halted in front of him.

"Has either of you taken any of the food?" Tancrede asked. He kept his voice low. His gaze traveled the ship.

Godfrey shook his head. "I haven't."

All of them turned to Landry.

"For much of the day, I couldn't bring myself to think about eating. But I did have the fruit Draper brought me."

"Yes, we've accounted for that," Tancrede said. "And I should have been more specific. I meant last night, before the storm."

Godfrey put up a hand, forestalling Landry's response. "What is this about?"

"When I went to retrieve the food I bought yesterday, I found a good deal less than I had expected. I know that Draper has taken several figs and apricots today, to help those suffering from the storm. But even so, there should have been more."

"You told me yesterday that you hadn't gotten much," Godfrey said. "That was why you had to ration last night's meal."

"I know that. But those rations could have lasted us for days. Long enough, certainly, to sustain us until we made landfall again."

A shiver went through Landry.

"And now?" Godfrey asked in a flat voice.

Tancrede gave a small shake of his head. "Now, I'd say we barely have enough to last through tomorrow."

Adelina watches the knights, panic rising in her chest until she struggles to draw breath. She cannot hear a word of what they're saying, but she knows they are talking about the food. She seeks out Egan with her eyes, finds him standing with Gawain and another man. They talk as well. Egan and the other man laugh at something. The knight doesn't, but he is always serious. None of the three seems aware of the conversation taking place among Godfrey, Landry, and the others.

She remains where she is, but continues to watch Egan, hoping to catch his eye. What are they to say if the knights ask about the food? What will he tell them?

"How are you feeling, my sweet?"

She whirls toward her father, wide-eyed, the way she might if caught in a lie.

His eyebrows go up and he grins. "I didn't mean to startle you."

"No, you didn't. I'm just—" She breaks off. He has asked how she's feeling, because earlier the up-and-down of the ship had made her quite ill. "I feel fine now," she says. "Thank you."

"I believe the knights intend to distribute some food in a short while. Are you well enough to eat?"

She cannot imagine ever eating again. Not because of how awful she felt earlier in the day, though that was very bad. But rather because of the guilt that has gnawed at her innards since the previous night. Even after the ordeal of the storm, she cannot get the taste of smoked meat off her tongue.

"I—I don't know. Maybe."

"All right," her father says. But she sees his concern in the lines around his mouth, the wrinkling of his forehead.

Landry lights the first torch, bathing the deck in warm light. Godfrey lights another. Tancrede steps forward to face the rest of them.

"Gather closer please," he says, motioning for all the passengers to join the Templars.

Adelina's father takes her hand and leads her forward with the others. She is shaking; she fears her legs won't support her. Again, she stares at Egan. Still he ignores her.

When they are all arrayed in front of the Templar, he says, "I am afraid I must share with you some disturbing news. Within the past day someone on this ship has stolen a large portion of our provisions. Much of the food I procured yesterday in the village has gone missing. Stores that should have lasted us for days now will likely run out tomorrow. The next day at the latest."

Silence. No one speaks. People regard each other with suspicion, even hostility. For a third time, Adelina faces Egan. He glances her way and their eyes meet. Then he looks forward again. His expression has not changed.

"I would know who has done this," Godfrey says, setting himself in front of Tancrede. His voice is like a hammer on stone. Adelina flinches at the sound of it. "Whoever has taken this food for him or herself has done so at the expense of every other person on the vessel. All will suffer for your deception, your gluttony, your selfishness. You cannot hide from God's judgment, and I will not tolerate your attempt to hide from us. Now, identify yourself."

No one speaks. Seconds stretch. Adelina's stomach knots like wet rope.

"None of us will eat, none will be allowed to retire for sleep, until the culprit steps forward. Of that you can be certain."

Nothing. Adelina looks at Egan again. He is already watching her. Guilt curves her shoulders. Bile rises in her throat. She cannot remain silent any longer.

"It was the child!" Egan points at her, his face distorted. One might think his accusation has caused him immeasurable grief. "I saw her last night, when the rest of us were abed."

"Adelina!" Her father stares down at her, clearly horrified.

"It's not true," she says.

"You saw her and yet you did not stop her?" Godfrey demands of the man.

"She's a child, a wisp of a thing. How much could she eat? That's what I thought to myself. She will have a few morsels and fall back asleep. We all see how thin she's grown. It never occurred to me that she could endanger the ship."

"You're lying!" she says, finding her voice. Her cheeks are aflame, and she is trembling even worse than before. But at least she can speak. "It wasn't me! It was you!"

He cants his head to one side, gives a frown that somehow conveys both disappointment and regret. She is furious and frightened and scared. She has never known an adult to lie with such ease, nor has she ever imagined that she would be the victim of such a man.

"Please, child," he says. "Do you deny that you ate anything at all last night, when the rest were sleeping?"

"Well—" She gasps for breath, eyes searching for a sympathetic face. But all the adults glare at her. Every one of them, including her father. None of them believes her. "Yes," she says, "I ate half a strip of smoked meat. You gave it to me after I woke up and saw you eating the food."

"More was taken than a strip of meat," Godfrey says, his saturnine gaze fixed on her.

"I know!" she points at Egan. "I woke up and he was eating. He saw me watching him and gave me some meat. He said it would be our secret."

"Why didn't you say something sooner?" Godfrey asks. "You would have known this was wrong. Why wait until now to say something?"

She drops her gaze, tears leaking from the corners of her eyes. One falls to the wood at her feet. Then another. "I was scared," she says, her voice hushed. "I—I thought I would get in trouble."

"Adelina," her father says again. He squats before her, forcing her to look at him. "I'm very disappointed in you."

"It wasn't me, Papa." The words are thick in her mouth. She can't stop crying. "It was him. I promise. I swear to—"

"Don't!"

She cringes back from a raised, rigid finger.

"Do not invoke God with lies! You know better than that. I taught you better, and so did your mother!"

Another sob escapes her. She spins away from him, eludes his attempt to grab her arm, and weaves through the rest of them to the passage leading down into the hold. The air below stinks of sweat and sick, but she doesn't care. All she wants is to be away from Egan and her father, and the rest of them. They think her a liar and a thief, and nothing she can say will convince them otherwise. Because she is both. Egan is worse. She knows that, even if they do not. But it doesn't matter what he has done. She shouldn't have eaten that meat. She shouldn't have allowed him to steal from the rest of them. She may not be guilty of all they believe, but she is guilty enough. She throws herself onto the blanket that serves as her bed, and she cries.

The girl's father gazed after her, shame, anger, and grief chasing one another across his features. Fearful as he was about the food they had lost, Tancrede sympathized with the man.

He remembered the look of disappointment on the child's face the night before, when she saw how little he could give her to eat. And, like Egan, he had noted several times in recent days how pinched she looked, how thin her limbs had grown. It didn't surprise him that she had acted on her hunger and her dissatisfaction with last night's meal.

And yet...

"What will you do with her?" Simon asked, lifting his chin and meeting Godfrey's glower.

"She is a child," the commander said, his voice tight. "We will not punish her."

"She stole from all of us!" said one of the older women. "We might starve because of her!"

A few others nodded their agreement.

"She was hungry," Tancrede said. "Who among us didn't make mistakes in our youth?"

"I will speak with her," Simon told them. "And I will make whatever restitution I can on her behalf." To Egan, he said, "I apologize for her behavior and her words against you. I know you were trying to protect her."

"Think nothing of it," the man said, with more generosity than most would have mustered under similar circumstances.

Again, Tancrede felt doubt crowding in.

Simon nodded to Egan, stepped to the hatch, and went below.

"We will distribute food shortly," Godfrey said, the words carrying. "Thank you all for your patience."

He turned away from the passengers, sent a grave look Tancrede's way, and retreated to the aft rail.

The passengers lingered on the deck, speaking among themselves. Egan kept to himself. He glanced at Tancrede, but wouldn't hold his gaze for long.

"An unfortunate turn of events," Landry said softly, sidling closer to him.

Tancrede nodded. "Indeed."

Gawain limped back to join them. "Poor child," he said, also keeping his voice low. "I cannot say that I blame her."

"What do you make of the man she accused?" Tancrede asked.

"Egan?" Gawain glanced back at him and shrugged. "I thought he was gracious with the father. And he proved himself useful earlier with the sail. Why?"

"No reason," Tancrede said. "Simply asking."

Gawain frowned. "Come now, brother. I don't believe that for a minute."

DAVID B. COE

"Just how much food was taken?" Landry asked, before Tancrede could reply.

Tancrede thought it an apt question.

"A lot," he said.

"More than a child could have eaten?"

"Egan said it himself: she's a wisp of a thing. How much could she eat?"

"Hungry as we all have been?" Gawain said. "She could have eaten a good deal. For that matter, any of us could have."

"You didn't see how much food was taken, brother," Tancrede said. "I did. It was enough to sicken the girl had she eaten it all herself. Egan, on the other hand..."

Gawain narrowed his eyes. "You doubt him?"

"I don't know what I believe," Tancrede said. "He was quick to make the accusation. Too quick, some might say."

"The girl admits that she ate some of the food."

Landry rounded on Gawain. "Yes, she does, which is more than Egan has done. She confesses to some wrongdoing, and that makes me more inclined to believe her denials."

"That makes no sense," Gawain said, throwing his arms wide.

Some on the deck looked their way, including Egan.

"Keep your voice down," Tancrede whispered.

Gawain leaned in closer. "The child's own father accepts that she is guilty," he said, lowering his voice as well. "If he believes she stole the food, why shouldn't we?"

"The father was humiliated," Landry said. "She stole. She hid that fact for most of the day. She admits this. Every person on board is in greater peril because food was taken. How could he not be ashamed? In such a position, how could he argue for her innocence?"

"What are the three of you discussing?" Godfrey asked, joining their circle. "And why have you not yet given out some food? It grows late."

Tancrede looked to Landry, who dipped his chin.

"We believe the girl might have been telling the truth."

"All three of you?"

Gawain's mouth twitched. He looked off to the side.

"Landry and me," Tancrede said.

"And does it matter that her father disagrees with you?"

To his credit, Landry did not flinch from the commander's glare. "Not really, no."

Godfrey appeared to consider this. "All right. How do you wish to proceed?"

"I want to speak with her," Tancrede said. "Below, without an audience."

"Of course, you're welcome do so. But I would be surprised if she told you anything different from what she said here a few minutes ago."

Tancrede took the measure of Egan again. The man still kept to himself. "I'd be surprised, too. That may be the point."

CHAPTER 5

Her father comes down into the hold and sits beside her. When he first arrives, Adelina expects that he will berate her. Instead, he merely strokes her hair and whispers words of comfort. She cannot stop crying. She cannot forgive him for believing Egan's denials over her own. But he loves her still, and this comes as a great relief.

She hears footsteps above them, and then on the worn wooden stairs leading below.

"May we speak with you?"

Adelina opens her eyes, sees through a blur of tears that two of the knights have come. Landry and Tancrede.

"Yes, of course," her father says.

"Forgive us, Simon," Landry says. "We wish to speak with your daughter."

Her father moves closer to her. "Sir Godfrey said she would not be punished."

"And so she will not be. But we wish a word with her. You may remain if you like, or you can leave us briefly. I assure you, no harm will come to her."

"I don't—"

"It's all right, Papa." Her voice quavers. She sniffs, wipes her eyes, and sits up. "I want to speak with them. Alone. I promise to tell them the truth."

Her father scowls, clearly hating this idea.

"Simon," Tancrede says, "she will be safe with us. You know this. And as you say, she has already been spared punishment. We merely wish to learn more about what precisely happened last night."

Her pulse quickens. Do they believe her? Is that why they have come?

"Please, Papa. Let me talk to them."

He lets out a long breath, stands. "I'll be right over here," he says, walking to the stairs.

Landry and Tancrede sit before her, both solemn. She crosses her arms over her chest.

"You know that it is a sin to lie, yes?" Tancrede says.

She nods.

"In your religion as well as ours."

"I know that."

"Good. Earlier you said—"

"Everything I said up there was true," she tells him, eyes locked on his. "I stole. Egan offered me a piece of meat, and I took it, because I was very hungry." Fresh tears run from her eyes and she swipes at them with an impatient hand. "But he gave it to me because I saw him stealing food, cheese as well as the meat. I don't know what else he took. But he was going through the food. That's what woke me up. He saw me watching him and told me how hungry he was and then brought the meat over to me and gave me half. He said it would be our secret. Neither of us would tell anyone." More tears fall onto her lap, but she ignores them.

"I know no one believes me because I'm a girl and he's an adult, but that's what happened. I swear it before God." Saying this, she chances a look at her father. He watches them from the stairs. She can't tell if he can hear what they've said.

"Why didn't you tell anyone what had happened?" Landry asks.

She wants to shy away from his appraising gaze, but she makes herself face him, and allows her tears to fall. "Because what I did was wrong, and I didn't want to get in trouble. I knew my father would be shamed."

"Did Egan threaten you? Did he say he would hurt you if you told us what really happened?"

Saying he had done these things might convince them. It would certainly excuse her silence in the day since Egan ate the food. But thus far, her lies have only made matters worse. More, she has promised her father that she will tell them the truth.

She shakes her head. "He didn't threaten me at all. He gave me food. That was how he made sure I wouldn't tell."

The knights glance at each other. After a moment, Landry nods.

"We believe you," he says, facing her again.

Adelina blinks. "You do? Truly?"

He grins. "Shouldn't we?"

She cannot help but smile in response. Her heart lightens, gratitude to these men overwhelming her. This feeling is better than any food she has ever tasted.

"What you did was wrong, Adelina. You saw someone stealing from all of us, making life more difficult for all of us, and you did nothing to stop him. Indeed, you partook of his pillage, which is even worse."

"I know. I'm very sorry."

"I believe you are." Tancrede stands and calls to her father.

He hurries back to them, appearing frightened. "What did she tell you?"

"She told us what happened," Landry says, standing as well. "And we believe her."

Puzzlement creases her father's forehead. "I don't understand."

"We think that Egan did steal the missing food. He gave Adelina a morsel to buy her silence, just as she told us earlier."

"You're sure of this?"

"A lot of food was taken, Simon," Tancrede says. "More, I believe, than Adelina alone could have eaten."

Her father shakes his head. "I wanted to believe her, but that man…" His expression hardens. One of his hands closes into a tight fist, and his dark eyes, normally so gentle, turn flinty. She has seen him angry many times before, but never like this. "*He* stole the food? And he was willing to let the blame fall on my daughter?"

"I'm afraid that's—"

Landry has time for no more than that. Her father tries to push past the knights, his hand on the hilt of the knife he carries on his belt.

Tancrede grabs his arm and pulls him back. "Simon, no!"

Her father struggles to break free. Landry helps Tancrede restrain him, and Adelina starts to cry again.

"I'll cut his throat!" her father says, snarling the words.

"No, you won't!" Tancrede says. "Leave this to us. We'll speak with Godfrey, and if we can ascertain the truth of what happened, he will administer justice. You have our word on that."

"What is that justice likely to be? A reprimand? Loss of one night's rations? If he did these things – if he ate our food and blamed Adelina for his crime – he deserves to be punished!"

"Trust us, Simon. Please."

After another few seconds, her father relents, ceasing his struggles and heaving a breath. He raises his hands for the knights to see. They release him.

"Forgive me," he says.

"We understand," Landry tells him. "But you should probably remain below while we speak to Egan."

"No. That I will not do. You want me to forego my own vengeance, and I will. I appreciate the sense in that. But I will have the satisfaction of seeing him confronted with his crimes." He puts an arm on Adelina's shoulder, and draws her to him. "We both will."

The Templars weigh this in silence. Eventually, Tancrede opens his hands in acquiescence. They start up the stairway to the deck, allowing Adelina and her father to follow them. But as they climb, Adelina sees her father touch his hand to the hilt of his blade once more.

A step behind Tancrede, Landry was conscious of Simon seething below him.

"I don't like this," he muttered, so that only his fellow knight could hear.

"Neither do I, but we haven't the authority to confine them to the hold. Besides, if it was my daughter, I'd want to see the man confronted as well."

Landry knew it would have been fruitless to argue, even if he hadn't felt the same way.

They went to Godfrey first. He stood at the rudder, seeming lost in thought. Draper and Gawain were deep in conversation nearby.

As they approached the commander, he roused himself. "Well?"

"The girl is telling the truth," Tancrede said. "I'm certain of it."

Landry nodded. "We both are."

He looked back, expecting to find Simon and Adelina with them. But the man and his daughter lingered by the hatch. Simon glared at Egan, who remained near the starboard rail, watching them all, wary and alert.

"How can you be so sure?" Gawain asked, coming to stand with them. "Is she so much more convincing than Egan?"

"Actually, yes." Tancrede addressed Godfrey again. "We have no proof beyond the amount of food that was taken, and the truth we heard in the girl's words, but I would stake my life on this. She's not innocent. She doesn't claim to be. But this was Egan's crime. She happened to witness it, and that is why he shared his bounty with her. I believe that's the only reason."

"You agree?" Godfrey said to Landry.

"I do."

"Very well. How should we proceed?"

Tancrede shook his head. "I don't know. But we should act quickly, and I believe we should mete out some punishment. If we don't, Simon is likely to take matters into his own hands."

"Not that I would blame him," Landry added.

Godfrey sent a dark look his way. "We will not act out of vengeance, or allow anyone else to do so. That is not justice, nor is it our way." He stared past them toward Egan. "But let's speak to him. The three of us, I think. Gawain, Draper, remain here. Keep an eye on the father."

"Of course," Draper said.

Godfrey, Tancrede, and Landry made their way to Egan. As they passed Simon and Adelina, Landry offered what he hoped would be a reassuring smile. Simon appeared unmoved.

The other passengers cleared out of their way, opening a space in the area near Egan. For his part, the man remained where he was. Landry saw that he carried a knife on his belt, but he kept his hands at his sides.

"What is this?" he asked, eyes skipping from one of them to the next.

"We have questions for you," Godfrey said. He nodded to Tancrede.

"Tell us again what you saw the girl do," Tancrede said.

Egan shrugged. "She was eating. She found the food you bought, and she ate as much of it as she could. I know she's small, but you should have seen her. I didn't want to say as much before – young as she is – but she was shoving food into her mouth. Handfuls of it."

"I thought you said you didn't worry about her eating too much," Landry said. "'A wisp of a thing,' you called her. You said that you let her eat because you thought she wouldn't take too much. That was a lie?"

"Well, no—"

"So, you're lying now."

"No, I'm not. She took a few handfuls, and I thought that would be enough for her. But... But she must have taken more."

"She claims it was you," Tancrede said. "She woke up to the sound of you moving about in the hold. When you saw that she was awake, you gave her a bit of meat to keep her from waking the others."

His bark of laughter sounded forced. "Well, of course she said that. What would she say? I caught her with her hand in the bag, and she knows it."

"So you didn't eat any of the food at all?"

"No! I've told you what happened. Her father believes me, as do the others. Why won't you?"

"No, her father doesn't believe you," came another voice.

Landry looked back. Simon stood directly behind him, knife in hand.

"Simon, this is not your fight," Landry said. "Go back to Adelina. We'll handle this."

"Not my fight? If not mine, then whose?"

Egan sneered. "I don't believe this," he said, eyeing each of the knights in turn. "You would believe her over me? A Jew girl over a Christian? Do those crosses on your chests mean nothing to you?"

Landry took a step toward the man, rage speeding his pulse. "This has nothing to do with their faith!"

"Of course it does," Tancrede said.

Landry pivoted toward his fellow Templar. "What?"

Tancrede's glare never wavered. "It has everything to do with faith. We know that Adelina has told the truth, because she swore to her God. We take her explanation on faith, because we sense the truth of it. There is holiness in a confession given freely, without evasion, and with God's forgiveness, which comes to those who acknowledge their sins." Distaste contorted his expression. "In the same way, there is evil in lies, in false witness. And just to be clear, you, sir, are no Christian."

Egan drew himself up, raised his chin. "I don't have to listen to this."

"No, you don't. You're free to swim back to Cyprus."

Landry stifled a laugh, which came out as an undignified snort.

"I will not be ridiculed!"

"If that is the punishment we choose for you," Godfrey said, "then yes, you will be."

"They're Jews!" Egan said, shouting the words as he pointed at Adelina and her father. The tendons in his neck bulged. "You would dare punish me and do nothing to her?"

Simon pushed Landry aside and attempted to lunge for Egan, leading with his blade. But Landry was bigger than Simon, and stronger, and despite the ache in his shoulder, he caught the man around the waist and wrestled him back.

Egan retreated a step, hands raised to ward himself. "You see? They're animals! You can't trust them!"

"I'll kill you, you lying bastard!" Simon bellowed, still struggling to break free.

Landry had half a mind to let him go. It seemed Tancrede's thoughts ran in a similar direction.

"Perhaps we should allow Simon to do as he pleases," said the lean knight, eyeing Egan critically.

Egan's cheeks blanched. "What do you mean?"

"Administering justice at sea is no easy matter," Tancrede said, more to Godfrey than to Egan. "This is why a ship's captain is generally accorded so much latitude. So perhaps it would make sense to allow the girl's father to choose a proper punishment for this one." He tipped his head in Egan's direction. "That strikes me as just."

Simon ceased his struggles. He was breathing hard, but he glanced at Landry. "Forgive me," he whispered for the second time that evening.

Landry released him. "Of course."

"I would be happy to administer justice," Simon said, raising his voice so the others could hear.

"No!" Egan wet his lips. "I mean, I've done nothing. You can prove nothing."

"That's true," Godfrey said. "Perhaps a duel is in order. A contest before God. Surely the just party would prevail."

Simon gave a decisive nod. "Gladly."

"No," Egan said again, just as quickly. "You—you can see the man is crazed with rage. It wouldn't be a fair test of honor."

"I believe it would," Godfrey said. To Tancrede, he added, "A fine idea, Brother Tancrede. You have our thanks."

Simon brandished his knife and advanced on the man. Egan backed away. He grabbed for his own weapon and fumbled it. It clattered to the deck and he dove to retrieve it. Scrambling to his feet again, he held the knife before him, his hand shaking violently.

"To the death?" Godfrey asked.

Tancrede lifted a shoulder. "Naturally."

Egan's gaze bounced between the knights and Simon, who continued to stalk him. "No, wait!"

"Perhaps you wish to make restitution in some way?" Godfrey asked.

"Yes! That's it!" Still he fell back, pursued by the girl's father.

"You would first have to admit your guilt, confess to all on this vessel that you lied about Adelina, and that it was you who stole the food, you who gave her the small bite she had to eat."

"Yes, fine! I confess it! Now call him off!"

"Say it now."

"I stole the food. It was like she said. She woke up and saw me. I gave her the meat to keep her silent!"

"Good. You must also agree to give us whatever valuables you have with you, so that we might, at the next opportunity, buy provisions to replace those you took from us."

Simon was almost on him now. He lashed out with the toe of his boot, catching Egan's wrist. The man's weapon flew from his hand, bounced against the ship's hull, and slid to the base of the rail.

"Anything! Just tell him to stop!"

Simon seized Egan by the collar and hauled him to his feet.

"Simon, hold."

The girl's father paused to glance back at Tancrede. He was no longer beyond reason, as he had been earlier, but Landry read a plea in the man's eyes. If the Templars allowed it, he would slay Egan without a second thought.

"Please," Tancrede said. "You don't want his blood on your hands, nor on Adelina's. He has confessed. All now know that she didn't do this thing."

"He wouldn't have admitted it," Simon said. "He would have been content to see her punished in his stead."

"Yes, and he will answer to God for that. Do not debase yourself for a man like him. Leave him to wallow in his misery."

Simon faced the thief again, one fist knotted in Egan's shirt, the fingers of his other hand tight on the hilt of his weapon. He stood thus for several seconds. All on the ship were silent. The only sounds were the taps of swells on the hull and the creaks of wood and rope.

At last, Simon thrust the man away. Egan fell to the deck, landing on his back with a thud and the *whoosh* of expelled air. He looked to the side, toward his lost knife. Simon stepped to the weapon in two quick strides, scooped it up, and pocketed it.

"An initial payment, earnest of your restitution," he said, and walked away.

Landry stepped past him in the opposite direction and the two exchanged nods. Reaching Egan, Landry pulled the man to his feet none too gently.

"I want to make myself very clear," he said. "You live by Simon's forbearance. If any harm comes to him, or to his daughter – if either of them suffers so much as a scratch between now and when next we make land and can rid ourselves of you – I will hold you accountable, and you will answer to my sword. Do I make my meaning clear?"

Egan's brows knitted, but he lifted a shoulder in what might have been acquiescence.

"I can't hear you."

"Yes," the man said, sounding sullen. "I understand."

"Good. Now get out of my sight."

KNIGHTFALL: THE INFINITE DEEP

Landry released him. Egan straightened his shirt and met the glares of the rest of the men and women on the ship's deck. Finally, he walked with as much dignity as he could muster to the hatch. He passed Simon and Adelina without saying a word or acknowledging them in any way, and descended into the hold.

Once he was gone, conversations sprouted all over the ship. Simon and Adelina kept to themselves. Simon lifted the girl into his arms and spoke to her in a whisper. Adelina buried her face against his neck and appeared to be crying. Landry and the other Templars allowed them their privacy.

Tancrede distributed rations from the food they had remaining, seeing to the Templars' needs last. Landry received a piece of root and some smoked meat, maybe three bites in all. It did little to satisfy his hunger, but of course he kept his complaints to himself.

When Tancrede finished handing out food, he stowed what remained near the rudder and rejoined the other Templars.

"We should return to sweeps. A few of us, at least. The sooner we make land, the sooner we can replenish our stores."

Godfrey shook his head. "I want all of you to get some sleep. After the storm and all that's happened since, we need rest most of all. We'll do no one any good if we're too exhausted to care for those in our charge. We can take up the oars again come dawn."

"But—"

"That is an order, Tancrede. Go. Sleep. More than any of us, you've earned it."

"Very well." Mischief glinted in his eyes. "But

when I awake, I intend to tell you just how much I disapprove of this command."

The other Templars grinned.

"The rest of you go as well," Godfrey said. "I'll take the first watch."

"No, I will," Landry said. "I'm not tired, and I won't be able to sleep."

Godfrey's small frown conveyed concern.

Landry made himself smile. "Too much excitement."

"Very well. Wake me in a couple of hours."

Landry settled himself along the rail near the ship's prow, away from the torches, where he could see stars shining in an ebon sky. The other passengers didn't retire immediately, and for some time whispered conversations continued in pockets along the deck. But none who remained awake approached Landry, and he was content in his solitude.

He was wearier than he had admitted to Godfrey, but he needed time to ponder the evening's events. He admired Tancrede and Godfrey for finding a resolution to the conflict that exonerated Adelina, punished Egan, and shed not a drop of blood. He was forced to wonder if he would have been capable of doing the same.

Egan struck him as the worst sort of villain: gluttonous, greedy, cowardly, and uncaring as to who might suffer for his sins. Landry would not have faulted Simon had he chosen to kill the man.

A part of him questioned whether it was just that Egan should pay so modest a price for what he had done. The man seemed to have no conscience. He would not bear the burden of his own guilt. Not as Adelina did for her own small transgression.

Yet, he also understood that Simon would have had to cope with guilt of his own had he taken Egan's life. Perhaps not immediately, but soon and for years after. Youthful though he was, Landry already had too much experience with meting out blood and death. He understood all too well the burdens they imposed. Tancrede had done Simon a favor by staying his hand.

Landry saw this now, but it had taken him some time to reach this understanding. Tancrede and Godfrey had gotten there well ahead of him. He wondered if Draper and Gawain had, too. Still, he took some consolation in grasping these truths at all. Perhaps, he thought, this marked the first stirrings of wisdom, the initial steps along a lengthy path.

He surveyed the sea, listened for sounds of any approaching vessels. Seeing and hearing no threats, he turned his gaze to the setting half-moon and waited for the passengers around him to descend into the hold or bed down on the deck. His stomach rumbled, and he allowed himself a rueful smile. He doubted that even Egan's closest friends on this ship, whoever they might be, would extend much charity to the man this night.

Landry woke Godfrey sometime later, and lay down between blankets on the deck. He slipped into a deep sleep, and might have remained that way well into the morning had a sharp word from Draper not roused him soon after sunrise.

Gawain and Godfrey were already with the Turcopole. All three of them stood facing the east, hands raised to shield their eyes from the sun.

Looking that way himself, Landry spotted a ship. Even from far away, he could tell that she was a good deal larger than theirs. More, she had three masts, all of them whole, and she was headed in their direction. Judging from the way her prow cut through the swells, it appeared she was moving at speed.

"Wake Tancrede," Godfrey said to Draper. "I would have preferred to let him sleep, but we require his seafaring knowledge."

Draper went below. Landry made his way to where his Templar brothers stood.

The Turcopole returned moments later with Tancrede in tow. Tancrede's auburn hair was awry, and his eyes were puffy. He looked exhausted. But his voice was crisp as he said, "We need as many people on sweeps as possible. Now." He cast a glance Godfrey's way. "You shouldn't have let me sleep so long."

"The ship only just appeared on the horizon. We woke you as soon as we perceived the threat."

Awakened no doubt by the noise above, several of the passengers emerged from the hold, Simon and Adelina among them. All reacted with alarm at the presence of the other vessel. Egan followed the others into the morning light. Rings like bruises darkened the skin beneath his eyes. He kept to himself, and none of the others deigned to speak with him.

The Templars, with the exceptions of Tancrede and Landry, went below and began to row. Several of the passengers joined them. But despite their efforts, their vessel felt sluggish and vulnerable. They needed to harness the same wind used by the other vessel. Without it, they would soon be overtaken.

"We have nothing for them to steal," Nila said. She

faced the Templars, a plea in her eyes. She wanted to be convinced of this. "They can board us, but what could they possibly take?"

Tancrede and Landry locked gazes for a second.

"They could be slavers," Tancrede said, the words wrung from him. "There's gold to be made taking men and women – and yes, even children – from a vessel such as ours."

Landry did not look at Simon and his child, having no desire to alarm them more than necessary. But others were less discreet. Simon spoke to Adelina in low, soothing tones. What reassurances could he offer her, though?

"If there are enough of them," Tancrede went on, "and they have skill with weapons, the nine of us might not be enough to protect you."

"Then what can we do?" Nila asked.

"We can remain on sweeps for as long as we have to," Landry said. "And we can pray to God that we reach some form of land before they reach us."

He looked back at the other ship. Already it was closer. They couldn't outrun it with so few oars. He cursed his injury, wishing he could row. But he knew that numbers hindered them more than anything else. He could have replaced any of those currently rowing, and it would have made little difference. There had to be some other way to evade capture.

The other passengers marked the approach of the ship with apprehension. Adelina clung to Simon, who stroked her hair, saying nothing.

Tancrede eyed the other vessel and frowned, his hand still on the rudder. "I don't like having the others on sweeps," he said. "If it comes to a fight, it would be better if most of us weren't exhausted from rowing."

"Is there anything we can do with the sail?" Landry asked. "Might we tie it to the prow in some fashion? Anything that might allow it to catch some of this wind."

Tancrede considered the sky, and then the front of the ship. "Given some time, I might be able to figure out something. But not while we're being pursued. For now, loath as I am to admit it, the oars are our best option."

"They can keep rowing," Landry said. "And you can tie the rudder in place. But maybe together, you and I can find another way."

Before Tancrede could answer, cries went up from the front of the vessel.

"What now?" Tancrede muttered.

Landry and Tancrede hurried to the prow. Landry's heart sank at what he saw there.

A second ship loomed before them. Also distant, and tacking at an oblique angle to their line. But Landry felt certain that those on this second vessel had spotted theirs.

Tancrede seemed to assume the same. He ran back to the rudder, and turned their ship, angling it away from both vessels.

"We can't outrun them both," he said, as if answering a question. "I'm open to suggestions."

Simon gazed at one ship, and then the other. "Do you think they're working together?"

"I would be surprised."

Landry agreed. The sails of the first ship each bore a black sword, the blade tip colored red. The sails of the second vessel were plain white.

"That could work to our advantage."

"Let them fight each other for the spoils," Landry said, "and in the meantime, we slip away."

"Something like that, yes."

"That will work for a time," Tancrede said. "But eventually one will prevail, and we'll face the same problem we had when it was just the one ship after us: we're hobbled, and they're not."

"Both ships might be, if they battle each other first."

"You're leaving a lot to good fortune."

"I believe we're due for some," Landry said. "Don't you agree?"

"I'm pretty certain it's not my decision to make," Tancrede said. "But yes, if the Lord were to welcome my thoughts on the matter, then I would say we're due for a good deal of luck right about now."

"Agreed," Landry said. "So, let's see if we can't create some good fortune of our own."

CHAPTER 6

Tancrede steered them to the east, off the lines of both pursuing ships. At least at first. It didn't take long for the other vessels to correct their courses and give chase.

Simon took Godfrey's place below, and the commander joined Landry and Tancrede on the deck.

"At least now we know that both ships are following us," Tancrede said, his tone as dry as dust.

Landry found three longbows and two dozen arrows in a back corner of the hold. These he gave to Tancrede and the commander. He believed himself a competent archer, but with his shoulder still on the mend, he hadn't the strength to draw a bowstring. Rather than keeping the third for himself, he called Gawain onto the deck. One of the women, Irène, took his place on sweeps.

Aside from the Templars, no one on the ship carried a sword. If the *Tern* was boarded, and they were forced to fight hand-to-hand, their passengers would be armed only with short blades. If that. Landry didn't give them much chance of surviving an encounter with either ship. A life of bondage was the best they could hope for.

By the time the sun had climbed directly overhead, both vessels were close enough that Landry could make out the features of some of those aboard. The ships were galleys, built for war. They were a good deal longer and sleeker than the *Tern*. Each was rigged with three sails, and long rows of oar holes on either side. The prow of the first ship, the sails of which were marked with those blood-tipped swords, had been carved to resemble a dragon, its neck reared back, like that of a snake ready to strike. The prow of the second had been fashioned after a sea eagle, the head carved to appear feathered, the beak broad and hooked. Both vessels cut impressive lines. A rounded merchant vessel like the *Tern* couldn't possibly outrun either ship. Given that they were forced to rely on oarsmen, they should have been boarded already. That they hadn't been was testament to Tancrede's skill at the rudder.

The first ship had been riding a direct wind and so was the nearer of the two. The second vessel had been forced to tack a crooked course in their direction. Yet, it wasn't far off.

"That second captain knows what he's about," Tancrede said, as he gauged the ships' positions. Landry heard grudging respect in his voice.

Gawain scowled. "Too bad for him that by the time he reaches us, he'll have nothing to do but pick over our bones."

"None of that," Godfrey said. "Good fortune, remember?"

Gawain's expression didn't change.

As they watched, the second vessel furled its sails and went to oars – at least thirty of them on each side. With the Mediterranean relatively calm, the ship actually gained speed, and followed a more direct course toward the *Tern* and the other ship.

"She'll be more maneuverable now," Tancrede said. "That other ship might have no choice but to go to sweeps as well."

"Why did they wait to do that?" Landry asked.

His friend shrugged. "It would have been a long voyage on oars, and they want to be able to fight when they reach us."

As the first ship bore down on them, bowmen took up positions along its starboard rail.

"Get everyone below!" Tancrede shouted. "Now!"

Those passengers who had lingered on the deck to monitor the progress of the ships rushed to the hatch, pushing and shoving in their desperation to take cover.

The vessel remained too far away for their archers, but in another minute or two, Landry and the other Templars would need to take cover. He retrieved his battle shield, strode to the rear of the ship, and positioned himself near Tancrede.

"What are you doing?"

"Guarding you, of course. What do you think?"

"I think I want a guard whose shoulder works."

Landry stared at him, then burst out laughing. Gawain glowered at them both. Godfrey frowned as well.

"In all seriousness, Landry," Tancrede said, "I don't want you risking your life to save mine."

"Without you, we're dead. It is that simple. So, yes, I will risk my life to protect you. What choice do I have?"

"I think they mean to ram us," Godfrey said from near the fore of the *Tern*.

It took Landry a moment to realize he referred to the second ship. But the commander was right. The second galley had closed the distance to their ship with alarming speed, and it appeared to be on a collision course.

"Is there anything we can do?" Landry asked.

Tancrede pulled hard on the rudder, turning the ship so abruptly that the rhythm of the rowers was broken. But even at her best, a small vessel like the *Tern* couldn't change direction immediately.

"She'll obliterate us," Tancrede said, keeping his voice down so that only Landry could hear. "A ship that size, at that speed... Brace yourselves!" he called to the others.

Anticipating assaults from both vessels, Landry grabbed hold of the rail with one hand, and readied his shield with the other.

But the second ship did not ram them. Rather, it slid by on the *Tern*'s port side and interposed itself between the Templars' ship and the other vessel. Bowmen rushed to the port side of this second vessel and without pause loosed a volley of arrows at the first ship.

Landry would have guessed that they were beyond range, but their arrows rained down on the first vessel, felling their archers, drawing screams, slicing through the ship's sails. They sent another salvo at the vessel, and a third, eliciting more cries. By the time the second ship had passed between the *Tern* and the first, it appeared to Landry that most of the men on the other vessel's deck had been killed or wounded.

Still, the second vessel wasn't done. Its oarsmen turned a tight circle and approached the first ship, drawing closer with this pass, but keeping it between the *Tern* and the other vessel. As it passed the galley, its sailors released another volley, this time of flaming arrows.

Some rained down on the deck. Others cut through the sail, and still others struck the ship's hull below the rails. Everywhere they hit, fires burned, blackening the wood. The sail was consumed by flame in mere moments, as if it were a dried leaf. Black smoke rose from the vessel. Men cried out and leapt overboard, some of them burning as well. As they flailed in the water, archers from the attacking ship finished them off with deadly precision.

As the ship continued to burn, an eerie silence settled over the scene, broken only by the pop and crackle of the burning hull. Landry heard no more cries, no more human sounds of any sort. The second vessel carved through the water, encircling the carcass of the first, perhaps searching for survivors. Landry had never imagined that one ship might conquer another with such ease. He thought this second vessel must be a pirate ship, or perhaps even a ship of war from some unknown country. Had the other vessel been an enemy, or a perceived rival for whatever spoils the *Tern* might offer?

The ship completed another orbit around the burning vessel before approaching the *Tern* once again and pulling abreast of her.

"What now?" Landry whispered.

"Well met, the *Gray Tern*," a man called from the aft deck of the other vessel. He was tall, broad in the shoulders and chest. Unruly black hair shifted in the wind, and a trim, dark beard lent a severe aspect to his angular face.

Tancrede looked to Landry and then Godfrey, and twitched a shoulder.

Godfrey responded with a shrug of his own. "Well met," he shouted in answer.

"Permission to board?"

Tancrede shook his head.

"We would have you state your business first."

Laughter greeted this, and not just from the one man.

"A brave response, given your complement of men, and the state of your vessel. But very well. We are the *Melitta*, a ship of fortune."

"Pirates," Tancrede said, exhaling the word.

"So," Godfrey called in answer, "when you ask permission to board—"

"A formality."

"At least he's an honest pirate," Gawain said.

"You have my word that no harm will come to any on your ship," the man went on. "But we did just save you all from an unpleasant fate, and we would speak with you before deciding on suitable compensation."

Godfrey nodded. "We would like to discuss this among ourselves first. With your permission, of course."

"Of course," the man said. He sounded amused.

Tancrede called below for those on sweeps to cease their efforts. At this point, further attempts at escape seemed pointless.

The *Tern* slowed. The other Templars climbed onto the deck. The passengers clamored to do the same, but at Godfrey's urging, they remained below.

The commander explained their situation as succinctly as possible, and in a voice meant to carry to those in the hold.

"If he wants the ship, it's his," Tancrede added when Godfrey was finished. "We can't stop him, and I have no desire to die trying. You saw what he did to that other ship. He has no reason to lie to us, and no reason to fear us. If he says he means us no harm, chances are he's telling the truth."

"Is this what you meant by good fortune?" Gawain asked, the irony in his words bordering on bitterness.

"Quite possibly, yes," Godfrey said. "Very well," he called to the *Melitta*. "Be welcome on our ship."

Before long, the *Melitta*'s oarsmen had steered their vessel close enough to the *Tern* to lash the ships together. Men set planks from the rails of the larger ship to those of the Templars' vessel. The bearded man, who Landry assumed was their captain, led a contingent of six bowmen and as many swordsmen onto the *Tern*. The captain approached Godfrey and sketched a bow.

"My name is Killias," he said. "I captain the *Melitta*."

"Godfrey. My pilot is Tancrede." He introduced the rest of the knights by name as well.

"Templars," the captain said, lifting his chin to indicate Godfrey's tabard.

"Yes."

"Shouldn't you be at war?"

Godfrey's eyes narrowed. "We were. Acre fell several weeks ago. We've been seeking a safe harbor ever since."

Killias nodded, seeming indifferent to events in the Holy Land, and at the same time surveyed the ship. "The storm do this?" he asked, waving a hand at the broken mast.

"Yes."

The captain faced Godfrey again. "You Templars are known for your wealth. So why do I have the feeling that you carry few riches on this ship?"

"We barely have food enough to last the day."

Killias gave a dry laugh. He walked the length of the deck, his boots clicking on the old wood. No one spoke a word. When he reached the stern, he exchanged nods with Tancrede and started back toward Godfrey. Landry watched the captain, and also kept track of his men, a hand on the hilt of his sword. As the pirate passed him, he glanced at the weapon and smirked. Landry bristled.

"Calm yourself, Templar. I meant what I said. None of you need come to harm."

He walked on, only halting when he reached Godfrey. He gestured toward the burning ship, which had started to sink. Smoke still billowed into an otherwise clear sky.

"Had you seen that ship before?"

"Never. We spotted her just after dawn and tried to outrun her."

"Folly. You never would have gotten away. She was the *Blood Dawn*, captained by a man named Tatius. We've had dealings with him. He's the sort who gives men of my profession a bad reputation. Without our intervention, you would have been attacked, boarded, plundered. Do you carry passengers?"

Godfrey didn't answer straight away. Clearly, he wasn't yet ready to trust the man. But after a pause, he said, "Yes. They're below."

"Women, children?"

"Several women. One child."

"Well, when you Templars and the rest of the men

on board were dead, the women and the child would have been taken, used most foully, and sold into servitude at the first opportunity."

"If we could pay you, we would."

"Your swords might have some value. Your armor as well."

Landry tensed. He sensed that Gawain and Draper had done the same.

"We can't part with those."

For a moment that seemed to stretch on perilously, Godfrey and Killias stared at one another. At last the pirate smiled.

"No, I don't suppose you can. To be honest, I wasn't trying to extract any sort of reward. This is my way of telling you that I'm glad the bloody bastard is dead. I would have killed him and destroyed his ship even if you hadn't been here in need of aid."

Killias wandered as he spoke, ending his peregrinations at the base of the broken mast, which he studied with some interest.

"But we were in need," Godfrey said. "We still are."

The captain looked up from the shattered wood. "Yes. An interesting circumstance. You tell me you are low on provisions, without riches, and I believe you. But you have access to wealth. Were we to offer aid – food perhaps, and passage to that safe harbor of which you spoke – might we be rewarded in time?"

Godfrey paused, seeming to choose his words with care. "You understand, our Order is vast, and I am a mere soldier. I have little influence, and less control over whatever wealth the Templars might possess. But I can make recommendations, put in a good word with those who wield more power than I."

Killias responded with another smirk. "Do all knights of your order sound like that when they speak of gold?"

"Like what?"

"Mealy-mouthed ministers in a royal court."

Godfrey's smile was wry. "Forgive me. Yes, if at all possible, I will arrange payment. I can't promise a certain amount. But I give you my word that I will make the effort."

Killias grinned without restraint. "Better, Templar. That was better."

"Are you done then?" A woman's voice.

Landry could do nothing but gape. One of the swordsmen from the *Melitta* was, in fact, a woman. She was smaller than the rest of her company, but not so much so that she had drawn his notice. She wore her black hair shorn as short as that of a man. Her dark breeches and ivory tunic were loose-fitting enough to hide her form. But as she stood before them, a fist on her hip, scorn in her brown eyes and pursed lips, Landry wondered how he could have overlooked her presence.

"You have something to say?" Killias asked, with more indulgence than Landry would have expected.

"I could offer discourse on the useless prattle of men that might last a week, but I believe all of us have heard enough. I would imagine these men and their passengers are hungry, and seeing as you offered, I believe we ought to feed them."

Killias regarded the woman for several seconds before sending a contrite look Godfrey's way.

"We *would* welcome a meal," the commander said.

"No doubt. Allow me to introduce my daughter, Melitta."

"Namesake of the ship," Landry said without thinking.

In the next instant, he found himself enduring the woman's scrutiny. "How clever." She sounded anything but impressed. "This one misses nothing."

"Forgive her," Killias said. "Her tongue can be a bit sharp."

"Which is more than I can—"

"Don't," the captain said, raising a finger.

She swallowed whatever she had intended to say. Landry thought it likely that the captain had spared him further ridicule.

"You should gather your passengers, Templar, and bring them over to our ship. We have food aplenty, and means to gather more, if you haven't yet grown weary of fish."

"We haven't had enough food in the past weeks to grow weary of anything. We have had no means by which to provide for ourselves."

"Then by all means, let us repair to the *Melitta*."

A sound from the nearby hatch drew Landry's attention. Simon and Adelina peered up at him from the stairway leading to the hold. Many of the others had gathered just behind them.

"It's all right," Landry said. "You can come up. We're in no danger now."

Simon led them onto the deck. He held Adelina's hand. She stayed close to him, practically hiding behind him.

"Shame on you, Templar," Killias said to Godfrey, his voice booming. "You never mentioned that you had such a beauty aboard your ship." He winked at Adelina. "This one could be royalty."

She tucked herself more firmly behind her father, but Landry thought he saw a small smile light her oval, sunburned face.

"You're her father?" the captain asked, approaching Simon. He towered over the man, and his proffered hand appeared to swallow Simon's.

"Yes, sir."

"You can call me Killias, or Captain."

He put an arm around Simon's shoulder and steered him and the girl onto the planks leading to the *Melitta*.

"She looks starved."

Landry turned and found himself beside Killias's daughter.

"She has had a hard time of it," he said, the first words that came to him. "Worse than most on this ship."

The woman gazed after her. "Where is her mother?"

"I don't know. I've never asked either Simon or her." He wanted to ask where *her* mother was, but didn't dare. Like most Templars, he had vowed chastity to God, and so he normally eschewed the company of women. As curious as he was about this particular woman, he knew he would be better off engaging her in conversation about only the most routine of matters. Any attempt at more intimacy might imperil his vows, and expose him again to her barbed wit.

She regarded him sidelong, her sly grin suggesting that she understood him and his reticence all too well.

"Don't worry, Templar. I've no intention of luring you away from your Order. I prefer my men worldly. Breaking in an innocent can be so tedious."

He felt his cheeks redden, opened his mouth to reply, then clamped it shut again, uncertain of what he meant to say.

The woman laughed and walked away from him, hips swaying. Once more, Landry wondered how he had failed to spot her when first she stepped onto the *Tern*. He checked to see if any had noticed their exchange. Draper, who missed nothing, stood nearby, watching him, faint amusement in his dark eyes. Landry scowled and followed the woman to her ship.

There is so much food that Adelina doesn't know what to put in her mouth first. She has seen feasts like this before. Not so long ago, she and her father partook of them in the Holy Land. Mostly they led a modest life, but even they found a way to eat like kings at Passover and Yom Teruah.

The food they bring her on the *Melitta* is nothing like what she ate on those days of celebration. But it is flavorful and abundant, and she cares about nothing else. They have so many kinds of fish – some blackened over an open flame, some steamed, some even smoked. There are pungent cheeses, boiled roots, smoked meats like those that caused so much trouble on their ship. There are more figs as well, like the one she ate during the storm to settle her stomach. She avoids these. The memory of that ordeal remains too vivid.

She stops when she feels full, waits a short while, and starts in again. She feels her stomach expanding, her appetite growing back to what it was before Acre.

They give her some sort of spirit to drink, well-watered, of course. She drinks enough of it that her head becomes pleasantly fogged. She has seen her father drunk once or twice, again on the holy days. This is what it must feel like.

"That is enough drink, I believe," he says to her now. But his tone is mild, and he smiles.

"I'm thirsty. I've been thirsty forever."

"And hungry as well?"

"Yes. I could eat and eat and never stop."

They both laugh at this. Adelina can't remember the last time she felt so happy. She doesn't even mind that Egan sits not so far away, alone, near the middle of this grand ship. He ignores her and her father, and they are content to ignore him as well. Still, there is a small part of her that feels badly for him. Yes, he stole and he lied, and he tried to blame her for all that he had done. But he was hungry, like her. She understands that, can almost forgive him.

"Do you mind if I join you?"

The woman from the other ship stands over them, sun shining on her tanned face. She is solemn, shy even. Adelina isn't sure yet whether she likes her. She is very pretty, despite her short hair and the clothes she wears, which are better suited to a man. Her face is square, her cheekbones high, her skin smooth. Adelina has only the vaguest memories of her mother, who died when she was little more than an infant. But when she imagines her, she looks like this, though with longer hair, and wearing a gown.

"Not at all," Adelina's father says.

He shifts closer to Adelina, leaving room on his far side for the woman. She sits, but looks past Adelina's father to Adelina herself.

"Are you enjoying your meal?"

"Yes, thank you."

A smile flickers across the woman's face. "You're very pretty."

"Thank you. So are you. But why do you dress like that?"

"Adelina!"

The woman laughs. "It's all right. I dress like this because I am a sailor aboard my father's ship. I can't very well wear a gown as I climb into the rigging or pull an oar below, can I?"

"I guess not."

Her smile fades, leaving her grave once again. "I am Melitta."

"Like the ship?" Adelina asks.

"Like the ship. My father named her for me."

"My name is Simon," Adelina's father says. "This is Adelina."

"I'm pleased to meet you both." She looks like she might say more, but she falters.

"How long have you been at sea?" Adelina's father asks, his voice surprisingly gentle.

Melitta drops her gaze, brushes something off her tunic. "A long time. Since I was a girl not much older than your daughter."

"You lost your mother?"

She nods. Adelina isn't certain how her father knew to ask this, but she thinks that this might be why Melitta has come to speak with them.

"How old were you?"

"Very young. I remember so little about her. I lived with my aunt for a time, while my father sailed. He was a merchant then, and returned to port in Athens as often as he could. But when I was old enough I told him that I wanted to sail, that I didn't like waiting on land while he sailed from one adventure to the next." She stares out over the water, squinting, her lips thinned. "He could have said no, but I think he saw how unhappy I was."

"When did you become pirates instead of merchants?"

She laughs again. Adelina likes her laugh. It is warm and musical and as free as the shearwaters gliding near their ships.

"A few years ago," she says. "We'd had our wares plundered several times already, but on this last occasion, one of my father's crew said something foolish and was killed by one of the men who had boarded us. After, my father vowed that we would never be boarded again. So, as you put it, we became pirates ourselves. Sailors of fortune, we call ourselves."

"A kind name for a less than kind profession."

Her expression ices over. "Do not presume to judge us. Life on the sea is uncompromising, no matter what we call ourselves. Yes, we plunder ships. But unlike the men aboard the *Blood Dawn*—" She looks back the way they have come. The other ship has sunk, leaving no trace. "Unlike them, we do not murder, or traffic in slaves, or allow women and children to be ill-used by coarse men."

"And the sailors on that other ship?" her father asks.

"That was war," she says, the words stark and hard.

They fall into a taut silence that stretches on and on, making Adelina squirm.

"I don't remember my mother much, either," she says at last, desperate for anything to fill the void.

Melitta shares a pained look with her father. "That must be difficult for you."

Adelina lifts a shoulder. "No more than it is for you."

She smiles at that. "You're a brave one, aren't you?"

"Yes, she is," her father says before Adelina can answer. "I think the two of you must have that in common as well."

Another glance passes between them, another smile. Color seeps into Melitta's cheeks, and, amazingly, into her father's, too.

"We're Jewish," he says, for reasons Adelina cannot fathom. "You should know this."

"And I am a pirate. Why should I mind that you're Jewish?"

Adelina understands little of this, but she says, "Some people mind. They mind a lot."

"People back in Acre?"

She doesn't answer right away, and she can't keep herself from peeking over at Egan.

"What is she talking about?" Melitta asks Adelina's father.

"It is nothing. A small matter, settled now."

"Tell me." The resolve in her face, the steel in her voice. She is implacable.

Slowly, her father relates the story of what happened in the *Tern*'s hold, and then on the deck. When he falters, or fails to remember some critical point, Adelina speaks up.

Melitta listens without saying a word. But the very nature of her silence shifts as their tale unfolds. By the time they finish, Adelina has grown afraid. The woman is more formidable in that moment than any of the Templars.

She points at Egan, who eats his fish and roots, oblivious. "That one?"

"Yes. But all is well now, Melitta. The Templars

have spoken with him, and he has apologized to Adelina and to me."

"Apologized?" Melitta repeats with contempt. "That sufficed?"

Adelina notices his hesitation. "Not at the time," he says, an admission. "But given a day to think about it, I see the wisdom—"

He has time for no more than that.

She stands, and strides to where Egan sits.

The man looks up at her, scowls. "Yes?"

Melitta grabs hold of him with both hands, pulls him up, and digs a fist into his gut. Egan doubles over and retches. She pounds her knee into his face. There is a sound like the crunching of shells underfoot, and blood sprays across the ship's deck. Egan topples to the wooden planks, but she hoists him up again. She punches him in the face. More blood. He falls back, smacking his head on the deck.

By this time, Killias, Godfrey, and Landry are converging on her. The captain shouts her name. Adelina has begun to cry. She doesn't know why the woman is doing this, but she knows it is her fault, that the story she and her father told has prompted this assault.

Melitta kicks Egan in the side. He folds in on himself, retches again, vomits onto the deck.

Adelina's father tries to shield her from the blood and sick and Egan's moans, but she stares past him, taking it all in.

The captain reaches Melitta, as do the knights. They pull her away from Egan. Her breathing is heavy. Blood stains her breeches and the knuckles on her right hand.

"What are you doing?" Killias demands.

"Punishing this man as he should have been punished by the Templars."

"Punished for what?"

"Tell him," she says, rounding on Godfrey.

"This is a matter that has nothing to do with you or your crew," Godfrey says to Killias. "We handled it as we saw fit, and to the satisfaction of those victimized by this man. Your daughter has no right—"

"He stole from them. He ate provisions that were intended for all on their ship. And then not only did he lie to conceal his crime, he tried to blame the girl." She points at Adelina.

She has never had anyone defend her with such passion, or such violence. She knows she should be horrified by what Melitta has done. But she isn't. Ashamed though she is to admit it, she wishes her father had done the same the other night. Melitta, who only met her this day, has done more to avenge her wounded pride than any of the Templars, more than her own father.

"We have dealt with this," Godfrey says, "in a manner that is consistent with the teachings of our Order."

"A man who steals and lies and defames another member of his crew comes under the lash. That is the law of the sea." To her father, Melitta says, "Tell them. This is the way of things."

Godfrey lifts both hands, a gesture of placation. "First of all, he is not a member of our crew, and neither is Adelina."

"Of course they are," Melitta says, speaking to him as if he were simple. "You have a complement of how many on your ship? Twenty? A few more? Every man, woman, and child is part of your crew. If you are boarded, every one of them will be a soldier. That is the way of the sea as well."

"Had he been a member of our crew," Killias says, "he would have been disciplined, just as Melitta describes."

"Perhaps. But he is a passenger on our ship, not yours. And your daughter had no right to attack him in this way."

"Shall we ask Adelina what she thinks?" Melitta demands of him. "Or Simon?"

Godfrey considers the father and daughter. Then he shakes his head. "No," he says, sounding more subdued. "I don't believe that would be to anyone's benefit."

"Because you know I'm right."

Godfrey spares her one last glance. He turns to Draper. "Do what you can for his wounds." To Killias he says, "I trust you have bandages and healing herbs on your vessel."

"We do. You shall have all you need to treat the man."

"Thank you."

Godfrey walks away. Killias raises an eyebrow and shakes his head. But he doesn't rebuke his daughter in any other way. Melitta glares down at Egan, who hasn't moved since she kicked him. She walks toward the rear of the ship. As she passes Adelina and Simon, Adelina reaches for her hand. Melitta slows.

"Thank you," Adelina whispers, and lets her go.

CHAPTER 7

While the captain's daughter leaned on the rail at the stern of the ship, ignoring the rest of them, Landry and Gawain helped Egan to his feet, guided him to a barrel, and had him sit. At the same time, a member of the *Melitta*'s crew accompanied Draper below to fetch bandages and herbs.

Egan's nose still bled. Landry was certain the woman had broken it. She might also have cracked a rib or two with her last kick. A cut high on his cheek seeped blood as well, and the man had a lump the size of a quail's egg on the back of his head. Blood and vomit were smeared on his shirt and breeches.

Yet Landry had the feeling that Egan was fortunate to have come through the beating as well as he did. Left to continue her assault, which she surely would have done had her father and the Templars not intervened, the woman might have killed him.

"She had no right," Egan murmured, the injury to his nose making the words thick and unclear. "I gave no offense to her or her ship."

Tancrede raised both eyebrows, but kept his thoughts to himself. Landry chose to do the same.

"What are you going to do to her?"

"Do to her?" Landry repeated. "What do you mean?"

"She assaulted me while I was under your protection. Look at me! Surely she deserves to be punished!"

"Here comes Draper," Tancrede said, waving to the Turcopole, who had just emerged onto the deck and now hurried toward them. "He'll minister to your injuries."

Tancrede started away from the man, and motioned to Landry that he should follow. As they passed Draper, he said, "Good luck to you."

"What?"

"Speak only of your ministrations to his injuries. Ignore anything else he might say."

Draper turned a half-circle as they continued by him. "What is he going to say?"

Neither Tancrede nor Landry broke stride.

"You'll be fine!" Tancrede said over his shoulder.

Godfrey and the *Melitta*'s captain spoke near midship. They stood shoulder to shoulder, facing in opposite directions, both with their arms crossed over their chests. Even seeing them in profile, Landry thought both men appeared displeased.

"He's going to be fine," Tancrede said, as they joined the men. "But he wants the woman punished."

The look Killias gave him could have rimed the sails of his ship. "That is not going to happen. Melitta was right in what she said. A man on a ship of mine – on almost any ship you would encounter on the Mediterranean – who did the things that man did, would have been disciplined. Six lashes at least. He might have been denied food as well."

"So you've told me," Godfrey said. "And as I've already told you, this is no ordinary ship. None of us chose to put to sea. Like the rest of our passengers, Egan was forced to flee Acre. He is here by chance, a victim of circumstance."

"How he came to be here – how any of you wound up on your vessel – is of no consequence. You are here now. He betrayed every one of you. The child might have been most aggrieved, but his crimes were committed against all on your ship."

"By that same logic, might we also say that your daughter's assault on him was an attack on all of us?"

Killias went still, like a dog on the hunt. "You are treading a most dangerous path, Templar."

Godfrey showed no sign of being cowed by the man. "I'm merely trying to point out that there is more than one way to view this situation. I see no need for any more violence. But perhaps if your daughter were to apologize for her..."

He trailed off in the face of Killias's laughter.

"You've met my daughter. Do you truly believe you can convince her to apologize for anything?"

"That is beside the point, Father."

The four of them turned. Melitta stood just beyond their circle. Landry hadn't heard her approach.

"Why should I apologize? What good would an apology do? What solace did that man's apology bring to Adelina? None at all. You know it to be true, or at least you would have had you cared enough to consider the matter. Having him apologize to the girl did nothing for her. But I would imagine it made you feel better about yourselves." She directed her glare at each of them. "Perhaps it assuaged the guilt you carried for believing him instead of her when he first accused her of stealing.

"I would suggest you all consider the matter closed. I will not apologize. I certainly will not allow myself to be punished. And I don't imagine your friend will dare attempt to avenge the beating I gave him."

"He's not our friend," Landry said.

Godfrey put a hand on his shoulder. "Landry."

"He's not. As you point out yourself," he continued, addressing Melitta, "he is part of our ship's complement, and so it is our duty to protect him. But he is no friend of mine, and I have not forgiven him for what he did to the girl, to all of us really."

She quirked an eyebrow and turned to Godfrey. "At least one of you talks sense."

The commander didn't respond to her, but he did face the captain again. "Perhaps it's best if my people leave you. We appreciate all that you have done for us. I believe we owe you our lives. But we would best be on our way."

"There is no need for that," Killias said, relaxing his stance. "Unless you have discovered a cache of food, or conjured one out of seawater and air, I believe you are better off remaining with us. In lieu of an apology, or a lashing for my daughter, however deserving she may be—" He grinned to soften this. "—you should allow us to help you repair your mast."

"Do you believe it can be mended?"

"Possibly. It might not hold up long in another storm, but if the repairs are done properly, it should withstand a light wind."

Godfrey smiled. "That would be most welcome."

"Very well." Killias marked the position of the sun in the western sky. "There is still food aplenty to be eaten. We will begin work on the mast with first light."

"Thank you, Captain."

Landry didn't know how many among the two crews had heard all that was said in their parley, but it seemed that every person on the *Melitta* let out a held breath. Some of those from the Templar ship returned to their meals. Others were content to mill about on the deck of the larger ship, confident that for this night they would be safe.

Simon approached Landry, uncertain to the point of diffidence. "I fear we may have caused you a good bit of trouble. I'm sorry for that."

"None of this is your fault. Or your daughter's. And all is well now. The two of you should enjoy your food, and take comfort in knowing that our ship may soon be seaworthy again."

"That's good news. But still—"

Landry stopped him with a raised hand. "All of us have had our fill of apologies and talk of contrition. It's time we moved on."

Simon weighed this, then tipped his head in agreement. "Very well. Thank you."

He moved off again, back to Adelina. A short time later, Landry noticed that Melitta approached them and sat beside Simon, as she had earlier in the day.

The sun dipped below the western horizon. The sky darkened and members of Killias's crew lit torches on the deck of the galley. Others brought forth bottles of the anise-flavored spirit Landry had tasted earlier. This time, they didn't bother to water it down. Drinking it diluted in order to survive was one thing. A Templar did not partake of such drink in its pure form. Still, Landry sniffed at the bottle before passing it on to one of Killias's sailors. Soon after, someone pushed another bottle into his hand. He inhaled from this one, too, enjoying the aroma.

"Careful, brother," Tancrede said, taking the bottle from him. "We wouldn't want the scent to lure you into partaking in more dangerous ways." He took a whiff of the stuff himself.

Landry grinned, and reached to reclaim the bottle. Tancrede held him at arm's length and made a show of sniffing it again.

"Careful, brother," Landry echoed, laughing.

Godfrey appeared on the far side of Tancrede and plucked the liquor from his hand. "I think you've both snorted enough." He handed the bottle to a passing sailor. "It's time we returned to our ship."

"Should we gather the others?" Tancrede asked.

"Just the Templars."

Landry surveyed the galley. A few of the women from the *Gray Tern* spoke and laughed with Killias's sailors. While he watched, one of them allowed a man to lead her down into the ship's hold.

Quietly, he and Tancrede approached their fellow knights and told them that Godfrey wanted them back on the *Tern*. The men complied without dissent. Simon crossed back to their ship as well, carrying Adelina in his arms. She appeared to have fallen asleep.

A man from the *Melitta* emerged from the ship's hold bearing a lyre. He settled himself on the port rail of his ship and began to pluck at the strings. Eventually he sang as well, his voice deep and melodic. The music blended with the now-familiar sounds of life at sea: the rhythm of swells lapping at the hull, the whine of stretched rope, and the complaint of old wood.

Landry remained above deck, his arms resting on the rails near the stern of the ship. Tancrede sat against the hull nearby. The Templars did not bother to light torches on the *Tern*. They had enough light from the moon and the flames that danced on the *Melitta*.

Not long after descending into the hold with his daughter, Simon emerged again into the night. Landry watched as he crossed to the planks that spanned the water between the two vessels and walked back to the larger ship. Melitta greeted him on the other side, took his hand, and led him down into the hold.

A pang of envy squeezed Landry's heart, catching him unprepared.

I have taken a vow of chastity. I have devoted my life and body to service of the Lord. Why would I be jealous?

"Because I am a fool," he muttered out loud.

Tancrede glanced his way but remained silent. Landry gazed at the sky, searching for familiar patterns in the stars. Before long, though, he looked to the deck of the galley again. He couldn't have said what he hoped to see.

They ignored him. All of them. The Templars, the sailors, the Jews, the woman and her father. They pretended he wasn't there. To be sure, the one Templar – the Turcopole – had tended to his wounds, and been polite enough as he did so. But after binding a pungent poultice to his bruised ribs, and cleaning the gash on his cheek, even that one left him to be with his friends.

None wanted him there. None would have condemned the woman had she drawn a blade and cut out his heart. On the contrary, they would have rejoiced as they dumped his corpse into the sea.

He had been humiliated, mocked, shunned, beaten. And he saw no path to redemption. Even whole of body, he was no match for any of the men on either ship. Good Lord, the *woman* had beaten him bloody. In the Holy Land, he had been a man of some means. He'd had standing, respect. But with Acre's fall he had lost everything. He was nothing now. An object of derision, an outcast among outcasts.

There was naught for him to do but sit alone, hunched over the bit of food they had allowed him. At least he had satisfied the hunger that plagued him earlier on their journey. Small consolation.

When the first bottles of spirit appeared on the galley, no one thought to offer one to him. The bottles orbited the vessel, always beyond his grasp, as remote as the moon. Women from the *Tern* who had said not a word to him since the incident with the girl threw themselves into the arms of these ignorant sailors. Mere moments before, the captain's whore of a daughter had taken the Jew below, leading him by the hand.

He longed for revenge, but had no idea how he might achieve it. He could sneak onto the *Tern* and take the life of the brat who had caused all of this. But even if he reached her – small chance of that, given he could hardly walk – someone would be there to protect her. The Templars would finally have the excuse they sought to run him through. Much the same would happen were he to sneak below and find the Jew and the whore, defenseless in the act of love.

No, there had to be some other way. He was not a man of violence. But he was canny. He always had been. There would come a time when cunning and fate would allow him to strike back at those who had shamed him. The Templars might despise him, but they would not leave him here with Killias's ship, nor would they abandon him on some barren rock in the middle of the sea. Their sense of duty, of Christian charity, wouldn't allow it.

They would provide for him, even as they continued to disregard him. Fine. Let them. That suited his intentions.

He nibbled what remained of his food, stood, limped to the planks, and then over to his ship. Once there, he made his way below. The Turcopole followed him, asked after his wounds, inspected his bandages. Maybe this one was better than the others. Maybe, when the time came, if there was some way to spare this one the worst of whatever retribution he devised, he would do so.

Not at the expense of his vengeance on the others, though. If the Turcopole had to suffer, so be it. He would not grant mercy to all in order to save this one. He wasn't worth it.

The Turcopole left him, and he curled up on his blanket. His ribs ached. The pain of his shattered nose radiated through his entire face, and the knot on the back of his head was tender.

But the hold was silent, save for quiet breathing.

He raised his head, peered through the shadows until he spotted the girl. She lay nearby – closer than he'd expected. She was sound asleep. Her father was on the other ship, as distracted as a man could be.

He sat up.

"Is something the matter, Egan?"

He started, his head whipping around in the direction of the voice. The young, dark-haired knight – Landry – sat on the stairs leading to the deck.

"No, I—I'm just trying to get comfortable."

The knight didn't say a word. He didn't smile or nod. He just stared.

Egan rolled onto his other side, groaning as he did, and lowered himself onto the blanket. But now that he knew the Templar watched him, he couldn't bring himself to close his eyes. He felt the man's gaze as he would twin sword-points pressed into his back, and he held himself still.

But he seethed.

You won't always be watching, Templar. And I swear, I will find other ways to strike back at you.

Cunning and patience. These he would need to have his revenge. As it happened, they were qualities he possessed in abundance.

Landry was still awake when Simon returned to the ship.

He remained in the hold, near the stairway, where he could watch both Egan and Adelina. Simon trod lightly on the steps, and appeared surprised to see Landry awake and keeping watch.

"Has something happened?" he whispered. Before Landry could answer, he surveyed the hold, taking note of where his daughter slept, and where Egan had bedded down. "Did he do anything to her?"

"No," Landry said. He nearly mentioned seeing Egan look over at the girl, and his sense that the thief meant her harm. But he had no proof of this, and no desire to trouble Simon without need. "I didn't like the idea of the two of them being down here without anyone watching over her."

In the shifting light from the torches on deck, Landry saw Simon's cheeks shade to crimson. He hadn't meant his words as a rebuke, but he understood how the man might take them as such, in particular from a Templar.

"I didn't mean—"

"I shouldn't have—"

They spoke in unison, broke off at the same time. Landry smiled. Simon didn't.

"I make no judgment," Landry said. "Nor did I mean to imply otherwise. I saw Egan go below. I followed. It was as simple as that."

Simon nodded, his color still high. "Thank you." He faltered, and Landry thought he might say more. But he crossed to Adelina and knelt beside her. After adjusting her blanket, he kissed her forehead and lay down near her. Landry regarded Egan. Convinced that the man slept, he climbed to the deck and found a place to sleep as well.

The night passed without incident. The Templars rose with the dawn and spoke their morning prayers. The crew of the *Melitta* stirred a short time later, and before long both ships bustled with activity. Again, Killias offered food to the knights and their passengers, and Godfrey accepted on their behalf, thanking the captain for his generosity.

The men and women on the *Tern* made their way

over to the galley. Egan lagged behind, but crossed over as well, his gait stiff, the bruises on his face stark in the light of day.

The morning meal was far more modest than that which they'd enjoyed the previous night, but it was still ample, especially when compared with what they had eaten in recent days.

After eating, the Templars, the strongest of their passengers, and a good number of crewmen from the *Melitta*, made their way to the *Tern* and commenced work on the broken mast.

The *Melitta*'s carpenter repaired the damaged spar, and oversaw the sealing of the spot where the spar had punched through the *Tern*'s deck.

Next, they worked on the mast itself. The wood of the mast had splintered badly, rendering both the bottom end of the broken piece and the top of the base unusable. The carpenter had men saw off these shattered segments. Using a hatchet, he notched the new ends so they would fit together.

The men under his supervision then took positions along the length of the broken mast, intent on lifting it high enough to fit it back onto the base. It promised to be a herculean task. Landry took his place among the company of men preparing to make the attempt, but Draper stopped him.

"Your arm is not ready," the Turcopole told him.

"It feels fine." A lie, but the wound pained him far less than it had.

Draper smirked, clearly not fooled by the statement. "I'm sure it does. Nevertheless, I cannot allow you to do this."

"I do not need your permission, brother."

"No, but you do need Godfrey's. Please do not force me to involve him. We have plenty of men, Landry. For once. Do not risk further injury for nothing."

What answer could he make to such a plea?

He stepped aside so that another might take his place, and joined Gawain at the rail.

"We've been reduced to spectators," Gawain said.

"Not by choice."

"No. Draper ordered me away. I didn't know he could do that."

Landry chuckled. "I'm not sure he can."

Gawain answered with a rare grin. "Yet, here we stand."

An older man coated the top of the base and the notched end of the mast with ship's tar. Then, amid grunts, and a few expletives from the crew of the *Melitta*, the men lifted the mast and set it onto the base. The notches fit together perfectly.

Several men encircled the mast, holding it up. Others scrambled among them, using hammers and nails to brace the junction of the two pieces with wooden boards. More men followed, securing these pieces with thin rope and coating the rope and wood with still more tar. At last, all stepped away from the mast. It held. Landry stepped forward and tested its strength. Godfrey and Killias did the same. It felt as firm as it ever had. It wasn't quite as tall as it had been, but it would do.

"I do not believe it can weather a storm," Killias said. "I would not even hazard raising your sail in a powerful wind. But for most days..." He paused to gesture at the clear sky, the open sea. "For a day like this one – it should serve you well."

"Thank you, Captain," Godfrey said. "Perhaps, then, we should take our leave."

"Certainly we can uncouple our ships. But I think it best that we escort you." At a questioning look from the commander, Killias said, "Well, you have depleted our stores. We're as much in need of a port as you are." He flashed a grin, drawing one in turn from Godfrey. "These are dangerous waters, Templar. For any ship, but particularly one as small as yours. I wouldn't wish to see you and your passengers come to harm, and thus waste all that food we've given you."

"We'll be grateful for your company, and your protection. I know that I speak for all aboard the *Tern* when I say that, before you found us, we were sorely in need of a change of fortune. Your arrival gave us that and more. You were an answer to prayers. We are in your debt, and will never forget all you've done for us."

"Well, the less you say of this to others you encounter, the happier I'll be. The *Melitta* has a reputation to uphold. It wouldn't do for my rival captains to learn of how soft I've become."

"Oh, they know, Father," Melitta said, drawing laughs from men and women on both ships.

Landry enjoyed the repartee with the rest, but he happened to glimpse Egan's bruised face as the laughter continued. What he saw there chilled him to his heart. The man's glower, directed at all of them – Melitta and Killias, Godfrey and the other knights, Simon and Adelina – conveyed pure venom. He hated every person on the two ships. Landry wondered what devilry a man nurturing such hatred might wreak.

Egan shifted his small, dark eyes in Landry's

direction. Realizing that he was watched, he schooled his features and looked away. But Landry had seen enough. For the rest of their voyage, wherever it took them, he would keep watch on Egan. Their survival, he believed, depended on no less.

Working quickly, the two crews removed the planks that had joined the ships. The *Melitta*'s men raised their sails. Under Tancrede's watchful eye, the knights of the *Tern* did the same with their sail and the newly mended mast. The sail billowed with a light gust of wind, and the ship surged forward. The mast groaned in complaint, but it held and the ship cut a path in the *Melitta*'s wake.

They headed north and east, their destination now the same as it was before the storm struck: Rhosus, on the shore of Cilician Armenia, near the grand city of Alexandretta. The journey would take them near Aleppo, a city that had, in recent years, seen even more bloodshed than Acre. Landry expected that they would approach Rhosus from due west, and thus avoid sailing too close to Mamluk-held territory.

While the ships sailed separately, they remained in close proximity, and sailors from both vessels used a skiff from the galley to shuttle from one to the other. In this way, romances that had bloomed the night before continued. Melitta joined Simon and Adelina on the *Tern*, much to the silent consternation of Egan, whom Landry kept under constant observation.

"Are you their guardian?"

Perched on the rail, Landry turned at the sound of the voice. Tancrede had strayed forward from the stern.

"Shouldn't you be steering the ship?"

The knight shrugged. "Thomas has the rudder right

now. As long as he follows the *Melitta*, we should be all right."

Landry nodded and swung his gaze back to Egan.

"He's been humiliated, Landry," Tancrede said. "Melitta took all the fight out of him. You don't need to watch him every moment of every day."

"Perhaps. You didn't see him earlier. He was... I fear there is more fight left in him than you might think, twisted now by his shame and his bitterness."

"He's but one man. What do you think he can do?"

"I don't know. He might not even know. Not yet. But we would be remiss if we ignored the danger." He glanced back, his eyes finding Tancrede's. "I have nothing better to do while I heal. I can spare some of my time to keep an eye on the man. But promise me that you'll do the same if my attention is elsewhere. There's darkness in him, Tancrede. I see it growing. Promise me."

"Very well. You have my word."

"Thank you."

Landry shifted again, and stretched his tender shoulder. All the while, he continued to mark Egan's every movement, every shift in his expression. He might have been wasting time and effort, as Tancrede insisted. But he thought otherwise. He didn't fear that Egan might seek vengeance. He *knew* it would happen, just as he knew that the sun would set in the evening and rise again come dawn. Landry's fear was that he would not be prepared to stop Egan when the time came.

CHAPTER 8

They sighted land two days later: Cyprus again. Killias wished to make land there, but at Godfrey's urging, they sailed past the isle and continued northward toward the land of the Turks. They encountered one other ship along the way. It appeared to be a merchant vessel. Upon sighting the *Melitta*, this other ship altered its course and fled, reminding Landry of what Killias had said two days before.

The Melitta *has a reputation…*

It seemed they had been more fortunate than they knew in gaining the friendship of Killias and his sailors. No doubt the captain meant what he said when first they met the ship. He wished to be rewarded by the Templars, and he would expect handsome compensation.

Not long after they navigated around Cyprus, they caught sight of a much larger landmass to the north and east, which they assumed must be Anatolia. Killias's galley might have reached her shores within a day, but the captain had his sailors keep pace with the *Tern*, prolonging their voyage substantially.

Landry grew ever more watchful as they approached the Turkish coast. He expected Egan to strike at Simon or Adelina before they made land. He didn't.

Indeed, the closer they drew to land, the more withdrawn he became, until he appeared to take no notice of the Templars or his fellow passengers. Except for those rare occasions when someone spoke to him directly, he said not a word. He took food. He tolerated Draper's ministrations to his injuries. When he wasn't asleep in the hold, he sat along the rail, staring out at the sea, seemingly oblivious of all that happened around him.

Observing this, Landry questioned what he thought he had seen earlier in their voyage. Had Tancrede been right all along? Had the beating Egan suffered at Melitta's hand been enough to knock the fight out of him? Eventually, as they neared land and Landry's thoughts turned to what they might find on shore, his vigilance slackened.

Late in the second day after passing Cyprus, they followed the *Melitta* through the Armenian Bay and into a moon-shaped harbor. Mountains loomed in the distance, their dry slopes gilded by the setting sun. The town along the water's edge was a good deal larger than the one they had seen on Cyprus. Stone buildings rose from the lanes, graced with elegant, domed towers and soaring archways.

The *Melitta* struck its sails and went to sweeps. At Tancrede's urging, Godfrey ordered the *Tern* to do the same. As before, Landry remained by the hatch so that he could relay instructions from Tancrede to those pulling the oars. Before long, they had steered the ship to a wharf and tied in. The *Tern*'s passengers gathered by the starboard rail, eager to be off the ship.

Godfrey called for them to wait, and led the other Templars onto the deck.

"We cannot know what we'll find here," he said. "I hope, and even expect, that we'll be safe, but after what happened at Cyprus we would be foolish to assume that all will be well. You can leave the ship – I have no authority to hold you here. But I would urge you to stay close, so that if something happens, we can protect you. We will try to secure food, and we will also inquire about where it might be safe to leave you permanently."

"Leave us?" Simon said. "Why wouldn't we continue to sail with you?"

"Because as long as you sail with Templars, you are on a ship of war. It isn't safe for any of you, your daughter least of all. I'm certain I speak for all my brothers when I say that we have no desire to part company. But it is for the best."

Displeasure creased Simon's forehead, and showed on the faces of many of the other passengers as well. But none of them argued. Egan held himself apart and gave no indication that he heard any of what was said. When the rest of the passengers disembarked, he walked with them.

After watching them go, Godfrey turned back to his fellow Templars.

"Do you know this town?" he asked Draper.

"I know of it, but that is all. My family has its roots in a village near Smyrna, more than one hundred leagues from here."

"Will you be able to speak to those who don't know French?"

Draper lifted a shoulder again. "Perhaps. There are many dialects in my language, and they vary widely from the western shore to the eastern. Still, I should be able to make out some, if not all, of what they say."

"Anything you can do to make them understand us will be helpful." Addressing all of them once more, he said, "Our first task is to replenish our provisions, food and healing herbs both. We don't have much that we can use as currency, but the Cilicians see their land as an outpost of Christendom, and they have long supported the Crusade and its warriors. Once we locate a church, we might prevail upon them to help us. They'll know that we can repay. Still, after the 'welcome' we received in Cyprus, we should be cautious. I would rather not linger in this town. The sooner we can reach Bagras, the better off we will be."

"I see a cross," Tancrede said, pointing toward the city. "I believe we should start there."

"Agreed."

They left the ship together, their tabards announcing them as Templars and drawing stares from people they passed on the wharf, and then on the stone lane fronting it. Landry's hand crept repeatedly to the hilt of his sword, but he resisted the impulse to draw his weapon. He and Tancrede flanked Godfrey. Draper and Thomas walked ahead of them. Gawain and the others strode behind.

As they marched deeper into the town, more people took notice of them. A few spoke, and though Landry understood nothing of what they said, he recognized the tone. Where he had expected hostility, he found instead curiosity, and even signs of friendship. The Templars' weapons and armor, and most obviously the blood-red crosses on their chests, left no doubt as to who and what they were. While in the Holy Land, Landry had grown accustomed to the hostility of men and women he encountered in lanes and marketplaces. It had been too long since his presence last drew smiles and words of greeting.

As he and his brother Templars marched on to the church, Landry allowed his hand to hang by his side, near his sword still, but no longer hovering at the hilt.

The church Tancrede had spied was modest, but as graceful in design as so many of Rhosus's other structures. Its façade consisted of three stone arches, the middle one tallest. A single tower rose above this middle archway, and was crowned by the stone cross they saw from the ship. Broad stone steps led to twin doors beneath the central camber.

Godfrey paused at the bottom of the stairway, eyes raised to the cross. "We shouldn't all go in," he said. "I don't want them to feel that they're under assault. Draper, Tancrede, Landry, you will accompany me inside. Gawain, you shall have command of the men who remain out here. We seek no conflict with anyone in Rhosus, but if a threat should arise, return to the ship and leave these shores."

"Without you?"

"We should be safe within the church."

"Very well," Gawain said, disapproval tingeing the words.

Godfrey led them up the stairs and pushed through the doors.

Within, the church was dimly lit and spare, but

welcoming. It consisted of a small nave, shallow transepts, and a simple square chancel. The altar, constructed of stone, stood at the end of the chancel, beneath a rounded window of milky glass. Candles burned at intervals throughout the church, illuminating the only adornments: brightly colored frescoes on either side of the altar, one a representation of Christ and His disciples, the other depicting the Savior on the Cross.

A few souls prayed in rough wooden pews, but otherwise the sanctuary was empty.

Landry and the others knelt at the doorway, whispered prayers, and crossed themselves before standing and making their way toward the chancel.

As they did, a priest emerged from the north transept. Short and rotund, he wore a coarse white robe, belted with a length of rope. His hair was dark and tonsured. Seeing the Templars, he stopped and crossed himself.

Godfrey placed a hand on Draper's shoulder and raised his chin in the priest's direction.

Draper addressed the man in his language. The priest smiled, nodded, and answered in what sounded like the same tongue. Then he said, "Be welcome, brothers," his accent warm and rich.

"You speak French."

"Some, yes. I am Father Dawid. How can we be of service?"

The easing of Godfrey's fears seemed to lift years from his face. "I am Godfrey. With me are Draper, Landry, and Tancrede. We need food, Father. And healing herbs. For ourselves, for our fellow Templars, and for the men, women, and one child who sail with us."

"Of course. And do you have need of a healer?"

"Brother Draper has tended their wounds," he said, indicating the Turcopole. "But we have been short of food since we set sail some weeks ago."

"You were at Acre?"

Godfrey straightened, clearly taken aback by the question. "Word of Acre's fall has reached you?"

"Yes, though only within the past day or two."

"We were there. We were driven out by the Mamluks, and only by the grace of God did we escape with our lives. We've been at sea ever since. Were it not for a small bit of food that we secured before being chased from Cyprus, and the kindness of a sea captain who happened upon us a few days ago, we would have starved."

"You were fortunate to have encountered such a captain. Most who sail these seas are pirates who care not for the well-being of others."

Godfrey merely smiled and said, "God has been kind."

"How many are you in all?"

"We are twenty-two."

Concern creased his brow for just an instant. "That is many. Our means are limited."

"You will be repaid and then some by the Templars," Godfrey said. "You have my word on this."

"Thank you. We'll do what we can. For tonight, we can offer you some coin to spend in our marketplace. Provisioning you for longer than that will be more difficult. Can you give us until morning?"

"Of course. Thank you, Father."

Dawid stepped to the north transept and vanished into a small chamber. He returned moments later, bearing a small purse that rang with coins when he handed it to Godfrey.

"It is not much, but it should suffice for this evening."

"Again, our thanks."

"Do you require shelter for tonight?"

"Thank you, but we can sleep on our ship." Godfrey paused, then asked, "Does our Order still hold the fortress in Bagras?"

Another frown crossed Father Dawid's face. "They do."

"You hesitate. Why?"

"I know what I am told. No more."

"And what is that?"

"That they hold it, but only just. Their numbers are few, and they are harried constantly by bands of mountain brigands, and, sometimes, by companies of Saracens."

"Then they will welcome us," Tancrede said.

"If you reach them. The road to Bagras is said to be very bad. Brigands prey on those who attempt any crossing of the mountains."

Landry couldn't suppress a smile. "I mean no disrespect, Father, but we are Templars. Highwaymen do not concern us."

"They should, brother. They roam in bands of twenty or thirty, and though they may lack your skill with a blade, they are rough, capable men. You take them lightly at your own risk."

Landry thought to say more, but Godfrey silenced him with a small gesture.

"Thank you, Father," the commander said. "We are grateful for your aid and your counsel."

"Of course. Will you pray with me before you take your leave?"

Godfrey's smile this time was genuine and open. "We would be honored."

The Templars followed Dawid to the altar, where they knelt in prayer while the priest offered a blessing. When he had finished, they rose and left the church. Gawain and the others awaited them outside. Godfrey, Landry, and their companions descended the stairs and, as Gawain and the other knights fell in step with them, started back through the town in the direction of the marketplace. Along the way, Godfrey related all that Father Dawid had told them.

"Brigands on the road do not frighten me," Gawain said. "And if the Templars at Bagras are under siege, they will welcome our arrival all the more."

"Landry and I said much the same," Tancrede told him.

"I don't worry about brigands any more than you do," Godfrey said, sounding impatient. "If it was only us, I would set out for Bagras as soon as we have provisions. But we have a responsibility to those in our care. I don't want them on the road with us. Not if what Father Dawid told us is true."

"You spoke of parting ways with them," Landry said.

"That is my intention. But I won't leave them here – or anywhere else, for that matter – against their will. If they don't wish to remain here, in this town, we may have to sail farther."

They came to the market a short time later and, using the coin from Father Dawid, purchased food and wine for the evening's meal. Then, as the sun set over Armenian Bay, they took their supplies to the *Tern*. Some of their passengers had returned already,

Simon and Adelina among them. Others, though, had not yet boarded the ship.

He kept to himself, conversing with no one, hiding from them all, though he remained in plain sight. It worked.

They thought him broken. They dismissed him the way they would someone insensate. Even the dark-haired Templar, who clearly had taken it upon himself to protect the Jew and his brat, appeared to have lost interest in Egan. Perhaps he no longer thought him a threat to any of them. Good. Let him believe this. He would realize his error soon enough. All of them would.

He shuffled off the ship behind the others, slowed by his injuries, and fueled by them as well. The others spread through the town, scattering like bugs. He made a point of not following the Jews. Instead, he limped after one of the old women. She didn't notice.

Soon enough, he fell behind even her, his ribs aching. Silently, he cursed the captain's daughter.

He continued through the market without stopping, searching for a place where the less reputable might gather. He found it on the southern edge of the town, along a stretch of shoreline that stank of dead fish, rotting seaweed, and human waste.

Men sat on a pier long neglected and worn gray by years of wind, sun, and rain. The vessels tied to its wooden bitts appeared as ill-used as the wharf. So did the men. Their clothes were tattered, their beards untended, their hair – those who had it – unruly. They passed a flask among themselves, cackling at jokes Egan could not hear.

Long before he was close enough to speak with

them, they took notice of him, pointing and elbowing one another. Their rough laughter drifted over the strand, causing him to falter, to wonder if he had been foolish to come here.

He halted, looked back the way he had come.

The men called to him, beckoned him on with waves and waggles of their fingers. He couldn't make out their words, and it occurred to him that they might not even understand him. One of the men held up the flask and pointed to it. More laughter greeted this.

Egan walked on. He had made his choice.

As he drew near, the men quieted and marked his approach. Two of them drew knives. Egan raised his hands and walked on, hoping they would understand that he did not want trouble.

He stepped onto the wharf, avoiding a space where a plank had once been. One of the men said something in a language he didn't know. His heart sank. He shook his head.

"French," he said.

The men traded looks. Most of them appeared perplexed by this. But one dipped his chin. He was tall, thin, with black hair that fell in a swoop across his brow. A wine-colored birthmark marred the skin surrounding one dark eye.

"A little," he said, his accent as thick as fog.

Egan blew out a breath.

Another of the men said something. His friends chuckled.

"He asks what was done to make you... make you look like that. Your face. The cuts. The—" He brushed at the skin near his eyes and nose on his own face. "The dark marks."

He wasn't sure how to answer. If he told them a woman had beaten him, they would mock him until midnight. And if he revealed what he had done, he would get nowhere with them. The answer, when at last it came to him, struck him as uncommonly clever.

"Jews did this. You know that word? Jews, yes?"

The man's expression darkened and he nodded before telling his companions what Egan had said.

"Do you know the Knights Templar?" Egan asked them.

The man went still. "Yes," he said, his mouth barely moving.

Another of his friends asked a question, but he put the man off with a raised hand. "What of Templars?"

"I have been voyaging with them. On a small ship. The *Gray Tern*." He broke off, unsure if the man understood him. "We are on a boat, yes?"

"The *Gray Tern*. Yes. Go on."

Egan wet his lips. "It is a small ship. Slow. There are only a few of the Templars. Nine." He held up nine fingers.

The man gestured for him to continue.

"The ship can be taken. It is weak. If you can find someone who will take it. Someone who—"

"Pirates."

Egan smiled. "Yes, pirates."

The man stood, and Egan fell back a step. He opened his hands. "No worry. Not hurt you. But take you somewhere. They will want to hear from you. Yes?"

A question from one of the others made the man turn. He said something, shook his head. His friend repeated the question, and the man cut him off with a sharp motion. But he pointed to one of the others.

This one was also tall with closely shorn hair.

The second man stood. The first walked past Egan and off the wharf.

"Come," he said.

Egan hobbled after him. The second man fell in behind him.

They followed the shoreline away from the town. By now, the sun had started to set. Egan did not wish to be with these men and whomever they were on their way to see after dark, but he saw no way to put this encounter off until morning without raising the men's suspicions. He walked after the man with the birthmark, his ribs aching, and he glanced repeatedly to the west, unnerved by the sun's rapid descent. He was conscious of the second man behind him, but he refused to look back and reveal how frightened he was.

"Where from you come here?" the first man asked over his shoulder.

Egan wasn't certain he wanted to answer. The more he considered what he was doing, the greater his doubts. He halted.

"It's getting dark," he said.

Both men stopped as well. The one with the birthmark frowned, and shook his head.

"The sun." He pointed. "It is setting." He lowered his hand.

"Yes. So?"

"I—I need to get back. It will be dark."

"Not far now," Birthmark said. He didn't wait for a reply, but walked on.

Egan remained where he was until the man behind him said something. He didn't understand the words, but the harsh tone made his meaning plain enough.

When Egan chanced a peek at this second man, he saw that he had drawn his blade. Egan resumed walking.

The distance proved greater than Birthmark had suggested. With every step Egan took on the uneven sand, the ache in his legs grew. The sun slipped below the horizon and as darkness fell, he despaired of ever finding his way back to the town.

At last, mercifully, they rounded a small bend in the shoreline, which opened onto another shallow inlet. A ship – a galley much like the *Melitta*, though even larger – was anchored offshore. Several skiffs rested on the sand. Beyond them, men sat around fires, talking, eating, drinking. Egan counted at least fifty. A cluster of women stood nearby, and as he watched, a man approached them, spoke to one woman, and placed something in her hand. She pocketed whatever it was – a coin? – took him by the hand, and led him away from the fires along the contours of the inlet.

Birthmark halted and turned. Looking past Egan to his companion, he spoke in their tongue. Once again, Egan did not understand most of what he heard, though he thought the man uttered the word "Templar." The second man offered no response, but when the first man finished speaking, he gave a curt reply and continued toward the gathering on the beach.

"We wait here," Birthmark said to Egan. "They interested, they come. If not…" He shrugged.

The uncertainty of this bothered him, but he could think of nothing to say, beyond asking what the man meant. And he wasn't completely certain he wanted an answer to that question. He waited, trying to follow the progress of the second man as he spoke initially to men arrayed around the nearest of the fires, and then moved on, deeper into the gathering. Eventually, Egan lost track of him.

In time, however, a band of several men left the fires and started toward where they stood. Egan's mouth went dry.

There appeared to be eight of them in all, including the man who had accompanied Egan here. Two carried torches. The man who walked at the fore, beside Birthmark's companion, was half a foot shorter than both the men who had accompanied Egan. Yet, something about him made him appear more formidable. He was broader, more powerfully built. But he also carried himself with a swagger that the other two lacked. Egan sensed that the other men – those following – answered to this one. He had thick, dark hair, a hooked nose, and dark eyes that put Egan in mind of a hawk. Gold rings flashed on several of his fingers, and a long, curved blade hung from his belt.

This man said something to Birthmark as he neared them. Birthmark nodded a response.

The man turned an appraising gaze on Egan.

"I am Gaspar," he said, his accent pronounced, but less opaque than Birthmark's. "And you are?"

"My name is Egan."

"Egan," he repeated. "You are French?"

"Yes."

"You are journeying with Templar Knights?"

He glanced at Birthmark and his friend. "Didn't they already tell you all of this?"

"I wish to hear it from you. Where you sailed from, how you came to be here."

He wanted to ask for something to drink. Wine. Or better, liquor. "We were at Acre," he said.

"We heard of the siege there. Is that when you left? When the city fell?"

He swallowed, nodded. He then proceeded to relate all that had befallen the *Tern* since its departure from Acre: the failed landing in Cyprus, the storm, the encounter with Killias's ship.

"You say she is called the *Melitta*?"

"That's right. Her captain calls her a ship of fortune."

Gaspar thinned a smile. "I am certain he does. They are pirates. Skilled ones at that, though not so powerful as to be a danger." He motioned for Egan to go on.

"There is little more to tell. They escorted us here. The Templars are buying provisions." Likely they already had, and were back on the ship, safe and comfortable. This he kept to himself.

"They will sail from here? With the *Melitta*?"

"I don't know what they intend. They might sail. They also spoke of a Templar fortress in the mountains."

"In Bagras."

"That's the name, yes."

"There are risks to either choice," Gaspar said, as much to himself as to Egan. A second later, he eyed Egan again. "You would like us to strike at them. On the sea or on the road. That is your purpose in being here, yes?"

His pulse quickened. "Yes. There are only nine of them. They shouldn't be difficult to defeat. You can kill the knights and take the people who are with them. Do with them what you will."

"Templars are always difficult to defeat, no matter how many there are. But you are correct: we can take their ship. First, though, I want to know why you do this."

Egan felt his cheeks burn, and he turned his head to the side, wishing he could hide from the glow of the torches.

"Your bruises. They came from the Templars?"

"Not precisely," he said, his voice dropping.

"From who then? Why?"

"Does it matter?"

Gaspar spread his hands. "You are betraying them. Or that is how it seems. Perhaps this is a trap, a way of luring us into danger. So yes, it matters a good deal. We will do nothing until you answer."

He kept his gaze averted. "There are Jews on our ship. A man and his daughter. She—she claimed that I did something. The others believed her, and the Templars punished me. When she repeated her tale to those on the *Melitta*, one of them beat me. I want revenge."

"The girl lied?"

Egan cursed himself for hesitating. He knew Gaspar would notice.

"You did something to this girl? Forced yourself on her, perhaps?"

His eyes snapped to the man's face. "Certainly not. I am no animal."

"Then what did you do?"

Again, his face blazed. "We were hungry. All of us. I—I took food. And I blamed her."

"Ah," the man said, with a wry grin and knowing nod. He said something in a different language. The men standing with them laughed. "I believe I understand," he said in French. "Humiliation does this to us. You suffered doubly. Once on your ship, and again on the *Melitta*. Is that right?"

"They're Jews."

155

Gaspar dipped his chin again. "Well, you will be avenged. Because of you, the Templars will be taken, and any with them will die, or be sold as chattel. Is that acceptable?"

For the first time since reaching the strand, Egan allowed himself a smile. "Yes."

"I am so glad."

Gaspar's gaze shifted, and he gave a single sharp nod.

Someone grabbed his shoulder from behind. Before he could turn, agony exploded between his shoulder blades. It spread like white fire to his chest. His back arched, blood belched from his mouth. He couldn't draw breath. His knees buckled and he dropped to the sand. Looking down, he wondered at what he saw. Something jutted from his chest. A blade, glistening with blood. His blood. He found Gaspar's eyes with his own. Wanted to ask a question, but couldn't form the words.

"You are a traitor, and not to be trusted. We will use what you have told us, but your life was forfeit the moment you resorted to treachery." He looked to the man behind Egan and nodded again.

The sword was withdrawn. More torment.

Egan tried to breathe, but only inhaled blood. His vision blurred, dimmed. His body gave out, and he could do nothing to stop the fall. The last thing he felt was the sand rising to cushion his face.

CHAPTER 9

"We do not wish to be a burden to you," Simon said. "But we have voyaged together for weeks, over many leagues, and through trials that would have overwhelmed others. Haven't we proven ourselves?"

Godfrey let out a sigh, his expression pained. Landry didn't envy him this exchange.

"You have proven yourselves again and again. Men and women both, from the oldest among you to brave Adelina."

The girl smiled, blushed.

"But still, there are limits to how far we can take you. Our ship is too slow and too fragile to carry us all the way to France. These waters are perilous, as is the road to Bagras. We have only bad choices before us. We will not abandon you, but we cannot remain with you indefinitely. At some point, very soon I'm afraid, we must part company. Our place is with our Order, wherever we may find them. And we cannot assure your safety."

"None of us has ever asked for such assurances."

A sad smile alighted on Godfrey's lips. "I know that. You are, all of you, too courageous to do so. Yet, we'd be remiss if we allowed any harm to come to you."

"Where would you suggest we go?" Nila asked.

"That is up to you. You need not all go to the same place. I believe some or all of you would be safe here, in Rhosus. But this is far from your homes, and may not be to your liking."

"That is what you would prefer," Nila said. "Isn't that so? You have spoken of going to Bagras, of joining the Templars there."

"We have. But it seems the road to Bagras is more dangerous than we thought. We cannot bring any of you with us there. So, if you wish to leave Rhosus, we will forego Bagras for another Templar stronghold. Somewhere to the west, perhaps."

"I have no desire to live among the Cilicians," Simon said, "or the Turks, for that matter." He glanced sidelong at Draper. "Forgive me."

"There is nothing to forgive," Draper said.

"Can you take us as far as Crete, or even Athens?" Simon asked. "From there, we might secure passage to France, or another of Europe's kingdoms."

Godfrey looked to Tancrede, a question in his sky-blue eyes.

"That's a long way," the knight said. "In waters we know to be unsafe."

"We can follow the shoreline," Simon said. "At the first sign of danger, you can make for the nearest port and leave us there. But at least we would be a bit closer to our destination."

Godfrey considered this. Tancrede gave a small hike

of his shoulders, seeming to indicate that he thought it a reasonable suggestion.

"The rest of you want this as well?" Godfrey asked. "You would go to Crete?"

"They're not all here," Landry said, keeping his voice low so only Tancrede and the commander would hear.

"Who is missing?" Tancrede asked.

Landry wrinkled his nose.

His friend scanned the deck. "Egan?"

"For better or worse, he is under our protection."

"For all we know, he's not coming back."

"He might."

"Would you?"

Landry knew he was on the losing side of this argument. He himself didn't much care about the man, but he did feel responsible for him.

"If he returns, he'll go where the others go," Tancrede said. "Or he'll remain here. I feel no need to offer him more options than that."

Godfrey had listened as they debated and now he looked a question Landry's way.

"Very well," Landry said.

The commander faced Simon and the others. "As I asked before: all of you would prefer Crete to this place?"

Every one of them signaled their agreement.

"Then so be it. Father Dawid should have provisions for us in the morning. Once they are on board the ship, we sail for Crete."

"Will the *Melitta* sail with us?" Irène asked.

Landry recalled seeing her slip into the hold of the galley a few nights earlier, in the company of one of Killias's crew. No one echoed her question, but Simon watched Godfrey with keen interest.

"We will speak with the captain. I would prefer to sail with their protection. The *Tern* is vulnerable on its own. But after all he and his crew have done for us, they owe us nothing more. It's their decision to make. That is all," he added after a pause. "We'll eat in a short while."

The passengers dispersed, as did most of the Templars. Godfrey, Tancrede, and Landry remained. Landry scanned the wharf in vain, searching for Egan.

"I would prefer to do this with the *Melitta*," Tancrede said.

"So would I," Godfrey said. "And I would rather chance the road to Bagras than any return to the sea."

"There are other fortresses," Landry said. "Perhaps we'll find one along the Byzantine coast."

"Perhaps. Come," Godfrey said, treading a plank down to the wharf, "we should speak with Killias."

Their conversation with the captain went better than Landry had imagined it might. Killias might have thought that the more aid he offered the Templars, the greater his reward would be. Whatever his calculation, he agreed immediately to accompany them on their westward voyage, stating that he had commerce he wished to conduct with merchants in Lamas, Anamur, Selinos, and several other sea towns along their route.

Landry wanted to ask what sort of business an avowed pirate would have with legitimate merchants, but he kept the question to himself. He was glad to have the galley as an escort. Nothing else mattered to him as much. Melitta, who followed their conversation from nearby, appeared pleased by her father's decision, leading Landry to consider that her wishes might also have made Killias more receptive to the idea.

In short order, the Templars walked back to the *Tern* bearing good tidings.

They enjoyed a pleasant meal aboard the ship. As the night deepened, Irène and two other women made their way to the *Melitta*. Later, after Adelina had fallen asleep, Simon did the same. To Landry's relief, the envy he experienced a few nights before did not resurface. Rather, his thoughts were consumed by concern for Egan.

When he spoke of this with Godfrey, the commander dismissed his worries much as Tancrede had.

"Why would he have stayed with us, Landry? He was hated by Simon and Adelina, looked upon with contempt by the others, and by us, if we're to be honest. Not to mention that he was humiliated by Melitta. He has no reason to rejoin us. He probably recognized that Rhosus is as fine a place for him as any we might find. He's not coming back."

Landry could not fault his logic any more than he could Tancrede's. But still, even after Godfrey left him by the rail, and on through the rest of the night until he finally fell asleep, Egan's absence gnawed at him, not because he cared what happened to the man, but because he feared what Egan might do now that his fate was no longer tied to that of the *Tern*.

When morning broke, and Landry found that the man had not returned to the ship during the night, he accepted that his friends had been right. Egan wasn't coming back. Still, his trepidation lingered and deepened.

After matins, the Templars crossed through the town back to the church they had visited the night before. Father Dawid awaited them there with a cornucopia of meats, cheeses, fruits, greens, breads, and wine, as well as additional coin with which to replenish their stores over the course of their voyage. Landry had been sure the priest would do his best to help them, but he had not expected that he and his flock could provision them so lavishly.

"We cannot thank you enough," Godfrey told him. "You have my word, as a Templar, that you shall be rewarded for your generosity, above and beyond whatever this cost you."

"You are kind, Brother Godfrey. We do this to honor God and your service to Him." A mischievous smile stole across his face. "But we will gladly accept those rewards, when they are bestowed. In the meantime, pray with me once again before you go."

"It would be our pleasure."

The knights entered the church and knelt before the altar as the priest led them in prayer. Then they gathered what Father Dawid had given them and made their way back to the ship, each Templar laden with some of their bounty. With the help of Simon and their other charges, they stowed the food and wine in the hold. As they did this, Landry's thoughts turned again to Egan. He had to admit that he would rest easier at night, knowing the man was not aboard the ship, and thus not a danger to Adelina or their precious stores.

Tancrede oversaw the preparation of the ship for departure. Godfrey sent word to the *Melitta* that they would soon be ready to leave port.

The morning had dawned clear and warm. A steady breeze blew out of the north, and the bay was calm. They could not have asked for a better day on which to commence their voyage. All of them were in high spirits, and why not? They had food, wind to fill their sails, and a destination from which they might eventually reach their homes.

Landry's shoulder had not pained him in several days, and so when it came time to row the *Tern* away from the wharf, he insisted on taking up an oar himself. Draper disapproved, but Landry didn't care. He did feel a twinge or two as they oared the ship into the bay, but he bore them in silence.

Once they were on open water, Tancrede had Victor and Thomas raise their sail. Within seconds of being unfurled it had swelled with wind, propelling the ship forward. The repaired mast held.

Ahead of them, the crew of the *Melitta* raised her sails as well, and together the two vessels cut through the placid waters of Armenian Bay toward the Mediterranean.

Adelina stands at the prow of their ship, her father behind her, both his hands on her shoulders. The sea sparkles before them, as if strewn with diamonds. Her hair dances in the wind, and occasionally, if a swell slaps the hull just the right way, a spray of seawater dampens her face. Each time this happens, she laughs aloud.

She has been of two minds about going back out to sea. She fears another storm. She does not wish to be driven below into the hold to endure again the sickening lurch of rough waters. On the other hand, her father tells her that they are headed to a land named Crete, a place of legend, of glorious art and ancient treasures. A place from which they can commence the final leg of their journey to France. Adelina thinks she could suffer through ten storms for that.

Mostly, she is happy that Egan is gone. She knows this is uncharitable of her. She tries to tell herself that she wishes him no ill, but is merely glad he is gone. She is not certain, though, that this is true.

As the *Tern* emerges from the bay and angles westward onto the sea, the water becomes somewhat more turbulent. Not enough to worry her or make her ill, but enough to drench her and her father with each rise and fall of the sea. They retreat to the middle of the ship.

Adelina wants to go farther back so that she can watch Tancrede work the rudder, but her father asks her to sit with him near the hatch.

Even after she does so, he does not say anything. His dark eyes scan the sea, and wind ruffles his brown curls. She senses that he wants to ask her something, but she waits, and he remains silent.

"Father?" she says after a time.

He answers with a nervous laugh, brushes a strand of hair from her brow. "You look so much like your mother."

"You've told me."

"So I have." He heaves a breath and glances ahead of them in the direction of the *Melitta*. "I'm wondering…" He breaks off with a small shake of his head. Laughs again. Adelina has never seen him like this.

"Are you all right, Papa?"

"I'm fine, yes. I—I wonder… what you think of Melitta."

Adelina frowns. "The ship?"

His laugh this time is stronger, more like his usual one. But his face reddens. "No, not the ship. The woman."

"I like her," Adelina says. "She's nice to me, and she... What she did to Egan..."

"She was your champion, wasn't she?"

The only one. She did more for me even than you did. "Yes, she was," is all she says.

"I believe, in her own way, she championed both of us. I'm grateful to her. And... and I care about her, Adelina. Very much."

Understanding breaks over her like a wave. She can do no more than stare at him, her mouth open. She is embarrassed and frightened and thrilled and too uncertain of herself to speak a word.

"She and I have... well, we have spent some time together, and we have talked about a good many things. Including you, of course. She is very fond of you."

Adelina's eyes well, and tears spill down her cheeks. She cannot say why she is crying. "Do you love her?" she asks in a quavering voice.

"I don't know," he says. "I might."

She wants to ask how he can be unsure of such a thing, but the words will not come.

He reaches for her and starts to say something more, but Adelina has heard enough. She runs from him, ducks down through the hatch and into the hold, and throws herself onto her blanket on the old wooden floor. There she balls herself up, much the way she did the night Egan accused her of stealing, and she cries until her throat aches. In time, she falls asleep.

Landry did not mean to eavesdrop, but it was a small ship and, as usual, he stood with Tancrede near the stern. Both heard much of what Simon said to the girl.

When Adelina broke away from him and sprinted down into the hold, Simon started to follow.

"Let her go," Tancrede said, sympathy in his voice.

Simon regarded them both, then looked toward the hatch.

"She will come back up eventually," the lean knight went on. "But she is not yet ready to hear all that you have to say to her."

The man dipped his chin in agreement and then shook his head, appearing to argue with himself. "I didn't think she would be so unhappy. She likes Melitta. I know she does."

"Liking her is one thing. Accepting her as her new mother? That is quite another."

Simon glanced up at that. "I never said that I intend to marry her."

"You said enough to lead her thoughts there."

"I suppose so. She has always been quick, just like her mother." He walked to where Landry and Tancrede stood, and leaned on the rail like a man weary from battle. "We've been alone a long time, Adelina and I. A girl needs a mother, as well as a father."

"Even if that mother is a pirate?" Tancrede said.

A reluctant grin split Simon's face. "Yes, even so." His smile fell away, his eyes darting between the knights. "Forgive me. I shouldn't burden you with these concerns. Especially since..." He trailed off, appearing discomfited.

Tancrede shifted the rudder slightly, keeping the ship in line with the *Melitta*. "Our vows of celibacy do not change the fact that we are men. We probably understand you better than you imagine. Isn't that so, Landry?"

Landry offered a weak smile, hoping this would suffice. Truth be told, he had never been in love, which might be why he was so jealous of Simon when first they encountered the galley and the captain's beguiling daughter.

"You would marry?" Tancrede asked, filling a lengthening silence.

"Maybe," Simon said. "I don't know. But we have spoken of Adelina and me remaining with her when the rest disembark at Crete."

"A girl on a pirate ship?" Landry asked.

"A merchant ship, actually. Melitta would give up pirating and she and I would sail and trade together."

"Still, life at sea might be hard on the girl."

"That was my thought as well. But Melitta tells me she was but a year or two older than Adelina when she began to sail with her father. It is not as far-fetched a notion as we would believe."

"Cousins of mine grew up on ships," Tancrede said. "There are worse fates for children."

Simon's expression brightened, and for some time none of them spoke. Tancrede continued to follow the bearing established by Killias. The sun turned a slow arc overhead. The wind remained steady.

Landry couldn't say what it was that made him look back. He sensed no danger, had no reason to believe they might be pursued. But as soon as he peered back, beyond Tancrede at the open sea behind them, he spotted the ship.

It appeared to be another galley, similar in shape and size to the *Melitta*. Its sails were struck; the vessel bristled with oars. Those within the ship seemed to row with purpose. It trailed the *Tern* by some distance, but given the way it carved through the swells, it wouldn't take the vessel long to overtake them.

"Tancrede," he said, and pointed.

His friend paid no attention to him. Rather, he whispered, "What is she doing?"

Landry whirled to follow the direction of his gaze. The *Melitta* was in mid-turn. As he watched, men struck her sails and others went to sweeps. Beyond the *Melitta*, Landry glimpsed a second vessel. Or rather, a third. Yet another galley, also on sweeps, also approaching at speed.

"There's a ship behind us, as well," he said.

Tancrede looked back, muttered an imprecation under his breath.

Godfrey strode in their direction, Gawain limping after him, and the other Templars following. "What's happening?" the commander asked.

"Nothing good," Tancrede said. "It seems we're being chased and headed off at the same time."

"We should make for land," Landry said.

Tancrede looked over his shoulder at the pursuing ship. "Yes, maybe. Let's see what Killias has to say."

By this time, the *Melitta* had completed its turn and was headed back in their direction. Moments later, she pulled even with the *Tern*.

"You see?" Killias called, indicating both ships with a gesture.

"Yes," Godfrey said. "Can we escape them by going to land?"

The captain considered both ships, a scowl on his angular face.

"*We* can. I fear you won't make it to port in time. Not unless we buy you a few extra minutes."

"What do you mean?"

"Precisely what I said, Templar. You sail for port. We shall remain here and rain arrows on both ships until you're safe."

"No," Godfrey said. "You'll all be killed."

"You underestimate my crew."

"Not at all. But those two ships are easily as large as yours, and if each has as many men, it will be slaughter."

"While the two of you quarrel like old peddlers," Melitta said from the galley, "those two ships are closing on us."

"You have a skiff," Godfrey said. "Would you be willing to part with it, at least for a time?"

"To what end?"

"Let our passengers row to land. We'll keep both vessels here until they are safe."

"And then what?"

"We are Templars. We'll fight. It's what we do."

"The women can take Adelina," Simon said, looking from Godfrey to Landry to Tancrede. "But the rest of us should remain. We can help you."

Godfrey shook his head. "You belong with your daughter, Simon. And even if you didn't, you cannot help us. We are trained for war. I admire your courage, but I cannot risk allowing you to remain."

"But—"

"Listen to him, lad," Killias said. He pointed a rigid finger at the nearer of the two ships. "Those men are killers. You and the others are more likely to get a knight killed as he attempts to save your life. Take your daughter and the others, and go to shore. Your courage will be needed and tested there."

"Please, my friend," Godfrey said, giving Simon

no time to argue. "Gather your daughter, get on that skiff, and go."

The commander pulled from his belt the coin purse given to him by Father Dawid. He pressed it into Simon's hands. "Take this. Provide for them. Keep them safe. That is the most important thing you can do right now. Please."

Simon pressed his lips thin, his face pale in the sunlight. At last he nodded and hurried below.

Adelina wakes to shouts from above. She cannot make out what any of the men say, but she hears anger in their voices, and fear. She hears her father's voice. He is as loud and strident as the others. This scares her. She sits up, pushes a hand through her tangled hair, and stands, intending to go to him.

She is still upset by the things he said to her earlier. But he is all she has, the only person in her world who can ease her fright.

Before she reaches the stairs, he is there. She runs to him, and he gathers her in his arms, lifts her.

"What's happening?" she asks, her words muffled against his neck.

"We're leaving the *Tern*."

She pulls back to look at him. "Why?"

"There are ships after us. Pirates, I fear. We need to row to land."

"What about the knights? What about Melitta?"

"They will stay and fight," he says. She can tell from his worried expression and the chill in his tone that he doesn't like this idea.

He carries her onto the deck. The Templars await

them, grim, their gazes fixed on two ships that come at them from opposite directions.

"You will be in our prayers," Godfrey says. He smiles at Adelina, strokes her cheek with a gentle finger. She decides that perhaps he is not so frightening after all.

The rest of passengers are already in the small boat that floats beside the *Tern*. Adelina's father places her in Landry's arms. Landry, in turn, lifts her over the side of the vessel and lowers her to Nila, who waits in the smaller boat. Her father swings himself over the rail, but hesitates there, his gaze finding Melitta. They stare at each other for a heartbeat, two. She touches her fingers to her lips. He does the same.

Then he is in the small boat with Adelina and the others. He and two other men row. Melitta watches them from the rails of her ship until a cry from Killias seizes her attention. She moves away from the side of the ship and Adelina loses track of her.

Adelina twists to look at one of the galleys converging on the *Melitta* and the *Tern*, and then the other. They are big ships, the biggest she has ever seen. Their prows are shaped to look like serpents and they cut through the water with a swiftness that frightens her. Shouldn't she and the others remain with the knights and Melitta? Shouldn't they fight the men on these two galleys? Melitta told the Templars that Adelina and her father are crew, just as the Templars are. Doesn't that mean that they should remain and stand with them?

She pivots back to her father, opening her mouth to ask as much. Seeing his expression, though, the lines etched in his brow, around his mouth and eyes, she swallows the question. If they could have remained, they would have. He would have insisted.

She looks back again, even more scared for her friends, the people who have kept them alive these past days. It occurs to her that she might never see any of them again. She clasps her hands, squeezes her eyes shut, and prays, hoping that God will honor a Jewish prayer to save Christian lives.

CHAPTER 10

Members of the *Melitta*'s crew leapt down to the *Tern*, all of them bearing bows and quivers. Better, Killias and Godfrey had decided, that both ships should be well armed for the coming encounter. Leaving the *Tern* with only the Templars to fight would have made it an easy target. Perhaps with another dozen men, trained archers all, they could fight off the galleys for a time.

But Landry knew this for what it was: an act of desperation intended to put off the inevitable. Both ships were about to be boarded, provided they weren't burned to empty husks, as the pirate ship was the day they first met the *Melitta*.

"If we can get close enough to burn them out, as we did the *Blood Dawn*, we have a chance," Killias told Godfrey. "That is, if they don't possess weapons more formidable than oil-soaked arrows. Their bowmen will do all they can to keep us at a distance."

"What do you want us to do?"

"Don't come too close to the *Melitta*. We want to

divide their assault. The *Melitta* probably can't withstand an attack from both ships at once. If you can draw one away, give us time to defeat the other, we can come to your defense before you're overwhelmed." He grimaced. "That's my idea, anyway." He eyed the two galleys. "If you have other thoughts, I'd welcome them."

"I have little experience with naval warfare," Godfrey said. "I'm a knight, not a sailor."

"Enough talk, father," Melitta called from her ship. "If we don't separate now, we'll be trapped together."

Landry checked the position of the ships. They were close now. He could hear their oars slicing into the surface of the sea. The sails of both galleys were furled, but Landry noticed black markings on the cloth of at least one of them. He wanted to ask if the marks meant anything to Killias, but this didn't seem the time.

"My daughter is right," Killias said. He proffered a hand, which Godfrey gripped. "Godspeed, Templar."

"And you, Captain."

The captain rushed to his vessel. Tancrede steered the *Tern* away from Killias's ship. Landry had never been more aware of how slow the *Tern* was compared with other vessels. It seemed they crawled across the surface of the sea.

"Perhaps some of us should row," he said, striding to Tancrede, who manned the rudder, as always.

Tancrede checked their position relative to the galley behind them. Before he could answer, though, one of Killias's sailors, a tall, yellow-haired man with bronzed skin and dark eyes, shook his head.

"Speed won't matter in this fight. Or rather, it will, but you can't row fast enough to outmaneuver a ship like that." He nodded toward the galley. "They have three sails to your one, thirty men on sweeps to your dozen. No, we need every man on deck, with a bow in his hands. That's our best hope."

"Do you know these ships?" Godfrey asked, approaching the sailor.

"Not on sight, no."

"What about those markings on the furled sails?" Landry asked.

The man narrowed his eyes, turned to stare at the nearer vessel. After a few seconds he blanched.

"You *do* know them."

"Only by reputation."

Godfrey said nothing. Landry waited for more.

"They're pirates, but I assume you'd gathered that much. If I had to guess, I'd say those sails bear black crosses. Which would make them Redman's ships."

Godfrey's eyes narrowed. "Redman?"

"Redman the Monk, they call him. Word is he was one of your kind once, a knight of some sort. Perhaps even a Templar."

"Why do I find that anything but reassuring?" Landry said.

"You're clever, I guess," the sailor said. "He's said to be ruthless, canny as a shark, and as good with a blade as he is with a rudder. Captain's done his best to avoid him all these years. I suppose our luck was bound to run out eventually."

The man said this last with a backward glance at the *Melitta*. Landry was sure he would have preferred to be on his own ship, among his comrades. He sensed as well that the sailor blamed the Templars for turning their fortunes where Redman the Monk was concerned.

Tancrede continued to guide the ship away from the *Melitta*. Landry chanced a quick look toward the shoreline. The skiff carrying Simon, Adelina, and the rest of their passengers appeared tiny and vulnerable on the gentle swells of the Mediterranean. They had put some distance between themselves and the *Tern*, but they were still a long way from land. The Templars and Killias's sailors had to occupy the galleys long enough for Simon and the others to reach the coast.

Gawain and Draper joined him at the rail.

"They've a long way to go," Gawain said.

"I was thinking the same."

"All the more reason to fight." As Gawain said this, he pushed a bow and a bundle of arrows into Landry's hands.

Landry tested the tension of the bow then set the arrows at his feet, leaning it against the hull within easy reach.

A shout went up from the *Melitta*. Pivoting, he drew a sharp breath to cry out a warning. Not that he needed to.

A swarm of arrows shadowed the sky above Killias's vessel. As the barbs reached their zenith and began their deadly descent, the sailors on the ship took cover beneath wooden shields. Moments later, the arrows struck, their impacts like the popping of a violent blaze. A few men screamed in agony. Two fell to the deck, where Landry could no longer see them. But for the most part, the shields protected them.

At a bellowed order from Killias, the men and Melitta took hold of their bows and loosed a volley of their own.

He had no chance to see more.

A warning from the tall sailor pulled his attention back to the galley bearing down on his ship. Arrows flew from the pirate ship. Landry tracked them, gripping his Templar shield, his knuckles so tight they hurt. Belatedly, he realized that Killias's men had brought their own shields.

As the arrows dropped, Landry ducked beneath his shield and awaited the impact. It came with the same rapid *thwack* he had heard from the other vessel. But he heard no shouts or cries. In this one assault, no one had been hurt.

"Damn!" Tancrede said.

Landry looked his way, then followed the line of his hot glare.

The sail. Arrows had sliced through it in two places.

The Templars and Killias's men unleashed a flurry of their own. Twenty arrows sailed over the water to the galley. The pirates blocked them with ease. Landry heard laughter and then the snap of bows.

He and the others shielded themselves again. This time, the impact of the arrows brought a snarl from one man. One of the sailors had taken a barb in his calf, but that was all. Landry didn't expect their good fortune could hold much longer.

The galley continued to close the distance between the two ships.

"Their ship is too big," Gawain said, as they loosed their arrows again. "And they have too many men."

"You may be right," Draper said. "But their size may not be such an advantage after all." He pointed a finger at the galley.

At first, Landry wasn't sure what the Turcopole was indicating.

"Draper, I don't—"

"Their oars. Or rather, the eyes in the hull where they're fixed."

Landry looked again, squinting against the glare of the sun off the water. The oar eyes were shielded, but the shields had been fixed at an angle, so that archers on a ship as large as the galley could not aim at their oarsmen. From the level of the *Tern*'s deck, there was a bit of space. A very little bit.

"That would be quite a shot," Gawain said. But he grinned as he spoke.

Landry gauged the distance and the angle. Difficult to be sure. But not impossible.

"You're not serious," Killias's man said, as all of them took shelter from another volley.

Arrows thudded into the deck all around them.

"They are getting close," Draper said. "If we do nothing, we will be boarded or burned within the next few moments. This may be our only hope."

"I don't know that I can hit a target so small."

"I have a silver piece that says you can't," Tancrede said. "Two of them if I make my shot."

The sailor flashed a quick grin. "You're on, Templar. The oarsmen," he called to his fellow sailors.

"Dunc, that's impossible," one of the men answered.

"Try it. One time. Then we aim for the deck again."

They nocked arrows, drew back their bows, and released them. As many arrows thudded into the shields or the side of the hull as threaded the holes. But several found their marks. Wails echoed from within the larger ship. Five oars jerked out of the water, and the galley veered away from the *Tern*. Tancrede steered them in the opposite direction, catching a gust of wind and putting some distance between the two vessels.

"You owe me a silver, Templar," the tall sailor said.

Tancrede smiled. "But only one."

Landry glanced at the other vessels. The *Melitta* and the second pirate ship continued to circle each other and trade attacks. From what he could tell, neither had gained a decisive advantage.

"They're turning back this way," Gawain said. "Should we try it again?"

Draper shook his head, clearly deflated. "It won't work a second time. Already they have replaced the lost oarsmen and shielded themselves from within.

"It was a good idea," Godfrey said.

Draper frowned. "A delay of the inevitable. Nothing more."

"It gives us time to think of another strategy."

Landry wanted to believe that Godfrey was right, but more arrows rained down on them in wave after wave. On those occasions when they had time to send back barbs of their own, their attacks seemed pitifully small. The galley closed in on them again. Landry could think of nothing they might do to get away or keep themselves from being boarded.

Another of Killias's sailors fell to the deck. This man didn't move again. An arrow jutted from his neck and blood stained the weathered wood.

Their shields looked like the backs of great barbed beasts. Arrows were embedded in the deck and the mast. The sail had been shredded. And still the assault continued.

The galley pulled abreast of their ship. Some of the pirates fired more arrows at them. But others used long iron hooks to grapple the *Tern* to their vessel.

Then they placed planks across the gap between the two ships, and the *Tern* was boarded.

Still gripping his shield, Landry straightened, dropped his bow, and drew his sword. His fellow Templars did the same, as did Killias's men.

The pirates were more skilled with bows than with blades. So were the sailors from the *Melitta*. Landry, Tancrede, Godfrey, and the other Templars, on the other hand, were renowned and feared throughout the world for their skill with steel. The numbers were not in their favor, but Landry preferred this fight to the peek and hide of fighting with bows.

Without a word among them, the Templars gathered together into a phalanx, instinct and the experience of a hundred battles guiding them. The pirates threw themselves at the knights, only to have their assault break upon the Templars' blades and shields like waves upon a rocky shore.

One man charged at Landry, gripping a scimitar in both hands. He was large, muscular, but reckless. He leveled a furious blow at Landry's head. Landry parried with ease. Shifted his weight. Delivered a strike of his own to the man's exposed side. The pirate collapsed in a bloody heap, innards spilling onto the deck. As easy a kill as he could recall.

But two men took the place of the dead one. Both big, both strong. Both wary now that they had seen their brother fall.

One chopped at Landry's head. The other swept a blow toward his gut. Landry raised his shield to block one, twisted his blade down to counter the other. His entire body quaked with the impacts. He leveled a strike of his own at the man on his left, pounded his shield into the face of the other man.

Both pirates fell back a step, then advanced together. Landry feinted, hammered his blade into the base of one man's neck. Blood arced from the wound. A backhanded blow severed the second man's arm. Landry finished him with a thrust to the heart.

He had no time to catch his breath. Two more pirates closed on him. This fight went much the way the last one had. He parried, absorbing their blows with his sword and his shield. And he lashed out, drawing blood, maiming, and then killing.

More pirates rushed at him.

Most of Landry's fellow Templars remained alive. He sensed Tancrede on one side of him, Godfrey on the other. Their breathing had grown labored, though. He knew nothing about the fates of the others, or of the men Killias had sent to their ship, or of the *Melitta*. He fought for his own survival. The longer he lived, the better the chance that his brother Templars beside him would remain alive, and the greater the likelihood that Simon, Adelina, and the rest would reach the safety of land.

He wiped sweat from his face with his arm. His sword and shield felt heavy. The pirates coming his way stepped over the bodies of their shipmates, and raised their swords to pound at him. These men were no more skilled than the others he had killed. But they had yet to break a sweat. They breathed normally. Their weapons probably felt light in their hands.

Like the men before them, they attacked him in unison, seeming to mirror each other's movements. As before, Landry tried to block one attack with his weapon and one with his shield. But they were

quicker than the men he had faced earlier. Or he was
slowing down.

His shield took the brunt of the attack from his
left. The strike on his right clanged off his sword, but
bit into his shoulder. He grunted, countered with a
downward sweep of his blade that hacked into the
pirate's leg. The man fell to one knee. Landry pushed
at the other pirate with his shield. His foe pushed
back. Landry staggered. The man on one knee struck
at him from that lower angle. Landry chopped with his
blade, blocking the attack. But the second man hewed
at him yet again. His shield arm almost buckled. The
first man stabbed up at him, seeking to disembowel.

Landry blocked this attack as well. Knocked the
man's sword away. Stabbed him through the throat.
He turned his full attention on the second pirate.
Already, though, another man advanced on him.
Others appeared to be waiting in line to get at him,
restrained only by the confined space aboard the *Tern*.

A brief exchange of sword blows and the pirate he
had engaged fell to the deck, his head cleaved in two.
The next men came at him.

"Tancrede?" Landry called, though he dared not
take his eyes off the men bearing down on him.

"Still here. For the moment." His voice sounded
ragged.

"Godfrey?"

"Alive, barely."

They had time for no more than that. Fresh assaults
opened gashes on Landry's hands, his brow. A careless
parry deflected a strike to his collarbone. An inch or
two higher, and the artery in his neck might have been
severed. In time, he lanced one man's heart, severed the

other's head from his neck. But he was relying now on his training, his knowledge of combat. His strength was spent, his reflexes grew more sluggish with each stroke of his sword. It was no longer a question of *if* he would die. It was only a matter of when. For all of them. There were just too many of the enemy. Skilled as the Templars were, they could not overcome these numbers.

"Enough!"

The voice cut through the clamor of battle like a dagger through parchment.

The pirates broke off their assault. Landry was too weary to take advantage. He let his shield arm drop, and leaned on his sword, his breath coming in great gasps. If his adversaries had chosen that moment to renew their attack, he would have been unable to defend himself.

"Surrender, Templars, and the lives of your friends shall be spared."

At first, he couldn't locate the speaker. When at last he spotted the man, he thought this must surely be the pirate of whom Killias's man had spoken: Redman the Monk.

He stood on the rail of the galley, clinging to a line from the mainsail, as comfortable on his perch as a falcon on a crag. Black hair hung to his shoulders, framing a tapered face. He wore a simple white shirt and plain black breeches, but rings of gold shone on several of his fingers. A curved blade hung from his belt.

Godfrey stared at the man before looking over the ship, and the carnage that had bloodied its deck. Landry did the same. Dead pirates lay everywhere; the Templars and their allies had exacted a toll on the marauders. But several of Killias's men had been killed as well. Only five remained alive. All were wounded. The golden-haired man – Landry had not taken the time to learn his name – bled from a dozen gashes. His nose appeared to have been broken. It was red and more crooked than it had been. Blood stained the skin around his mouth and chin.

Most of the Templars remained alive. Most, but not all. It took Landry a second or two to figure out who was missing.

"Victor," he whispered.

Tancrede hissed through his teeth, then muttered a prayer.

"Do you surrender?" the dark-haired man called from his perch.

"Why should we?" Godfrey demanded, adjusting his grip on his sword and eyeing the men he had been fighting.

"Because if you fight on, your deaths are inevitable. And those who fight with you will perish as well. Surrender, and we will spare all of you."

Godfrey's brow creased, drawing a laugh from the pirate.

"You don't believe that we intend to let you live."

"The thought that you might be lying has crossed my mind."

"Think, Templar. We are familiar with your Order, and the riches you hold. There is far more profit in allowing you to live than in killing you here. If we must, we will take your lives, take your ship, and pursue those you sent to shore. There might be some profit in that as well. But we would prefer to keep the eight of you alive. For a time, at least."

"Trust them not," said the yellow-haired sailor. "They're cutthroats. Nothing more."

"Perhaps. But if we continue this fight, we're all doomed."

"We're doomed no matter what!"

"Maybe. Maybe not." Godfrey shifted his gaze back to the pirate. "I take it you're the man they call Redman the Monk."

The man threw back his head and laughed.

"You've heard of the Monk, have you? No, I am not he." He gestured at the other ship. "He is aboard the *Poniard*, slaughtering your friends."

Against his will, Landry turned toward the other two ships. The larger galley still pursued Killias's ship. A storm of arrows pelted the *Melitta*. He couldn't tell if any of those aboard still lived.

"My name is Gaspar of Cadiz," the pirate went on. "I command the *Gold Prince*."

"You work for this Redman?"

"We are… associates." He smiled.

"Meaning you answer to him."

The smile vanished. "No more questions. No more talk. Do you wish to live, or shall we butcher you like pigs and take what we can from your ship? Quickly, Templar. My patience runs thin."

Godfrey faced Landry and Tancrede. "Thoughts?"

"If we surrender now, we live to fight another day," Tancrede said, his voice low. "And we save the lives of Killias's men."

"I'm not so sure," Gawain said from behind Landry. An angry gash on his cheek wept blood. "I don't trust him any more than does our friend here." He lifted his chin in the direction of the yellow-haired sailor. "We've cut down a lot of them. He may be as reluctant to continue this fight as we are.

I say we fight on. If we die, so be it."

"We've already lost one Templar and seven of Killias's men," Godfrey said. "And there must be fifty more pirates on that ship. We can't win. We would be throwing away our lives."

Landry sensed Gawain bristling, but the knight said nothing more.

"Well?" Gaspar asked.

Godfrey took a long breath. "Very well." He dropped his sword and shield.

One of Gaspar's crew hurried forward to claim both. Following their commander's example, Landry and the other Templars dropped their weapons as well. With obvious reluctance, the surviving men from the *Melitta* did the same.

"A wise choice, Templar." To his own men, he said, "Bring them aboard. Bind them with care. Kill the others."

Godfrey's eyes went wide. "*What?*"

Gaspar's men wasted not an instant. One plunged his sword into the chest of the yellow-haired sailor. Two of the other sailors died the same way. Pirates slit the throats of the remaining two. Landry, Tancrede, Godfrey, and the other Templars tried to fight back. But surrounded and disarmed, they could do little. In seconds, Landry found himself confronted by five sword tips, all leveled at his chest.

"You gave your word!" Godfrey shouted at the man.

"I staked out a position in a negotiation. I make no apologies for doing what was necessary to secure the result I desired." He turned and hopped off the rail. "Bring them aboard," he said over his shoulder.

The pirates forced them onto the planks and across to the galley. There, men bound their arms behind their backs, tying them at the elbows and wrists.

They started to herd the Templars below into the hold, but Gaspar stopped them.

"In good time. For now, they can remain on deck and watch the destruction of their friends."

Landry stared once more at the other two ships. Their only hope now was that somehow Killias might defeat Redman's vessel and then rescue them from Gaspar. It took Landry no more than a glance to understand that this would not happen.

The *Poniard* had pulled even with the *Melitta* and had started to board her. Killias and his crew fought valiantly, but their ranks had been decimated by Redman's archers. They were soon overwhelmed.

The pirates didn't kill the survivors, as Landry expected. Instead, a man strode to the stern of the *Melitta* and waved a hand, indicating that the *Gold Prince* should approach.

Gaspar had his rudder man steer the vessel closer.

As they neared the two ships, another man walked to the aft deck of the *Poniard*. He was older than Gaspar, bald, tall, and muscular. Like the captain of the *Gold Prince*, he wore a white shirt and black breeches, but he bore no jewelry that Landry could see. A dark beard and mustache sharpened his features.

"Greetings, Templars," he called.

"That is Redman," Gaspar said, somewhat unnecessarily.

"You are just in time," the bald man continued. "I must decide the fates of your friends. I would know your minds."

"This can't end well," Tancrede said under his breath.

"I can kill them all, or I can take them and sell them to slavers. I am inclined toward the latter, but I believe it might be safer to take their lives and be done with it. What say you?"

None of them spoke. Godfrey had gone pale. Landry knew he would be punishing himself for surrendering to Gaspar.

"Come now," Redman said. "Surely you have an opinion on the matter. You can't be completely unconcerned when it comes to their fortunes. Do you care so little whether they live or die?"

"Slavery or death," Killias said. "That is no choice at all. But if we must choose, we will take death."

"Bravely said." Redman walked to where the captain stood. Killias was flanked by pirates, each of whom held a sword to his chest. "Who would have believed that a pirate would display so much more courage than Templars? I grieve for the Order, so far has it fallen."

He glanced back at Godfrey and gave a small shrug.

A blade flashed silver in his hand, and with a quick, violent motion he slashed Killias's throat.

Blood fanned over the captain's chest, forming a crimson bib. His eyes rolled back and he dropped to the deck.

"Death it is," Redman said.

Melitta screamed. She struggled to run to her father, but two men held her back.

Redman stared down at the captain for a second or two, then strolled back in the direction of the Templars. "Now then, I repeat my question. The captain chose death. Shall we assume his crew intend the same choice?"

Godfrey hung his head, though only briefly. "We were told that you were once a Templar. I refuse to believe it."

"Believe what you will, Templar. But I *was* a knight, and I freed myself from that particular yoke." He grinned. "By the grace of God." He shifted his eyes to Gaspar. "Take them below. Put them in the cage. We'll deal with these—" He waved a hand at Melitta and the rest of Killias's crew. "—and then we'll be on our way."

He turned and advanced on Killias's daughter. Landry and Tancrede struggled against their bonds, but to no avail. Pirates shoved them toward the hatch of the *Gold Prince*. The last Landry saw of Melitta, she stood with tears on her cheeks but her chin held high, unbowed before Redman the Monk.

CHAPTER 11

The cage was what it sounded like: an iron prison set in the recesses of the *Gold Prince*'s small hold. Each of the Templars was led by two pirates into the pen. When all were inside, another of Gaspar's men secured the cage door with a lock, also made of iron, that was the size of Tancrede's fist.

The hold itself was set near the stern of the ship, and separated by a wall from another forward hold. Tancrede assumed that the galley's crew slept and ate in that other area. It had to be larger than this one. The air in their cramped hold was still and hot, and it stank of sweat and piss, rot and vomit. Tancrede breathed through his mouth until he started to grow accustomed to the stench. Aside from a few small slits in the wood, which allowed in a bit of light and too little fresh air, the hold had no openings save the hatch. Rat droppings dotted the uneven floor. A half-decayed rat carcass lay near the back corner of the cage.

Gawain toed the carcass, clearly disgusted. "It seems

we have pets." He kicked the carcass out of the cage.

Tancrede still bled from wounds on his head, neck, and arms. But several of his fellow Templars were worse off than he. Thomas had suffered the most grievous injury, a blow to his leg deep enough that Tancrede could see bone. It bled profusely. Sweat shone on Thomas's long face. Dark, damp hair clung to his brow, and his breaths came shallow and quick.

"I could help him if they would let me," Draper said, frustration tightening his voice. "We need to stop the bleeding, and he requires a poultice to prevent infection. Otherwise he could lose the leg."

The wound on Gawain's face needed attention as well. Tancrede had little confidence that these pirates would allow them any treatment at all. He rarely had cause to question Godfrey's leadership, but in this case the commander had chosen poorly. Gawain had spoken true: a fight to the death would have been preferable to this.

He didn't say as much, of course. He didn't have to. Godfrey's guilt weighed on him, curving his shoulders, haunting his pale eyes. The commander spoke not a word. He stood near the door to the cage and stared out toward the hatch, as if he might will Gaspar to come to them.

Landry, on the other hand, stalked the perimeter of their prison, scrutinizing every joint in its construction, and every plank of wood beneath their feet. As he completed a circuit around the space, Tancrede joined him.

"What do you see?"

The young knight shook his head. "Very little," he said. "No weak points in the bars. No rotted planks."

A bitter smile flitted across his lips. "And even if there were, with our arms bound like this there isn't much we could do."

"They'll have to untie us eventually," Tancrede said. "Unless they intend to feed us themselves."

"What if they don't plan to give us any food at all?"

"Gaspar said—"

"Gaspar is a liar. We know as much already. I would guess that this fallen monk is no better."

"They've gone to a lot of trouble to take us as prisoners," Godfrey said, the words flat, empty of emotion. "We have to assume they want us to live."

Landry looked like he might argue further, but in that moment the smells reached them. Lamp oil, wood smoke, the char of human flesh.

"One of them is burning," Gawain said. "I suppose it's too much to hope that Melitta managed to avenge her father."

Tancrede shared a grim look with Landry before bowing his head and muttering a prayer for the crew of the *Melitta*. Not long after the stink of smoke reached them, the motion of the galley changed. Where it had bobbed in place, it now seemed to be turning.

"We're moving," Landry said.

Gawain moved to the bars nearest to one of the openings in the hull. "Apparently," he said. "The question is, does that bode ill or well?"

Tancrede crossed to stand beside him. "They may be going after the skiff."

Footsteps sounded overhead. Someone descended into their hold. Gaspar.

He wrinkled his nose as he stepped away from the stairway.

"I see you're settled in," he said.

Godfrey made his way to the front of the cage. "One of our men is wounded. He requires healing."

Gaspar's expression remained mild. "We have wounded as well. When our healers have ministered to all of them, they will assess the condition of your man."

"We can heal our own," Godfrey said. "Give us the bandages and herbs we carried on our ship, and allow us to use them."

The pirate shook his head. "That would mean untying you, and I have no intention of doing so. At least not while you're aboard my ship." Amusement flickered in his dark eyes. "Don't look so unhappy, Templar. Were I to untie you, I would also expect you to row. As it is, you have free passage."

"Do you intend to have your men spoon-feed us then, like mothers caring for their children?"

"No. I see no need to feed you at all. You are knights. Surely you are accustomed to the hardships of war? You can go without meals for a time. I doubt any of you will starve."

Gaspar took hold of the lock and gave it a tug. The prison rattled, but the lock did not give. After a quick perusal of the cage, he nodded to himself and started back toward the stairway.

"Where are you taking us?" Godfrey said.

The pirate turned. "Do you know these waters? Are you familiar with the lands adjacent to them?"

Godfrey hesitated.

A smile crossed the man's face. "I thought not."

He left them without saying more, climbing onto the deck and walking overhead. A few seconds later Tancrede heard laughter from above.

Not long after, the rhythmic splash of sweeps reached them from outside the ship, and the galley surged forward. For Tancrede, who had remained on deck for even the worst of the storm they had endured, riding over swells and troughs while in the hold proved uncomfortable. It hadn't occurred to him that he might be bothered by the motion of a ship, but he couldn't recall when last he had been confined to a hold for more than a few moments.

After they had been under way for some time, Landry asked, "Are you all right?"

"I'd be better above."

"Now you know how the rest of us felt on the *Tern*."

Tancrede didn't feel well enough to acknowledge the gibe. He sat in that spot nearest to the opening, wishing for just a moment or two above, the touch of a cool breeze, the scent of sea air. His arms, back, and shoulders had begun to ache from being bound for so long in such an awkward position, and his wounds still throbbed.

After a while, Thomas lost consciousness. Tancrede doubted he would wake again. The movement of the vessel remained steady, and from what he could see through the gap in the hull, the sun still shone. A small blessing, that. He would have found rougher weather unbearable.

An hour passed, maybe two. Tancrede couldn't gauge the time.

"We haven't encountered the skiff," Landry said, breaking a lengthy silence. "We would have slowed and we would have heard... something."

"Maybe the Monk got them," Gawain said.

"Maybe. Or maybe they reached land before either ship overtook them. I choose to believe that."

Gawain dipped his chin. "Then I will as well."

Sometime later, as the sky visible to them from within the cage began to darken to azure, the rhythm of the oars, which had hardly wavered at all, slowed noticeably and then ceased altogether.

The Templars exchanged glances.

"Do you think we've reached land?" Landry asked.

No one answered.

With the galley no longer moving at speed, the up and down motion of the vessel grew more pronounced. Tancrede guessed that they were stopping for the night, which meant his stomach would only suffer more. He kept the thought to himself, preferring not to speak. In addition to his other woes, his bladder ached. He sensed, though, that their captors wouldn't even allow them the dignity of relieving themselves.

Darkness fell. Food aromas drifted into their hold from the other hold. Despite feeling ill, Tancrede's stomach rumbled. But no one brought them food. Nor did the pirates bring light of any sort. The dead space just outside the cage came alive with scrabblings and scratches. The rats.

"Gaspar!" Godfrey called, startling him.

When this first cry brought no response, Godfrey shouted for the pirate again, and then a third time.

At last, the stairs creaked beneath bootsteps.

"What are you bellowing about, Templar?"

"My men require food and drink. One of us still needs healing. And we must be allowed to... to step out of this enclosure and see to our basic needs."

"I've told you already, you will not be fed, at least

not until we reach land. Our healer is weary from the day's labors. If circumstances allow, he will see to your man tomorrow. As to the rest, you will remain where you are, as you are. If you must piss yourselves, or shit yourselves, be my guests. You wouldn't be the first to befoul the cage in that way." He laughed at this and left them.

For a long time, none of the Templars spoke. Finally, Godfrey cleared his throat.

"Pray with me, brothers."

Tancrede closed his eyes and tucked his chin.

Godfrey began with the Creed of the Apostles, an assertion of faith. After that, he led them in the Angelus, and finally in Vespers. Even after this, though, he was not finished.

"By your Grace, Lord, we are Templars, devoted to your service. See us to salvation. Deliver us from the wickedness that surrounds us. Redeem us so that we may continue to serve you through your son Jesus Christ. Protect those who we sent to shore. Minister to your servant, Thomas. And grant rest to those lost this day. Amen."

"Amen," the others echoed.

"Sleep, brothers," Godfrey said. "Tomorrow brings new hope."

They arrayed themselves in the available space, propping themselves against the bars as best they could. Tancrede didn't believe there was any possibility he would sleep. But in time he dozed off. He jolted himself awake every so often, only to drift again into slumber.

Still, the night seemed to last an eternity, and when at last he opened his eyes to the golden glow of morning, his aches had redoubled.

Draper shifted onto his knees, grunting his discomfort, and crawled to Thomas, whose youthful face had turned gray.

"He lives," the Turcopole said. "Though only just. I fear he won't last another day."

Voices and movement on the deck, and in the other hold, told them that Gaspar's crew was up and about. But no one brought them water. The healer did not come to check on the wounded Templar. Before long, with the splash of oars, they were under way again.

Tancrede peered out through the opening, trying to locate the sun and thus determine the direction in which they were headed. He thought they might be sailing east, back the way they had come the previous day, but he couldn't be certain.

More hours dragged by, marked by hunger and cramped muscles, and the stifling heat of their prison.

Late that day, the ship slowed again. Men above shouted, and for the briefest of moments Tancrede thought that perhaps the *Gold Prince* was under attack. Soon enough he realized his error. Laughter and song told him that Gaspar's men were celebrating, not dying.

Even as bitter disappointment flooded his heart, footsteps on the stairway drew his gaze. Gaspar led several men into the hold. He carried no weapon himself, but the pirates with him gripped swords.

"Bring them up," the captain said, halting beneath the hatch.

His men unlocked the cage and ordered the Templars to their feet. When they struggled to comply, the pirates hoisted them up by their bound arms. The pain stole Tancrede's breath, blinded him. He staggered against the bars, then righted himself.

"What about this one?" one of the pirates asked, nudging Thomas with the toe of his boot.

"Him, too." Gaspar sounded bored.

"He won't wake up. I think he's dead."

"He is not dead," Draper said, planting himself in front of the pirate. "We have told you again and again. He needs healing."

"If he won't wake up, kill him."

"No! He needs water and bandages and a poultice!"

The pirate looked back at Gaspar, who shook his head. The man tried to push past Draper, no doubt intending to kill Thomas.

Draper tried to keep himself between the pirate and Thomas. For a few seconds, he succeeded. Finally, the sailor pounded Draper with the hilt of his sword, bloodying the Templar's nose and knocking him to the floor.

He stepped over Draper, and stabbed Thomas through the chest. Blood stained the knight's tabard, but otherwise, he didn't move or make a sound.

"Bring the rest," Gaspar said, and climbed the stairs to the deck.

With the pirates prodding them, the Templars shuffled out of the cage, and ascended the stairway into the blazing light of day. Tancrede could barely open his eyes for the glare, but he welcomed the cool air and the sounds of the sea.

Two of the pirates emerged onto the deck as well, bearing between them the body of Thomas. They carried him to the starboard rail and without pause, without even a word, dumped the knight's body over the side. Hearing the splash, Tancrede closed his eyes and whispered a prayer, his gut turning an unsettled somersault.

As his eyes adjusted to the daylight, he realized that the *Gold Prince* had been joined by Redman the Monk's ship. The former Templar stood on the rail of his vessel, which lay just off the port side of Gaspar's.

"A shame about your fellow knight," Redman said. "I had hoped to capture all nine of you. Now we're down to seven. I shall have to take care not to kill any more of you."

"You could start by feeding us," Godfrey said. "Allowing us something to drink."

"In good, time, Templar. You appear to be in fine health for now. As I'm certain Gaspar has told you already, we have no plans to unbind you while we're at sea. I know how Templars fight. The danger is too great.

"But don't despair. We'll have you on land before this day is through. Then you'll be given a morsel to eat, and water to drink." He opened his hands and smiled. "You see, I'm not a barbarian. I am a man of business. You are now an asset, one I intend to use to my advantage. I have no intention of permitting you to die."

Something about the way he said this chilled Tancrede's blood... *Permitting you to die.* It seemed that he expected them to wish for death before long. If Godfrey heard the same threat in Redman's words, he gave no indication of it.

"Why, then, did you bring us up here, if not to give us food?"

"I thought you would want to leave your cage for a time. But if I was wrong—"

"No," the commander said. "I was... curious. That's all."

The Monk answered with a thin smile.

"What happened to the rest of the *Melitta*'s crew?" Godfrey demanded.

"Is this curiosity as well?"

"Concern for the lives of friends."

"You need not concern yourself with them anymore. They are beyond your help."

Landry caught Tancrede's eye and gave the smallest shake of his head.

"Then we will spend our last breaths avenging their lives," Godfrey said. "You will answer for what you did to them."

"Bravely said, Templar, but we both know your threats are empty. You cannot eat or drink or even scratch an itch on your nose without leave from me. You are mine to do with as I please. If you believe otherwise, you are lying to yourself."

"And if you believe that you will profit from this venture, you're doing the same. One of the men on the *Melitta* claimed that you were once a Templar. I doubt that very much. A knight of our Order would know better."

Redman's smile melted, leaving his expression impassive. Except for his gray eyes, which were as hard and sharp as chips of flint.

"Throw them overboard."

For the span of a taken breath, no one on either ship moved or spoke. Tancrede had time to think that the Monk meant only to intimidate them. As Godfrey said, he had gone to great lengths to capture them alive. Why would he kill them now?

But then Gaspar snapped his fingers, pointed at the Templars, and gestured toward the water.

Men seized Tancrede, lifting him off the deck. Somewhere nearby, several of his fellow knights roared in rage. Tancrede fought the men who held him, kicking out with both feet, writhing in their grasp. But they bore him to the nearest rail, and without faltering tossed him over.

He tried to twist his body so that he would hit the water back-first. Instead, he hit on his side, the surface of the sea slapping his face, battering his abused shoulder and arm, robbing him of precious breath.

The brine closed over him. The force of his impact carried him deeper, away from the glimmering surface. He couldn't swim, of course – not with his arms bound. He kicked, desperate to rise. His chain mail weighed him down, as did the soaked mantle and tabard. Lungs burning, pulse laboring, he continued to kick until mercifully he did start up toward the sun.

When at last he broke the surface, he gasped for air. One breath. Before he could take another, a swell hit him, filling his mouth and throat with water. He sputtered, spat, inhaled again. Another swell washed over him. The muscles in his legs burned. He didn't know how long he could keep himself afloat. He strained against the ropes that held his arms and wrists in the vain hope that the water would loosen them. It didn't.

He took one last breath, went under again. He kicked, but his legs were too tired, his clothing and armor too heavy.

There was no dishonor in this surrender. They were prisoners. There was no telling what Redman would have done to them had he allowed them to live. This would be an easy death, an end to an ill-fated venture.

He stopped kicking, watched as the dancing light on the sea's surface receded.

Forms splashed into the water above him and followed him down. Men took hold of him and hauled him back toward the surface. Others grabbed him as he came up. Moments later, they heaved him back over the ship's rail and dumped him unceremoniously on the deck of the *Gold Prince*.

Gasping for breath, and coughing up mouthfuls of salt water, he lay on the damp wood with his eyes closed. He was aware of others nearby, panting as well. After a time, he opened his eyes. Gawain and Brice lay closest to him. He saw Landry, Godfrey, and Draper as well. Lifting his head, he spotted Nathaniel, yellow hair lank, water running from his beard. They were all there. Except Thomas and Victor, of course.

"Let that be a lesson to you, Templar," the Monk said. He hadn't moved from the rail of the *Poniard*. "I can kill all of you whenever I wish, with merely a word to my men. Do not challenge me. Do not mock me or insult me. Do not anger me in any way. Not if you care for the men under your command." To Gaspar, he said, "Return them to the cage. No food. No more time on the deck. And they've had their water for the day."

Men laughed at this.

Again, Tancrede was lifted by members of Gaspar's crew. They set him on his feet but kept their grip on his arms as they guided him back down into the rank hold and to the cage.

He leaned against the bars and slid to the floor, wincing at the lingering agony in his arms. Once all the knights had been forced back into the prison, a pirate locked the door. Redman's men filed up through the hatch, leaving them alone.

"I'm sorry," Godfrey muttered.

"You have no reason to apologize," Tancrede said.

"Don't I? I made us surrender when we should have fought. I allowed them to murder Killias's men. I nearly got every one of you killed just now."

"Well," Tancrede said, "when you put it that way…" He allowed himself a peek at the commander, who looked back at him. After a moment, they both laughed. The others began to laugh as well.

Soon their mirth subsided. Tancrede closed his eyes again and leaned his head back against the bars. Sometime later, he startled awake, unsure of when he had fallen asleep or of what had awakened him.

"The ship has slowed," Landry said. "I hear birds. I think we're near land."

"We are," Gawain said. He stared through the bars at the gap in the hull. "I see trees."

The ship glided on, its movements gentler now that they were near to shore. In time, they stopped completely. The ship thudded with activity. Men walked in every direction on the deck above them and splashed into the water on both sides of the ship. Tancrede couldn't be certain, but it sounded to him as though the other ship had anchored nearby.

Still they remained in the cage, ignored for now. Without the movement of the ship and the wind of the open sea, the hold grew even hotter than it had been.

By the time the pirates entered the hold to retrieve them from the prison, Tancrede couldn't help but be thankful. He knew better than to think that their circumstances would improve much on land, but he hoped never to see the cage again.

The pirates placed Tancrede in one skiff with Gawain and Brice. The others were transported in a second vessel behind them. The men rowed their boat onto a broad strand and ordered them out of the skiff.

Standing on the hot sand, Tancrede studied their surroundings, seeking any path to freedom. That notion didn't last long. He saw no people, no buildings, no signs of humanity at all. There only was sand, and water, and a jungle thick with palm trees, huge ferns, and other shrubs.

The pirates didn't waste time. They looped a rope around his neck, and then around the necks of his fellow Templars. They pulled the loops tight, until the jute chafed his skin and he had trouble swallowing.

"That ought to hold them," one of the men said, grinning at his companions.

Another of the pirates took the lead end of the rope and tied it to his belt. He then started across the sand toward the trees beyond. The Templars had no choice but to follow. A second pirate brought up the rear, his end of the rope also secured at his waist.

They entered the jungle through a small gap in the trees and followed a sandy path away from the shoreline. It wound through copses for a time before angling up across a hillside, and down into a shallow dale. It leveled off for a short distance, but then climbed and dipped again. It continued thus for what felt like leagues. They walked and walked, the path climbing and descending and winding ever farther from the lagoon where they had landed.

Such a journey would have been routine for him, for any Templar. But with the rope at his neck, with his arms bound, with his last meal and sip of fresh water a distant memory, Tancrede struggled to keep his feet. His head ached and his vision swam. He stumbled several times, though on each occasion he righted himself before he fell to the ground. He would have begged for a respite if not for his pride, and his certainty that the pirates would deny him any mercy.

At one point, Gawain did fall. The pull on the rope jerked Tancrede backward and made him gasp for air. Several of the Templars behind him cried out.

The man leading them glared back. "Up, you!"

"He's hurt," Tancrede said, rasping the words.

"I don't give a damn. Either he keeps on, or we kill him here. His choice."

"Then give me a bit of slack."

"Why?" the pirate asked, eyes narrowing.

"Just do it!"

The man hesitated, but then seemed to decide that the sooner Gawain was up, the sooner they would reach their destination, wherever that might be. He took two strides in Tancrede's direction. Tancrede stepped back toward Gawain, but he couldn't quite reach.

"Another step."

The man scowled.

"What the hell are you about up there?" the pirate at the rear called.

The first man took another step back, allowing Tancrede to reach the younger knight.

Gawain was on his knees, his head hanging low. "You plan to pick me up?" he asked, breathless.

"If I could, I'd put you on my back."

Gawain raised his gaze to Tancrede's, his eyes welling. He nodded. "I know you would. I'd do the same."

The knight forced himself up – no small feat without the use of his arms. He stumbled a bit but then steadied and dipped his chin a second time. "Thank you, brother."

"I didn't do anything."

"We both know better."

They shared a smile and Tancrede turned back to the lead pirate. "On then. What are you waiting for?"

The pirate frowned. Gawain gave a huff of laughter.

They walked for at least another hour. The jungle began to darken, the air to cool.

Ahead of them, the forest thinned. Tancrede saw more of the sky through those trees remaining in front of them. Eyeing the canopy, he stumbled over a change in their footing.

The dirt path had intersected a cobblestone road. It was in some disrepair, dotted with loose, split, and missing cobbles, but still it seemed utterly out of place here on this seemingly deserted isle. They turned onto the paved lane and continued their climb.

As it turned out, the road was nothing compared to the next surprise. As they rounded a broad turn, they came within sight of a huge fortress, easily as large as any temple of the Order that Tancrede had ever seen. Like the road, the structure showed signs of age. The outer wall was pitted and scarred, likely from past battles. The towers beyond the wall were similarly marked, and sections of walls and buildings were streaked white with bird droppings.

As they neared the structure the enormous twin oak doors of the main gate swung inward, opening onto a broad dirt space. This inner courtyard was filled with wooden huts and cruder shelters created with canvases and rope. Cooking fires burned in several stone rings. Dozens of men occupied the space, as well as women, and even a few children. Dogs ranged among the shelters and fires.

As the pirates led the Templars into the fortress, the people paused in their tasks to regard them. Seconds later, almost in unison, they all turned their attention back to what they had been doing before.

The pirates pulled Tancrede and the others on, through the common area, past the large central structure of the compound to a second, smaller stone building. There was an ancient grace to the central tower and the outer wall. The main building was crowned by a crenelated turret that must have offered a striking view of the surrounding terrain. Similar towers stood at each corner of the outer defense. The building to which the pirates had led them, however, was little more than a stone box. Its door was constructed of iron rather than wood. A few small, square openings, guarded with iron bars, marked the exterior. Otherwise nothing distinguished the structure, or mitigated its austerity.

The pirates and Templars halted before the building, and one man produced a key that opened the iron door.

"What is this place?" Godfrey asked, regarding the door, the walls, the barred windows.

"This," came a too-familiar voice, "is your new home."

All of them turned. Redman stood behind them, flanked by half a dozen armed men.

"Quite possibly, the last home any of you will ever know."

CHAPTER 12

The pirates ushered the Templars inside and down a narrow stone stairway. As they descended into the bowels of the structure, the fetor that reached them made the hold of the *Gold Prince* seem ambrosial by comparison. Even the smoke from oil-soaked torches couldn't mask the reek: a noisome mix of must and dirt, of excrement and urine, of rotting flesh, sweat, fear, hopelessness, and death. Landry gagged.

Menacing shadows from the torches followed them down the stairway. The steps were uneven, worn to a treacherous polish by centuries of use. More than once, Landry almost lost his footing.

Their descent ended in a round chamber surrounded by small cells of stone and iron. A dark corridor led off from the chamber. Landry wasn't sure he wished to know where it led.

The pirate with the key opened the doors to three cells. Redman, who had followed them down, stepped to the middle of the chamber.

"You will sleep and eat and spend your days here," he said, his voice echoing. "Except for those times when I have need of you elsewhere."

"Meaning what?" Godfrey asked.

The pirate answered with an enigmatic smile.

"Put them in," he said to his men.

The nearest of the pirates removed the rope from around the Templars' necks, and shoved them into the cells. The doors were low, and Landry had to duck through. Landry and Draper were placed together in one cell, Tancrede and Gawain in another. The third held Brice, Nathaniel, and Godfrey. Redman's men shut the cell doors, which clanged ominously.

The locks appeared every bit as formidable as the lock that had held them on the ship. Landry had no doubt that the bars were as sturdy as well.

"When will you untie us?" Godfrey asked.

"When I'm ready. That is also when you'll be fed, so don't bother to ask."

"You promised us food and drink when we reached land."

"You are on land. You will have food and drink in time. I promised no more than that."

"What do you want with us?"

"Do you really have to ask, Templar? I know the Order. I am aware of the vast wealth you control. The riches of the Temple have funded crusade after crusade, and what do you have to show for it? Acre has fallen. You have no territory or strongholds left in the Holy Land. But you still have your gold. That is what I want."

"So you do intend to ransom us."

The bald man scowled with disgust. "You lack

imagination, like too many of the men I knew when I was a knight."

A bell pealed in the distance, the tones reaching them through the tiny openings in the stone walls. Redman canted his head and smiled again. "Supper," he said. "I'm afraid we must leave you now. Until tomorrow. Or the next day."

He started up the stairway, signaling with a small gesture that his men should follow. No one remained to guard them. If Landry needed further proof of the impossibility of escape, that was it.

"They could at least pretend they're afraid we might break out," Tancrede said from his cell, watching the men leave.

"Do you see any weaknesses?" Godfrey asked.

Landry didn't. Between the stark stone walls and the iron door, the cell struck him as impenetrable. There were small piles of straw in two corners of the cramped space, and a stained moth-eaten blanket balled up on each one. Other than that, the cell was empty. The only possible weaknesses in this ancient prison were the door locks and the barred openings in the walls ten feet above them. And these didn't appear weak at all.

"I see nothing," Draper said. "No way to escape, unless we can master the locks themselves."

"We should try," Godfrey said. "As soon as we have use of our arms again."

"And when do you suppose that will be?" Gawain asked.

The commander didn't bother to respond.

Landry lowered himself to his knees, then sat back against the stone. Draper did the same on the other side of the cell.

The last thing Landry wished to do was think about how hungry he was. But the evening bells still tolled, announcing the pirates' meal and making it all but impossible for him to think about anything else. As the sky grew ever darker, and the air continued to cool, he became aware of insects buzzing near his face, and of others, vermin from the straw and blankets no doubt, crawling over his skin. When they began to bite, he shook himself and shrugged violently. That did little to dissuade the tiny beasts. He stood and paced around the enclosure.

Draper joined him a short time later, but neither of them remained on his feet for long. As vexing as Landry found the bugs, he was too weary to stalk about in circles.

Gradually, the other knights settled down for the evening as well. They didn't speak much. There was little to say. As on the ship, they heard the pirates laughing and singing. Occasionally dogs bayed.

The moon rose late, its light a broken square shining on the wall opposite the high windows. An owl screeched repeatedly. Landry slept as much as he could. His body begged for rest, but his aches made deep slumber impossible. When at last he did fall asleep for more than a moment, he dreamt of falling into the sea, his arms bound, his clothes and chain mail dragging him down. He woke gasping for air, sweat soaking his face and neck. Draper still sat across from him, moonlight shining in his dark eyes.

"You are all right," the Turcopole said, the words empty and yet oddly comforting.

Landry shifted, making himself as comfortable as possible, and soon fell asleep again. Still, when morning came, he felt no more rested than he had the night before.

The pirates ignored them throughout that day and the one after, much as they had aboard the *Gold Prince*. The Templars received no food or drink. They remained trussed up like animals. Landry sensed his body weakening. His hunger consumed him. His throat ached with thirst. His head pounded and the cell appeared to shift and spin whenever he opened his eyes. Every muscle hurt. More, the thought of their captors enjoying yet another meal only a short distance away enraged him, filled him with envy.

Redman and Gaspar must have considered this constant neglect a tactic, a way of breaking the Templars' spirit. Landry wanted to believe that the pirates' disregard would have no effect on them, but by the morning of the third day, he knew better. For good or ill, the pirates would come for them eventually. *They've gone to a lot of trouble to take us as prisoners...* They spoke of profit, of opportunity, of the Templars being assets. They had something in mind for the knights. Landry feared what that might be.

But as their confinement stretched on, he grew eager for almost any interaction with their captors. Every noise from the surrounding compound made him sit up in anticipation – the clang of that distant bell, the whistle of the wind in the bars overhead, each creak and shudder of the ancient prison, every scrabbling on the stone floor by some unseen creature. The noises infected his mind. On occasion, they drove him to his feet and to the small barred opening in the door to their cell. His heart thudded and his stomach clenched with an odd blend of trepidation and relief.

On each occasion, when he realized once again that no one had come for them, he registered the empty chamber as both reprieve and frustration.

He and Draper did not speak. Neither did Gawain and Tancrede. Landry heard Godfrey murmuring to the young knights in his cell, but he could not make out what the commander said.

Days in this dungeon were cool – a small mercy. Night brought colder air, against which the threadbare blankets were nearly useless. The sky beyond the iron bars remained unrelentingly clear. Late in the afternoon of that third day, Landry thought he heard a distant rumble of thunder. He and Draper stared at each other before straining to look out the high window. Landry thought he could make out a few dark clouds. He listened for more thunder. Even a passing shower might offer a few drops of clean water.

But after the promise of that distant growl, he heard nothing more. The day waned and those few clouds passed them by. Landry hung his head and took several long breaths, fearful that he might weep. Despondency threatened to overwhelm him. He was drowning in it.

"Courage, my friend," Draper said, pitching his voice so that the others would not hear. "God is testing us. By His grace, we will endure and be redeemed. This cannot last forever."

Landry did not meet his gaze, but after composing himself, he nodded.

The evening unfolded as had each of the preceding ones. The bell announcing mealtime mocked his hunger. His cell darkened and grew cold. Every pulse of blood renewed the dull agony in his shoulders and bound arms.

Somehow, though, he slept. All of them did.

How else could Landry explain what awaited them the following morning?

A small bowl of water and a platter of food had been placed in the cell. There were no utensils, of course, and even if there had been, neither he nor Draper had been untied. No doubt the pirates wanted the Templars to abase themselves by eating and drinking like animals.

Landry twisted himself up onto his knees and crawled to the food and drink. Draper did as well, reaching the platter at the same time.

The platter held some sort of thick stew. Overnight, fat had congealed on top of it. But it smelled edible. More than that, truth be told. Landry's stomach growled.

"What do you suppose it is?" he asked.

Draper raised an eyebrow. "Do you really care?" He indicated the plate with a jerk of his chin. "Go ahead. I will start with the water."

Rather than eating, Landry stood and moved to the door.

"Do the rest of you have food?"

"Yes," came the reply from the far cell. Nathaniel's voice?

He heard Tancrede and Gawain rousing themselves.

"We do as well," Gawain said.

"Did you hear them bring it?" Tancrede called.

"No. Did anyone?"

No response.

"It's edible," Brice said, the words thick, as if he were speaking around a mouthful.

Landry returned to the platter. He tried to reach for it, but stopped himself. Even if he could have lifted a handful, how would he have gotten it to his mouth?

"It is all right, Landry," Draper said. "Eat it as you must. We do what is required to survive." He smiled. "But save some for me."

Landry nodded. Feeling ill-at-ease, he bent over the platter and took a small mouthful of the food. The meat in the stew was gamey and stringy, and the spices gave it a bitter flavor. He didn't care. He plunged his face into it, gulping down mouthfuls. In mere seconds, he knew he had eaten his share. Though tempted to keep eating, he forced himself to stop, and raised his head. Draper was watching him.

"It is decent?"

"No, I don't think you'll like it. Perhaps I should spare you the horror of having to eat it."

Draper laughed. "You are wearing a good deal of it."

Landry tried to lick clean his lips, mustache, and beard.

Walking on their knees, they traded places. Landry lapped up water like a cat. Draper ate much of what was left on the platter before offering what remained to Landry.

"You're certain?" Landry asked, already approaching the food once more.

"You left me more than half. I have eaten my share."

Landry wasn't sure he believed this, but he didn't stop to question the man's generosity. He thanked Draper and proceeded to lick the platter clean.

"Do you see, Gaspar?" he heard as he finished. "Even the mighty can be made to resemble beasts. It takes only a bit of time."

Landry's head snapped up again. Draper had

stopped drinking and was facing the door. Gaspar and Redman stood together by the opening, leering at them. Redman's sharp beard gave him a devilish look. Gaspar's eyes gleamed like black gems. Several men loomed behind them, grinning as well.

Redman whispered something to the men. One of them nodded his understanding and led the others out of Landry's sight. He and Draper scrambled to their feet and pressed themselves to the door, so that they could see the chamber beyond their cell.

As they watched, the pirates unlocked the door of the far cell, pulled Godfrey out, and locked it shut again.

The Monk drew a knife from his belt. Landry shouted a warning, convinced that the pirate meant to kill Godfrey. Redman paused, grinned in Landry's direction, and cut the bonds holding the commander's arms and wrists.

At the first movement of his hands, Godfrey cried out and dropped to his knees. He brought his arms forward slowly, gritting his teeth. His arms remained at the same odd angle they had been in.

Two of Redman's crew stood over Godfrey, swords pressed to his neck.

"I would have them cut the bonds from all of you," the Monk said. "But if any one of you threatens my men with so much as a frown, I will give the order to have your commander beheaded. Do I make myself clear?"

None of them answered.

"I said, 'Do I make myself clear?'"

"Yes," Tancrede said.

The others murmured their assent as well, the sounds echoing like a chorus.

Redman nodded to the other pirates, and groups of them approached each cell.

Draper and Landry backed to the center of their enclosure as the pirates entered. The man who cut the ropes from Landry's arms made no effort to be gentle. He jerked Landry's arms up. Landry gasped at the anguish that jolted through his shoulders and back. The man then sawed at the ropes for a few seconds. When they fell away, the pirate scooped them off the ground and left the cell. The man who removed Draper's bonds followed him out and relocked the door.

Landry remained as he was, swaying in the middle of the cell. Even if Redman hadn't threatened Godfrey's life, he would have been unable to strike at any of the pirates. His arms were as stiff as tree limbs. Every attempt to move them brought torment. Even the act of lowering them so that they hung at his sides was too painful to bear. Moans from the others told him that they suffered as he did.

He held himself still except for his arms, which he attempted to ease down just a bit with each breath. After some time, he also tried to rotate his wrists. This brought new waves of suffering.

He couldn't say how long it took him to bring his arms forward to something approximating a normal position. Even after he had, he could only move them slowly. The thought of merely lifting his hand to his face made him quail. Wielding a sword seemed something he had done in a different lifetime.

"Where is Godfrey?"

Brice's voice.

Landry lurched to the door. This brought another spasm of pain, but he barely noticed. He peered out at the round chamber and then at the door to Godfrey's cell.

The pirates were gone. The cell doors were all locked. Two Templars stared out from each barred opening. Even the last, where there should have been three men.

"Where did they take him?" Brice asked. Panic widened his eyes, making him appear even younger than usual. He held tight to the bars on his door.

"Did they put him back in your cell after they cut our bonds?" Tancrede asked.

"I don't—I don't think so, no."

Brice turned to Nathaniel, who shook his head.

"They didn't," the second Templar said. "I failed to notice at the time. But now I'm sure. That's when they took him."

"What do we do?" Brice asked.

Tancrede's face was a mask of concern. "What *can* we do?"

Landry and Tancrede exchanged glances.

"Redman!" Landry bellowed, the echo ringing like a hammer on steel. "We would speak with you!"

After several minutes, Landry tried again. This time, Tancrede joined him. But their shouts went unanswered.

They called for the Monk repeatedly throughout the morning and into the afternoon, but all their efforts were in vain. The pirates did not return, nor did Godfrey. Landry and the others grew ever more worried. During the same interval, Landry gradually regained control over his arms and hands. They throbbed still. He knew they would for days. But he no longer felt quite so powerless.

Not until late in the day, toward dusk, did the pirates bring Godfrey back. Gaspar led them; Redman was nowhere to be seen. Two men trailed the captain of the *Gold Prince*. They were bald, hulking, so similar in aspect and build that they might have been brothers. They bore Godfrey between them. The knight's feet dragged on the stone floor and his head lolled, wheaten hair hanging over his eyes, so that Landry could not get a clear view of his face. There could be no question, though, that he had been abused terribly. His tabard, mantle, and armor had been removed, and his body bore terrible marks: bruises, gashes, and what appeared to be burns. His flesh and his breeches were stained with blood.

The pirates lay him inside his cell and locked the door once more.

"What have you done to him?" Landry demanded.

Gaspar led the men back toward the stairs.

"What did you do, you bloody bastard?"

The pirate halted in mid-stride. After a moment, he turned and walked back to Landry's enclosure, halting just beyond Landry's reach.

"Call me that again," the pirate said.

Landry gripped the bars and pressed his face to them. "You're a bloody bastard. And so is Redman the bloody Monk. Now, what did you do to our commander?"

"Nothing that we won't be doing to you and your friends, too." A dark smile exposed yellowed teeth. "With pleasure."

He walked away, signaling to the other pirates that they should follow.

"How is he?" Tancrede called to Brice and Nathaniel once Gaspar and his men were gone.

"Alive," Brice said, his voice unsteady. "That's about all I can say."

"Describe what you see," Draper said, grasping the

bars beside Landry. "What have they done to him?"

"He's been beaten, and worse. There's blood all over his face. Bruises around both eyes and his nose. One of his hands has been... it's swollen and purple. He's a mess." Brice's voice broke on the last word. "There are marks on the rest of him as well. Wounds everywhere."

"Is there any water left in your bowl?" Draper asked, his tone steady, reassuring.

"A bit, yes."

"Try to give it to him. He needs to drink. He'll have lost blood."

"All right." For some seconds the knights said nothing, though Landry heard them moving in their cell. "Most of what we're giving him is dripping onto his chest or the floor."

"Is he drinking any?"

"Some, yes."

"Good." Draper sighed. "That's good."

"Now what?" Nathaniel asked.

Draper eyed Landry sidelong and lifted a shoulder. "Let him rest," he said. "There is nothing more we can do for now."

The Turcopole crossed to where he had been sitting against the stone wall. Landry remained as he was and stared at Godfrey's door, hoping the commander would wake soon, fearing that he might never.

Night fell, and the bells rang. Just hearing them should have rekindled Landry's hunger. What he had eaten that morning wasn't enough to count even as a morsel, much less a meal. But he couldn't think of food, or rest, or anything else other than Godfrey.

For nearly as long as he could recall, Godfrey had been the most important person in his life. He had few memories of his own father or mother. Godfrey had taken him on as an apprentice when he was but a boy, and had been as close to a parent as Landry had known.

He remembered one incident from his childhood – he couldn't say why this particular memory came to him now – when Godfrey taught him to ride.

"Slowly," his master had cautioned, setting him in the saddle and showing him how to grasp the horse's reins.

But of course, Landry had never done anything slowly. He kicked his mount to a trot, and then to a gallop. Within seconds he had lost control of the beast. Its gait jarred him. He started to slip from the saddle. He lost his hold on the reins and grabbed for the horse's mane.

He fell hard and tumbled to a halt. His shoulder hurt, as did his temple. When he dabbed at the bump there, his fingers came away bloody.

He heard a footfall behind him, and then, "I told you to go slowly, didn't I?"

Landry turned to look up at him. "Do you ride slowly?"

Godfrey's expression didn't change, but he shook his head. "Not always, no."

"Do other knights?"

Godfrey smirked. "No."

"Then why should I?"

Godfrey offered a hand. When Landry took hold of it, the master hauled him to his feet. But even after Landry was standing, Godfrey didn't release him. "Because you still have much to learn. And because I might not always be here to pick you up."

"Where would you go?"

"It's not a matter of... You need to learn patience, Landry, and control. Not of the horse, but of yourself. And not only to avoid falls and scrapes, but because others will come to depend on you. You must justify their faith in you, and God's faith in you as well."

"*God's* faith in *me*? I don't understand."

A rare smile from the knight greeted this. "I know. But you will in good time."

A low moan pulled Landry from his recollections.

"He's waking up," Brice said.

Draper was on his feet almost before the last word crossed the knight's lips. "Give him more water."

"We've only a little left."

"Let him have it all."

Within a few seconds, Landry heard coughing and a deep voice he would have known anywhere saying, "Enough. That's enough."

"Godfrey?" he called. "Let them give you the water."

"Landry. All of you. I'm all right."

"Yes," Tancrede said. "We saw that when they brought you back. You've never looked better."

"How long have I been here?"

"A few hours," Tancrede said. "They returned with you near to twilight, and it's been dark for perhaps two hours." A pause, and then, "What did they want with you?"

"I'm still not entirely certain." His voice was weak, the words halting. "They asked me questions about the Order, about the wealth we control, and how we might gain access to it. I tried to tell them that we are but one Temple. In Paris, to be sure, but a single Temple nevertheless. Our resources while considerable are not limitless. But Redman..." He paused for a few seconds. "He is filled with malice and greed. He believes we can make him rich beyond all imagining and he is determined that we shall do so, or die."

Silence followed. After a minute or two, Tancrede asked, "Where did they take you?"

"Down the corridor that leads from the central chamber. It was a long way. And the place where it ends... I had heard about such rooms, but I had never seen one myself. I never care to again."

A shudder ran through the words.

"I fear they will take all of you there eventually," he went on. "I wish I could tell you that you will be spared, but his avarice is like a disease. It poisons his heart and his mind. He will not rest until he has what he wants, or until we manage to escape." *Or until we're all dead.*

The words hung in the rank air, unspoken, but heard by all.

CHAPTER 13

Landry didn't sleep that night. He sensed that the pirates would soon be back – for him or for one of the others – and he wanted to be awake when they returned. To be prepared, or to bear witness.

He stood at the door, gazing out at the empty stone chamber, and flexing his arms and wrists, working out the lingering stiffness and pain. Draper snored softly behind him.

"Can't sleep?" came a whisper from the cell next to his.

Tancrede stood at his doorway, eyes shining with torchlight.

"I probably could, but I'm not willing to. You?"

"I feel the same. They'll be coming for me soon enough. I want to be ready."

"You think you'll be next?"

"I do. I'm older than the rest of you. Except Draper, maybe, but they'll assume that I know more, because I'm French and he's a Turcopole. They'll

225

take me, and then I would guess they'll take you."

"If your logic is correct, it won't be me. Gawain is older than I am. Draper's a lot older."

"True, but you shouldn't have angered Gaspar today."

Landry shrugged, looked away. "Let them take me. Better me than Brice or Nathaniel. Or Gawain, for that matter. They'll ruin his leg forever."

They fell silent. Tancrede eyed his door and pulled on the bars, seeming to test their strength.

"What do you suppose this was?" he asked.

"This building, you mean?"

"The whole place. Seems it could have been a Templar fortress. This part of the world was full of them at one point."

"That could explain how the Monk found it. If he really was a Templar."

"You doubt me?"

Landry's gaze snapped to the stairway. Redman stood at the base, several men behind him.

"The man's as quiet as a cat," Tancrede muttered.

"You're right," the pirate said, crossing to Tancrede's door. "This fortress did once belong to the Order. I found no treasure here, of course. They must have taken it when they fled. The Templars are thorough in that regard. Still, I did find much else of interest. And now it's your turn to learn exactly what it was I discovered." He nodded toward the door.

One of his men hurried forward, unlocked the door, and pulled Tancrede into the outer chamber. By this time, the others had awakened. Draper joined Landry at their door. Gawain took Tancrede's place. The young knights and Godfrey watched from the gap in their door. Godfrey's bruises and the dried blood still on his face gave him a ghoulish aspect.

"Strength, Tancrede," he called, as the pirates led him away along that shadowed corridor. "By His grace, you shall endure."

Redman laughed at this. "'His grace.' A meaningless phrase, clung to by an order bereft of honor. Let's see how much *His grace* allows your friend to withstand. Not much, I'd wager." He followed the pirates and Tancrede into the darkness.

"Pray with me, brothers," Godfrey said.

Landry crossed himself, closed his eyes.

"Lord, give strength to our brother, Tancrede. See him through his ordeal. Reward his courage, and his faith in You. Preserve him from the wickedness of those who would torment him. Bring him back to us, and grant us the wisdom to find our way home from this place. Amen."

"Amen," the rest intoned.

Over the next few minutes, most of the others retreated into their cells. Landry remained by his door. So did Godfrey.

He could see the commander more clearly now. Godfrey's injuries distorted his features. His eyes were mere slits within the swollen skin.

"You should sleep, Landry," he said. "You can do nothing for him from here. His fate is in God's hands now."

"No. It is in the hands of demons. Of men whose evil seems limitless."

"By God's grace—"

"God has forsaken us, Godfrey! Can't you see that? Look around you! Look at what has become of us! Acre has fallen! The Grail is lost! And we are captives in a place no one knows exists! God's grace is lost to us."

"You forget yourself, brother," Godfrey said, ice in his words. "You believe you know what God does and does not do? You would presume to judge Him, or declare that you can speak to His grace with more authority than the Lord Himself?"

His cheeks burned as if he had been slapped. "No! I merely—"

"You have lost faith, Landry." Godfrey's tone softened slightly. "I understand. It happens to all of us at one time or another. But you must find your faith again. Because before long, you will go where I have gone, and where Tancrede is now. And you will not survive that place in the absence of faith. Do you hear me?"

"Yes, Commander."

"Pray on it."

He swallowed, nodded. Turning away from the door, he faltered. Draper watched him. Neither of them said a word. Landry retrieved his blanket, draped it over his shoulders, and sat against the wall. His hand shaking, he crossed himself again and prayed. He began with the Apostles' Creed, though he and the others had, as usual, recited this together earlier in the night. As he finished, he thought he heard a cry from far off. He listened and soon heard it again. A scream. Tancrede, in torment.

You see? he wanted to shout to Godfrey. *Where is God's grace now? Tancrede is being tortured!*

He kept this to himself. Squeezing his eyes shut, he recommenced his recitation. The Creed again, and again, and yet again. The words filled his mind, but failed to block out the horrors of Tancrede's suffering.

He finished the Creed one last time and turned to the Angelus. Once. Twice. Five times. At some point, he realized he could no longer hear Tancrede, but this did not bring any solace. His friend had passed out, perhaps. Or died. Or been silenced by some brutality.

When Landry was done with the Angelus, he started Glory Be, and then a prayer of contrition.

But they were words and little more – noise in his mind to overwhelm his fear.

"Lord, where has my faith gone?" he whispered, tears running over his cheeks and into his beard.

He resumed his prayers, reciting one after another, until eventually he fell asleep.

When he awoke sometime later, he was ashamed. The last time he had drifted off while praying, he was a boy, newly taken on as a squire by Godfrey.

He intended to start the prayers again, but stopped himself at the scrape of a footstep outside his cell. Leaping to his feet and stepping to the door, he saw the two bald pirates supporting Tancrede, while another opened the door to the knight's cell.

Tancrede looked even worse than Godfrey had. Blood glistened on his face, his neck, his naked chest. His bruises were so severe they rendered him almost unrecognizable. One of his legs hung at an odd angle. Landry feared it was broken.

He wanted to berate the men, but knew it would do no good. This was Redman's handiwork, and he was nowhere to be seen.

"Bring him water," he said instead.

The nearest of the men startled at the sound of his voice, but recovered quickly.

"We don't take orders from you. If Redman wants him to have water, he'll have it."

"And if he dies? Who will Redman blame for that?"

The man's face fell. He glanced at one of his companions.

"Maybe a little water couldn't hurt," he said. "Redman doesn't have to know. He's right: if this one dies, we'll be blamed for certain."

The second man hesitated, then nodded. They set Tancrede in his cell and locked the door. One of the men ran up the stairs, and came back only a few moments later bearing a small flask that Landry assumed contained water.

He entered the cell and reemerged seconds later.

"It's in there, in the bowl," he said to Landry. "His friend can see to the rest."

Landry didn't reply.

"Gawain?" Draper called from beside Landry. "Can you give him the water?"

"I can, but I doubt he can swallow it. He's in a bad state."

"Do what you can," Draper said.

"You the Turcopole?" asked the pirate with the key.

Draper didn't answer right away. For a few seconds, he only stared, like a man incapable of speech. Then a quiver went through him and he lifted his chin.

"I am."

The pirate unlocked the door to their cell. "We're to bring you next."

Landry and Draper backed away from the door as they opened it. One of Redman's men leveled a sword at Landry's heart. The other beckoned to Draper. Draper crossed himself, half turned to Landry. Their eyes met. Landry knew he should say something, but he had no idea what. His emotions were too roiled, too conflicted. He had convinced himself that Tancrede would be proven right, that he would be next in Redman's torture chamber.

He *should* have been the next one to go. Draper was a good man, honorable, brilliant, as brave as any knight in their Order. But he was more scholar than warrior. He didn't deserve this. Landry should have said as much. He *wanted* to say as much. Yet, he couldn't bring himself to utter the words. Fear for his friend warred with a shameful sense of reprieve.

"Pray for me, brother," Draper said. "As you have for the others. As I will for you."

Landry nodded, his throat tight. Draper followed the men out. The man with the sword waited until Draper and the other pirate had exited the cell before backing out himself and shutting the door.

"Courage, Draper," Godfrey said. "Remember that you are a Templar, by the grace of God."

"By the grace of God," Draper repeated.

They led the Turcopole down the corridor. Landry watched until the knight and the pirates escorting him melted into the shadows and he could see them no more. He pressed his brow to the bars on the door, then looked toward Godfrey's door. The commander was there, already watching him.

"Tancrede is alive," Godfrey said. "Draper will return to us as well."

"Alive, yes. Thank God for that. And please the Lord you'll be right about Draper. But is that enough? Are we to accept this fate so long as none of us dies?"

"Of course not. That's not what I meant." He

paused. "Forgive me for what I said before. I was... I might have been too hard on you."

"I prayed, Godfrey. I swear I did. Hearing his screams, though—"

"It's not enough to pray. You must believe, as well. And more than that, you must trust. If it is His will that all of us should die here, you must have faith that there is a reason. Believing in God's purpose when we are victorious – that's easy. Any man can do that. A Templar trusts in the Lord when all other hope has forsaken him. That is the true test."

Landry knew this, of course. For most of his life, he had lived as squire to a Templar and then as a Templar himself. He had never been tested like this, though. Before their capture by the pirates, he had thought the loss of Acre the darkest moment of his life. Yet even at its worst, the battle for Acre had not brought him so low, or shaken his faith so completely.

Still standing at the door, he crossed himself and began yet again to pray.

"God, by your grace, grant us the strength to endure.

"God, by your grace, grant us the will to resist.

"God, by your grace, grant us the courage to keep faith."

He repeated the phrases one after the other, yet another litany that carried him through the dark of that night. Several times, he nearly broke the cadence. Once, when a wail from Draper spiraled into the night, like the howl of some wild jungle beast, he stumbled, fell silent.

"God, by your grace," Godfrey intoned, taking up the chant, "grant us the strength to endure."

On the second invocation, another voice twined with the commander's. "God... by your grace... grant us the... the will to resist." Tancrede. A miracle. His words were as thin as parchment, as weak as starlight in this rank dungeon.

Still, they were enough.

With the third line, Landry found his own voice again and spoke the litany with them. He did more than speak it. He felt it. He believed it. If Tancrede could cling to his faith after what had been done to him, how could Landry do any less?

Gawain, Brice, and Nathaniel joined them as well. Again and again, the six knights repeated their prayer, their words blending into a single supplication. The prison resounded with it. Landry wanted to believe that Draper might hear them and draw strength from the sound.

More important, though, in those moments stretching to an hour or more, Landry knew beyond any doubt that God heard them. How could He not? And knowing this, he knew as well that they would find a way out of this hell on God's earth. How many of them might make it, he dared not predict. But they would not be broken by this place. He would not allow it. Neither, he knew, would Godfrey or Tancrede or any of the others. Sensing the strength of his brothers, drawing upon it, he felt his own strength return, and with it his hope, his faith, his trust in the Lord.

Landry and the others only broke off their litany when the two hulking pirates appeared with Draper held between them. The third pirate, the keyholder, walked behind.

Like Tancrede and Godfrey before him, Draper was

insensate, feet dragging on the stone floor, head hanging, his face a mask of blood, his neck and torso darkened as well. His long hair was matted with it. Both of his eyes were swollen shut and his lips were split.

The first pirate opened the door to Landry's cell, pulled out his sword, and forced Landry to back away from the opening. The other two dropped Draper in the middle of the enclosure, turned as one, and without so much as a backward glance stalked out into the round chamber.

Landry was certain they would take him then and subject him to the same sort of beating they had given his friends. They didn't. They locked his door and started up the stairs.

"He needs water!" Landry rushed to the door, bracing his hands against the cold iron. "You brought some for Tancrede. He needs it as well."

"He'll have none," said one of the bald men. "Giving it to the other was a mistake. Not one we're likely to repeat."

They continued up the stairs and left the building.

Landry scrabbled to his friend's side, rolled him onto his back.

"Is he alive?" Gawain called to him.

Landry lowered his head to Draper's chest. The knight's heart beat an inconstant rhythm.

"Only just."

He scanned the man's body, squinting in the gloom. Draper had been beaten almost beyond recognition. One hand – his sword hand, of course – was mangled, swollen, misshapen. No doubt the pirates had broken the bones. Two of the fingernails on his other hand had been ripped out. Burns and cuts formed a grisly lattice across his chest and sides and back. Redman had been thorough beyond imagining. Only a monster, a devil who enjoyed inflicting severe damage on the human form, could have done all of this.

Landry's stomach gave an uneasy lurch.

When the pirates brought back Godfrey, Landry had been sure Redman had done his worst with the commander. Seeing Tancrede, he'd known he was wrong. What they'd done to Draper was worse even than what Tancrede had endured. He gave his friend the tiny bit of water that remained in their bowl. He wasn't certain that Draper swallowed any of it.

"They'll kill one of us before long," Gawain said from his cell, giving voice to Landry's own thought. "For all we know, they intend to kill all of us."

"Faith, brother," Godfrey said.

"Faith?" Gawain repeated. "After what they've done to Tancrede? To you? To Draper?"

"Yes, even so. Landry and I—"

"I heard what you said to him. I understand faith, Godfrey. All of us do. But we need more than prayers and faith and hope. We need a plan. We need a way out of here. Because we can trust in the Lord all we like, but the fact is, I don't want to die here."

"You believe I do?" Godfrey asked.

"No. But I believe you're... more at peace with your own mortality than the rest of us. That's admirable, a fine quality in a warrior. But I don't want to be at peace. I want to escape. And if I can kill a few of these cutthroats on the way out, so be it."

Landry couldn't help but smile in the darkness. He placed his own blanket beneath Draper's head, and covered Draper with the one from the Turcopole's pallet. Satisfied that he had done what little he could for the man, he stepped to his door.

Gawain and Godfrey stood at the gaps in their doorways.

"You're both right," Landry said, drawing their gazes. "We can maintain our faith without surrendering to this fate. That's what I intend to do." To Gawain, he said, "I expect one of us will be next."

The knight nodded, tight-lipped. "Probably."

"We need to do more than survive." He glanced toward the stairway to make certain Redman wasn't watching them. Lowering his voice, he went on. "We have to take the opportunity while we're out of these cells to learn what we can of this place. And if possible, we need to start plotting our escape."

"How?"

"I have no idea."

A smile touched Gawain's lips. "That's quite a plan you've developed."

"I'm still working on it."

"I'm glad to hear it," Godfrey said. "If that was it, complete, I'd be alarmed."

They all sobered.

"We cannot afford to be patient," Gawain said, looking first at Godfrey and then at Landry. "I meant what I said before. It's merely a matter of time before one of us dies at their hands. If all of us are too hurt to fight or even walk, we'll never get away. So, this plan of yours needs to take shape now. And yes, if they take me first, I'll look for a way out."

He pulled away from his door. Godfrey and Landry remained at theirs.

"Something changed for you."

Landry nodded. "I don't know what. Perhaps your words from before, or Tancrede praying with us despite his wounds. Whatever it was, I feel... clearer. I'm sorry I lost faith."

"You needn't apologize to me."

"I disagree. Master."

Godfrey smiled. "It's 'brother' now, as you well know. But thank you."

The pirates came for him as the first silver glow of dawn touched the barred window high overhead.

Landry had prayed through the night, forgoing sleep, preferring not to be roused from a dream to the nightmare of torture. He should have been tired, but the strength he had rediscovered while reciting the prayers with his fellow Templars sustained him.

When Redman's men opened the door to his cell, Draper woke. He groaned and tried to sit up, only to gasp when he put weight on his wounded hand. Landry knelt beside him.

"Landry," he whispered, his lips so swollen the name was almost unrecognizable. "They have come for you now?"

"Yes. I suppose that means you get to eat all of this morning's breakfast."

Draper essayed a smile, exposing bloodstained teeth. He clasped Landry's hand with his good one. "Keep faith, brother. We will be with you."

Landry laid his other hand over Draper's. An odd calm had come over him. He dreaded leaving the cell, and knew how he would suffer in the hours to come. But he had purpose now, a determination to defeat these men who meant to torment him. That began now. He would show them no fear.

He extracted his hand from Draper's grip, straightened and followed the pirates out of the cell. Redman and Gaspar both waited for him there. Gawain and Godfrey watched from their doorways.

"I hope you don't mind," Redman said. "Gaspar requested that he be allowed to join us this morning."

The captain flashed a spiteful smile. "We started a conversation the other day, you and I," he said. "I have looked forward to continuing it."

A frisson of apprehension chilled Landry momentarily. He quelled it, and held the man's gaze.

"Of course you have," he said. "Just know that in time, I will have my say as well."

Gaspar glared.

Redman, though, laughed appreciatively. "I admire your courage, Templar," he said. "Misplaced though it may be. Come along."

He pivoted and started down the dark corridor. Landry had no choice but to follow.

As he passed Godfrey's door, the commander spoke his name.

Landry slowed.

"Keep His grace foremost in your mind," Godfrey said. "And keep a prayer on your lips. You'll be all right."

"If only it were so simple," Gaspar said from behind.

His eyes still locked on Godfrey's, Landry put a fist to his chest and walked on.

Before he had taken ten steps, he was swallowed by the darkness of the hallway. A sharp point pricked his back between the shoulder blades.

"Just walk, Templar," Gaspar said. "Any attempt to fight or flee will end with my blade in your heart. Understand?"

On they went, the click of their boots on stone too loud in the closed space. And then, for a second or two, it wasn't. As the sound changed, so did the flow of air in the passageway. It was subtle, and as quickly as Landry noticed it, it ended. That moment was enough, however. He had no doubt that a second corridor ran off from this one. Of course, he couldn't know where it led, but this was a start.

A short time later, they came to another round chamber. It was lit by torches mounted in sconces, and unlike the round chamber at the base of the stairway, this one had no openings in its walls and no prisoner cells surrounding it.

Courage had carried Landry this far, but he recoiled at the sight of this place. He tried to mask his reaction, but he couldn't keep his eyes from roaming the chamber, alighting on one implement of torture after another: a cage edged on the inside with iron spikes; a table of iron and wood with manacles at either end and a daunting array of gears in between; a large hearth glowing with red embers and bristling with brands, pokers, and spikes; and more blades, cudgels, and axes than Landry cared to count.

"Welcome, Templar," Redman said, all pretense of mirth gone. "You have seen what the objects in this place can do to a man. You can imagine, I'm sure, what we intend to do to you."

Landry continued to scan the chamber, fear clawing at his heart. He allowed some of that fright to show on his face, hoping it would mask a second truth.

DAVID B. COE

Scared as he was, he had not forgotten the purpose
he embraced during the night. He couldn't ignore
the cages and tables and weapons, but he searched
for tools he might use. After only a few seconds, he
thought he spotted one.

"Gaspar here would like nothing more than to
put you in that cage." Redman indicated the spiked
enclosure near the hearth. "I believe he pictures
himself skewering you with a sword while you bleed
from a hundred punctures in your flesh." He wrinkled
his nose. "Not a pretty thought." A pause, and then,
"Despite my friend's thirst for your blood, I would be
willing to spare you."

Landry looked his way, knowing the Monk would
expect as much. He knew the precise position of the
object he had spotted, and exactly where he would
have to step if he was to have any chance of securing it.

"All you need to do is tell me how we might gain
access to the gold held in your Temple. It really is as
simple as that. Tell me that and you can return to your
cell, whole, unbloodied."

"And if I don't tell you? If I don't know?"

"If you don't tell me..." He waved an open hand
at the contents of the chamber. "And if you claim
you don't know, I won't believe you and I'll be very
unhappy. Both of us will be."

This might have been a path to freedom, a way
to end the beatings and contrive an escape. He could
reveal what he did know about the riches in the Paris
Temple, claim that he was willing to lead them there
and hand over the Templars' gold, provided Redman
ended the torture and freed all of them.

He didn't believe, though, that Redman would ever

240

let them walk out of this place. The pirate would gladly lie about his intentions to gain whatever knowledge he thought Landry possessed, but he would kill them in the end, or at the very least keep them here. He wouldn't be so easily gulled.

More than that, telling the pirate anything about the Temple would have been a violation of the oaths Landry took upon becoming a Templar. It would have been a betrayal of his brothers – not just those in the cells here, but all of them, every man who had ever donned the tabard of the red cross. He would sooner take his own life than turn his back on the Order. Clearly, given the beatings they had endured, Tancrede, Draper, and Godfrey had made the same choice. He would do no less.

But he would also do his best to take advantage of the situation in which he found himself. His gaze flicked downward again, to the item he had spotted on the dungeon floor. He tried to make it seem that he was avoiding Redman's gaze.

"Last chance, Templar," the Monk said. "You can save yourself, or you can suffer as your friends have. Those are the only choices before you."

"I—I cannot help you. I know nothing."

Redman's lip curled into a sneer. "Fool. Put him on the table."

He sensed movement from the men behind him, knew this would be his sole opportunity before the torture began. One man grabbed his arm. Landry twisted out of his grasp. The other man reached for him as well. Landry hammered an elbow into his gut. As the first man took hold of him again, he fought, allowed himself to fall to the floor. He smacked his head on the stone, and his breath left him in a rush. But he fell on top of the object he had seen.

The pirates grappled for him. Landry fought like a man possessed, lashing out with feet and fists. Or rather, one fist. In the midst of his frenzy, he snaked one hand beneath him. For one panicked moment, he could not locate the object. One of the pirates kicked him in the side. He retched. Another pounded a fist into his cheek, leaving him addled.

He worked his other hand down a few more inches. Just as they lifted him off the floor, he felt it. Iron. As long as his little finger, tapered to a point, squared edges. As the pirates carried him to the table, he slipped it into the waist cinch of his breeches, beneath his hauberk. It took him no more than a second or two, and then he was flailing again. The pirates fighting him didn't appear to notice. Surrounded as he was, and in the throes of his struggle, Redman and Gaspar could not see.

The men slammed him onto the table, stealing his breath again. Before he could fight himself free, they locked manacles around his wrists, and then his ankles.

Helpless now, he sagged back against the wood and iron. The worst was about to begin. But he had the object he sought. Time would tell if it was enough.

CHAPTER 14

They started by beating him.

Once he was secured to the table, they used some means he could not see to tilt the table up. Redman deferred to Gaspar, who seemed to relish the chance to deliver those first blows.

He hammered his fists into Landry's jaw, his cheek, his temple, his nose, his mouth, his eyes. Within moments, Landry was bleeding so profusely he could barely draw breath. His vision swam. With each blow, he saw white lights popping before him. Consciousness began to slip away.

"Enough," Redman said. "We don't want him passing out too soon."

Landry forced his eyes open. The pirate stood directly before him.

"I don't suppose you would care to end this now? We needn't go on. Just tell me: where in the Paris Temple will we find your gold?"

Landry turned his head to the side and spat a

gob of blood. "I don't know."

A weak smile lifted the corners of Redman's mouth. "No, of course you don't." He stepped back. "Remove his clothing."

Fear seized Landry's heart. Not at the prospect of the torment that would surely follow, but at the possibility that they might find the sliver of iron he had claimed and hidden.

The pirates unfastened the manacles at his wrists, but not those at his ankles. This put his mind at ease a little.

They stripped off his mantle, tabard, mail, and jerkin, leaving him naked to the waist. Then they bound his wrists again.

By this time, Landry's vision and thinking had cleared somewhat. He watched Redman cross to the hearth and pull on a leather glove. The pirate considered the implements there, at last choosing an iron pike. The metal smoked as he removed it from the flames.

"Are you certain, Templar?" Redman asked, turning and approaching him. "You know nothing at all about your Temple's riches."

Landry stared up at the vaulted stone ceiling. "I am certain."

"As I suspected."

At the first touch of the searing iron to his chest, Landry let out a bellow that was torn from the pit of his gut. He gritted his teeth, breathing hard through his nose. He smelled his own flesh burning.

Redman removed the pike but only for an instant. Before Landry could inhale a second time, he pressed the iron to his chest again. Landry roared.

"You mark all of them so," Gaspar said. "Why?"

Landry tucked his chin to look at what the Monk had done to him. The second burn cut across the first, forming a cross on his chest that mimicked – mocked – the Templar cross.

Redman approached the hearth, shoved the pike back into the flames, and claimed a crude, iron blade. "They are Templars," he said, walking back to the table. "I mark them as such. It's as simple as that. They must never forget, even in the depths of their misery, why they suffer. I want them to rue the day they took their vows."

"Never," Landry said, huffing the word. "By the grace of God, I am—"

His scream swallowed the rest of what he meant to say. Redman had carved into his gut with the hot blade. Not so deep that he spilled Landry's innards. Just enough to bring this newest agony.

"You were saying?"

"By the grace of God," he wheezed, "I am a Kni—" Another scream. He hoped his friends couldn't hear him. They would be praying for him, he knew. Perhaps the prayer he and the others had spoken earlier.

God, by your grace, grant me the strength to endure.

God, by your grace, grant me the will to resist.

God, by your grace, grant me the courage to keep faith.

He heard the invocation in his mind, and not merely in his own voice. Godfrey was there as well. Tancrede and Draper, too, weakened both, but strong in their faith. He heard Gawain and Brice and Nathaniel. Somehow, they had come to him, to carry him through this ordeal.

The iron blade bit into him a third time, ripping

another wail from his throat. Still, the prayer sang in his mind.

"You can spare yourself more of this," Redman said. Somehow, he was at the hearth again. Gaspar was with him. "Where is the Templar gold, and how do I get it?"

"I don't know," he said, his denial a rasp.

"A pity."

It was much worse after that. Redman allowed Gaspar to use the pike and blade on him, as well as a brand and a second, more refined searing blade.

Then they turned to the cudgels, using them on his shoulders, his elbows, his knees, and midsection. They might have asked him again about the gold. Landry couldn't be certain. He descended into a haze of anguish. Pain was everything. Sound, sight, smell. It assaulted every inch of skin, every expanse of bone and muscle.

He tried to hold to the thread of prayer repeating in his mind. Even that, though, receded as the torture went on. He thought he could hear the words still, but their meaning was lost to him. All that mattered was the next burn, or blow, or cut.

The last thing he remembered was one of them – did it matter anymore who did this to him? – attacking his hands, first with a hammer, then with hot needles under the nails, and finally with pincers that ripped out his fingernails. At some point in this final assault, darkness took him.

"Landry."

His name reached him from a great distance.

"Landry, drink this."

He tried to turn away. Even with consciousness a

KNIGHTFALL: THE INFINITE DEEP

distant shore, he sensed what awaited him there. Pain, dull and sharp, everywhere. He wanted no part of it.

"Wake up, Landry. You must drink."

Another voice, but he couldn't make out the words.

"Very bad," this nearer one said. "They nearly killed him. They might have yet. It is hard to say."

Murmurs again, and then, "I am trying. He has gone very far." A pause. "Landry, please."

The voice was moving away now. He had turned from it after all.

He opened his eyes to shadow, to a faint flicker ahead of him, and a speckled square above. His eyes fluttered closed, but he forced them open a second time. Stars shone outside the high window. The flicker came from the door. Torchlight through the gap framed the shape of Draper's head.

"I'll have that water now."

That, at least, was what he tried to say. It came out as a garble. Draper turned and strode to his side.

"Lord be praised," the Turcopole whispered. "He's awake."

Draper reached for something, and then, with a hand that was swollen and purple, dripped water between Landry's lips. Landry swallowed, parted his lips for more.

"We thought you were lost."

"How long?" Landry asked, hoping Draper would understand.

"They brought you back near to midday. It is night now, though not for long. It will be dawn soon. They just took Gawain."

Draper gave him more water. At a call from beyond the cell, he raised his gaze and left Landry's side. He was back in moments.

"They want to know... Did you find anything? Learn anything?"

The memory came to him in a rush. He tried to move a hand to his waist, but neither hand seemed capable of movement.

"I did. Found something. Learned a bit. Have an idea."

Even in the gloom, he could see Draper smile. "That is well done, Landry. Well done indeed. It is far more than I managed."

As his eyes grew used to the darkness, he noticed what he had missed before. Draper's face was a mess. Of course. He had survived his ordeal in the torture chamber as well. Before long, all of them would, unless he recovered in time to spare Brice and Nathaniel. Assuming they hadn't been brutalized already.

He drank more water. With some effort, he succeeded in raising his hands in front of his eyes. Both were swollen. It pained him to move the fingers of his off hand. His sword hand didn't work at all.

"They will recover in time. As mine will. But we won't be fighting anytime soon."

"Redman and his men will kill us before we've healed. We can't afford to wait."

"We can't prevail if we don't."

"We have to, Draper. The alternative is giving up, and I know you won't do that."

Draper gave a breathless laugh and a shake of his head. "No, I will not."

Landry lowered his off hand to the spot on his waist where he had secured the sliver of iron. "I have something here," he whispered. "Something I found in that chamber where he takes us."

"What is it?"

"A nail, perhaps. Or a broken spike from the cage they have there. It's long, and thin, and it might just allow us to open the locks on our doors."

Draper gaped with such amazement one might have thought Landry had sprouted wings and flown up to the barred window. "How did you do this?"

He made himself smile, though even that hurt his cracked lips. "By the grace of God."

"Did you find anything else?" the Turcopole asked, his voice dropping as well.

"Nothing I could take with me. There is a second corridor that turns off from the first. I don't know where it leads, but I believe there is a reason Redman keeps that corridor dark. He has torches burning everywhere else. Why not there, unless he wishes to conceal something? That second corridor could be what he is hiding."

The mere act of speaking exhausted him. He closed his eyes and immediately felt himself drifting toward slumber.

"Rest now," Draper said. "That is what your body needs most. Mine as well. Maybe when the sun rises they will bring us more water and food. They don't yet have from us what they want. That may keep us alive for a time."

He wanted to agree, and to thank him for his ministrations, limited though they were in these circumstances. The words wouldn't come, though. Sleep claimed him again.

When next Landry woke, daylight streamed into

the cell. Draper slept on his pallet of straw. He heard nothing from the other cells.

Every part of him ached. The swelling around his eyes limited his vision. But he was thirsty and hungry. He took both as good signs. Grinding his teeth against the pain, he forced himself to sit up. He tried to stand, but his right knee hurt too much. In the end, he dragged himself to the door, and with the hand that had been wounded least pulled himself to his feet.

Landry left the sliver of iron where it was, hidden, but he peered out into the round chamber. Seeing no one, he slipped his arm between the bars of the gap in the door. Without the bulk of armor and cloth, he had no trouble fitting his arm in that space. He was less certain he could reach the lock.

He stretched his arm down, sucking in his breath at the pain in his shoulder and back. At first, he couldn't reach the lock. He pressed himself to the door, adjusted the angle of his arm. Because the window in the door was so small, he had to do all this blind, and even then, reaching as far as he could, he felt only the rough iron surface of the door.

Frustration. Rage. Deepest disappointment.

"To the right."

Whispered words from the next cell.

Landry withdrew his arm and gazed through the gap. Tancrede stood at his door, daylight making his wounds even more horrific than they had appeared at night.

"You look terrible," Tancrede said.

"That makes two of us."

"Five. Draper, Godfrey, and now Gawain."

"He's back?"

The lean knight nodded and glanced back into his cell. "He's asleep. He looks as badly off as the rest of us." He regarded Landry again. "You were reaching for the lock?"

"Yes."

"You were even with it, but too near the middle of the door. Try again, to your right."

Landry did as Tancrede instructed, straining against the door again.

"Farther right."

He reached, and his fingertips brushed the edge of the lock.

"That's it," Tancrede said.

Shifting his stance and adjusting his arm again, Landry reached a second time. This time, he managed to cover the face of the lock with his hand. If he had been holding the sliver of iron, he could have worked it into the keyhole. Perhaps this would work after all.

Landry withdrew his arm from between the bars.

Tancrede watched him still. Godfrey had appeared at his door as well.

"So, you can reach it," Tancrede said. "Why would you want to?"

"That's my question as well."

Redman stood on the stairs, a few steps from the bottom. He descended the rest of the way into the dungeon, trailed by Gaspar and several pirates.

"What were you doing?"

"I thought perhaps one of your men had neglected to secure the lock. I hoped that if I could reach it…"

Landry trailed off. The Monk was shaking his head.

"My men are not so careless. Now tell me what you were doing."

At Landry's hesitation, Redman snapped his fingers and pointed at Godfrey's cell. Two of the pirates strode to the door, opened it, and pulled the commander into the center of the chamber.

Redman forced Godfrey to his knees, produced a knife, and held it to the commander's throat.

"Tell me now, or he dies."

Landry couldn't bring himself to answer. He had managed to secure that slender piece of iron, on which he had pinned all the hope he had left. He would not speak of it. He would die before he surrendered it.

Redman moved the blade. Blood from Godfrey's neck trickled over the steel.

"All right," Landry said. "I was... I was going to provoke you into taking me back to the torture chamber."

Redman slanted a wary look at him. "Why?"

"The spikes in the cages there. I thought one might fit in the lock. If I could make you take me back, I might contrive to break off a spike."

The Monk eyed him for another moment, then studied the locks on their doors.

"Go back there," he said to another of his men. "Check all the spikes you see in every cage. If any are weak, or loose, break them off and dispose of them. If I find even one that these men could possibly take, I'll have your head."

The pirate muttered, "Yes, sir," and hurried down the corridor toward the dungeon.

Redman shoved his knife into the sheath on his belt, pulled Godfrey to his feet, and shoved him back into his cell. A pirate locked the door. As he did, Redman crossed to Landry's door, halting a pace from it. Had Landry reached through the bars, he might have taken hold of the man's throat. He knew better than to try.

The Monk stared at him for several seconds, the time stretching uncomfortably. At last, without breaking eye contact, he said to his man, "Open this door."

Landry tried to mask his response, and resisted the urge to check the position of the hidden piece of iron. He prayed that it didn't show in any way.

By now Draper was awake. He sat on his pile of straw, his gaze fixed on Landry.

The pirate opened the door and Redman strolled in. He walked around the small space, pushed at the straw of Landry's crude pallet with the toe of his boot.

Rounding on Landry, he said, "Remove the rest of your clothes."

To his credit, Draper didn't react at all. Landry pulled off his boots and rolled down his breeches, taking care to gather the piece of iron in folds of the cloth. He stepped out of them, leaving the breeches on the stone floor and standing naked before Redman.

The Monk kicked at the breeches as he had at the straw. Landry held his breath.

The sliver of metal remained hidden.

Redman picked up Landry's boots, turned them upside down, and shook them. When nothing came out, he dropped them beside the breeches.

He circled the cell a second time. Pausing in front of Draper, he ordered the Turcopole to his feet and kicked at the straw of his pallet as well. At last, he returned to where Landry stood. He gave a small shrug, looked about again and then, without warning, dug a fist into Landry's gut, the blow landing on one of the dark bruises from Landry's time on the torture table.

Landry doubled over and collapsed to his hands and knees. Pain from his hand shot through his arm, and he fell over onto his side.

"That was a dangerous thought you had, Templar," Redman said, looming over him, orbiting him. "Any attempted escape from this place is bound to fail. And that failure will bring with it the worst sort of punishment for you and your fellow knights. The treatment you've received thus far will seem gentle by comparison. You believe the lock on your door is the only thing holding you here? You're a fool. I have two hundred men, weapons, walls of stone, doors of iron and oak. And you think you can defeat a lock and be free." He kicked Landry in the small of the back.

Landry groaned and weathered a wave of nausea.

The Monk laughed and left the chamber. The door closed and the lock clicked shut.

"The rest of you, be warned. Your friend is a misguided idiot who very nearly got all of you killed. There will be no escaping this fortress. Any attempt at such on your part will result in summary execution. You will leave this place when I allow you to leave, and not before."

Landry listened for his footsteps on the stairway. Only when he could no longer hear them, did he try to raise himself off the filthy floor.

"Are you all right?" Draper asked, kneeling beside him.

"I'm no worse than I was."

He sat up and reached for his breeches. The piece of iron remained where it had been, nestled in the folds of cloth near the waist of the breeches. Landry removed it and handed it to Draper. Then he dressed himself and staggered to his feet.

Draper turned the metal over in his bruised hands. "You believe it will work?" he whispered.

Landry lifted a shoulder. "We can only hope." Draper handed it back to him and he hid it again in his breeches.

"He has a point, you know. The locks are only the first obstacle. Getting away from this place in our current condition..." He shook his head. "I do not believe it is possible."

"I'm afraid that doesn't matter, brother. He intends to kill us. As soon as he gets what he wants, or realizes that he never will, he'll slit our throats and toss our corpses to the dogs."

Draper didn't argue.

"The question becomes: do we allow ourselves to be killed, or do we die fighting for our freedom?"

"When you phrase it that way, it does not strike me as a difficult choice. I do not know if you remember, but you woke during the night, and we spoke about—"

"Waiting for our injuries to heal, or fighting now. I do remember."

"I take it you still believe we should fight now."

"I believe it's our only choice."

Draper narrowed his eyes. "I do not recall you being so reckless in Acre or before. I thought as a man matures, he grows less rash, not more so."

"I wouldn't want to be like all the other knights." They shared a smile.

"Gawain is awake," Tancrede called from his cell.

They moved to the door, making room for each other at the window.

"Can he speak?" Landry asked.

"I can speak." Gawain's voice, weak but clear.

"What did you see there, brother?"

"I believe there's a second corridor."

Landry and Draper eyed each other.

"I think so, too," Landry said. "Anything else."

"Your armor and clothes are still in the dungeon. I noticed this when they removed mine. I saw no weapons, but the rest is near."

"If we can escape the cells, that dungeon should be our first destination." Landry said this softly, so only Draper could hear. He kept his eyes on the stairway, lest Redman surprise them again. He also didn't want Brice or Nathaniel to hear. It wasn't that he mistrusted the knights, but through his own carelessness he had revealed to the Monk that he and his fellow Templars were seeking a means of escape. He didn't want to share with the young knights any information they might reveal under torture.

"After the dungeon, that second corridor." Draper kept his voice low, too. "When?"

Footsteps prevented Landry from answering. The pirate that Redman had sent to the torture chamber emerged from the corridor. Seeing Godfrey, Tancrede, Landry, and Draper all standing by their doors, he halted, eyes narrowing.

"What are you doing?"

"Conversing," Godfrey said. "Unless we're prohibited from doing even that."

"Conversing about what?"

"The weather, of course," Tancrede said.

"Did you find those spikes?" Landry asked.

The pirate grinned and held out his hand. A half dozen pieces of iron, all of them similar to the one he already had, rested on the man's palm.

"Too bad, Templar. Your plan might have worked, had you managed to keep your mouth shut." He chuckled and crossed to the stairway.

"When are we to be fed?" Landry asked, stopping the man.

"You got food and water during the night."

"Yes, we did. How many meals have you eaten today? How many more will you have?"

The pirate frowned, his gaze skipping from one face to the next. "I don't know," he said. "It's not my decision."

"We need water," Draper told him. "Even if you don't bring us food, we have to have water. Without it, we can't heal." He pointed to the next cell. "Gawain, our friend whom Redman tortured most recently. He needs water now. We all do."

"Like I said—"

"It's not your decision," Landry repeated. "Yes, we know. But we'll die without it. Think about that."

The man hesitated, nodded, and finally climbed the stairs.

Once they heard the outside door open and shut, Godfrey asked, "What was that all about, Landry?"

"You don't want water?"

Godfrey said nothing, but stared his way.

"I have an idea," Landry said at last. "That's all I'm prepared to say for now."

"You don't trust us?" Gawain called.

"I trust you with my life, brother. But the less any of you know, the less chance of Redman extracting the information with his torches and blades."

Silence met this.

After a few moments, Godfrey said, "Yes, I understand. Good, Landry."

"What about me?" Draper said, whispering again. "I know more than I should."

"I have faith in you, brother," Landry said.

Draper nodded. "As I said before. Reckless."

Landry had to smile.

CHAPTER 15

The pirates brought them no food or water that night. Nor did they take Brice or Nathaniel to be tortured. For reasons beyond Landry's understanding, Redman and his men ignored the Templars for a time. Landry took this as a sign from the Lord that he should attempt his escape this night.

His bruises and gashes felt no better late in the day than they had that morning. His muscles were stiff and sore. The ache in his hands pulsed with every beat of his heart and reached deep into his bones. After stretching and fisting his off hand throughout the afternoon, he found that he could move his fingers with a minimum of discomfort. His sword hand remained swollen and tender. He thought it likely that at least two of his fingers were broken, and maybe his thumb as well. Like all Templars, he had trained to fight with both hands. But he was far better with his right than his left. He knew they couldn't get away from the prison without a battle, and he dreaded the coming encounter.

Godfrey led them in prayer at sundown and into the evening. When they finished, they fell into a heavy silence. Back in their Temple, it would have been normal for them to turn to wordless contemplation after Vespers. Here, it felt odd.

Landry listened for the pirates. Voices and laughter reached him from beyond the prison walls. Dogs barked, and he thought he heard strains of music, someone picking at a lute or lyre.

He moved to the door, placing his feet with care. For now, he didn't even want Tancrede or Godfrey to know what he was doing. The risk of being discovered by the pirates was too great.

Pulling the splint of iron from within his clothes, he snaked his arm through the bars and reached down for the lock. Once more, he was working blind, and because of his injuries, he had to do this with his off hand as well.

This time, he found the lock itself with ease. Grasping the sliver between his thumb and forefinger, he used his third finger to locate the keyhole. He tried to insert the iron piece, but on his first try, he scratched it across the face of the lock. Shifting his hand, he jarred the lock as well, making it clang against the iron door.

"What was that?" Gawain asked.

He heard steps in the next cell. Pulling his arm back in, he looked over to the adjacent door. Tancrede was there.

Landry shook his head.

"It's nothing," Tancrede said to Gawain. "Probably a rat."

Landry grinned. Tancrede stepped away from the door, and Landry tried again.

He reached through the bars and down, leaning against the iron door, shivering slightly with the cold. This time he used extra caution feeling for the lock and managed not to bump it, or make it shift against the door. When he tried again to insert the sliver into the keyhole, he missed on the first attempt. With this as well, he took care not to make any sounds that might alert the others to what he was doing.

On the second try, he found the keyhole, but this was no guarantee that he would prove successful. He had gotten in some mischief as a youth, breaking locks with objects not much different from the scrap of iron he'd found in the torture chamber. But in the past fifteen years he'd had little experience with locks, and even less with undertaking such a venture with his off hand, and without the benefit of seeing what he was doing.

He tried to shift the mechanics within the lock, pushing and twisting the iron sliver in one direction and then another. He knew what he was listening for – that memory from his childhood remained clear – but this was a more formidable padlock than any he had mastered as a boy. His hand began to cramp. His palm sweated, making his fingers slick. At one point, as he adjusted his grip on the piece of iron, it nearly slipped from his grasp. He paused, took several long breaths, and resumed his efforts.

"Landry!" Tancrede's whispered voice.

He stopped again and listened. Footsteps on the stairway.

With haste, Landry withdrew his arm. He retreated to his pallet, hiding the iron spike as he did.

Voices echoed in the chamber. The door to his cell

opened. One of the pirates placed a fresh bowl of water and some scraps of bread and meat on the floor.

"I don't suppose you'd care to leave us a key?" Draper said with a grim smile.

Landry shot a quick look at his friend. Draper, though, kept his gaze on the pirate.

The man answered with a mocking smile. "You mean like this one?"

He raised his key for Draper to see: a wave of his hand, a blaze of torchlight on the iron he held. This was enough to give Landry a look at the key: the shape, the length, the angle of its teeth. Then the pirate turned, left, and locked their door again.

Landry cast another glance at Draper and nodded his approval.

While the pirates fed the Templars in the other cells, Landry and Draper shared what they had been given. By the time they had finished, Redman's men were gone.

Landry approached the door again. Tancrede and Brice were at the other two doors. He faltered, unsure of what to do.

"Let us help you, Landry," Tancrede said.

"Help him with what?" Brice asked. The beginnings of a beard shadowed his jawline, and his dark hair, once neatly shorn, hung over his brow.

Tancrede didn't answer, saying instead, "Some things we have to do alone. I'm not certain this is one of them."

"If they're tortured," Landry said, hoping his friend would know who he meant, "they might speak of this. They might not be able to help themselves. And then this one hope will be gone."

"You don't trust us," Brice said, his voice flat, an accusation in his dark blue eyes. He remained unbruised, unbloodied. "Nathaniel and me. That's who you're speaking of, isn't it?"

"Try to understand, brother. These others – I've known them for some time now. I've known Godfrey since I was a boy. I only met the two of you in Acre, and while I admire your courage, and your strength, I don't know – I cannot know – how you might endure what Redman intends to do to you."

"This is another test of your faith, Landry," Godfrey said, joining Brice at the far door. "You must have faith in God, of course. But you must also have faith in your fellow Templars, not just those you know well, but all of them. Let all of us help you. Tancrede is right. You cannot do this alone."

He placed the sliver in the swollen palm of his sword hand and wiped his other hand dry. "Very well," he said. Grasping the piece of iron between his thumb and first finger again, he checked the stairway. Satisfied that it was clear, he slid his hand through the bars and held up the scrap of metal for his brothers to see.

"I found this when they took me to be tortured. If you can't see it, it is a piece of iron, a spike or perhaps a nail. I believe I can use it to defeat the lock on my door. And then on your doors. Forgive me for not revealing this sooner. I sought only to preserve this secret."

"Have you tried using it on the lock yet?" Gawain asked, appearing beside Tancrede.

He was as badly wounded as Tancrede; they looked like twins of a brutish father.

"Once, yes." He smiled. "I'm the rat you heard."

Gawain's eyes shifted to Tancrede. "Try again," he said.

Again, Landry reached through the gap in his door and to the lock. He couldn't deny that it was easier not worrying about the noise he made. In moments, he was working the sliver in the lock again.

"To the side more," Brice said. "The left. Your left."

Landry shifted his hand and tried again.

"Up," Gawain said.

Landry frowned, but altered his approach again. For several seconds he worked the lock, but to no avail.

"More to the left."

"To the right."

"Higher."

These instructions all came at the same time. Landry pulled back from the door enough to glare out at his fellow knights.

"You're not helping."

He went back to work. The others remained silent. For a short while.

As they began to offer advice again, Landry looked back at Draper and rolled his eyes.

"Remember the key," Draper said.

Landry nodded and closed his eyes, picturing the key he had glimpsed in the pirate's hand. Holding to that image, his eyes still shut, he turned the sliver of iron between his fingers and altered his angle of attack yet again.

Minutes passed. He sensed the impatience of the others, but did his best to ignore them. Something caught on the tip of the iron, and he thought the lock might open. But the metal slipped. He tried the same approach a second time, and a third. He was getting close. He knew it. One more twist and—

Ti-clack!

He opened his eyes and stared back at Draper. The Turcopole raised an eyebrow.

"That sounded promising."

"Landry?" Godfrey said, his tone almost reverent. "Did it open?"

He removed the iron from the lock, and held it to his palm with his ring finger. Then he felt for the shackle. It had opened from the body. Landry slipped the lock free of the joint holding the door shut.

"Landry?"

"Yes, it's open," he said, keeping his voice even. He drew his arm back through the barred opening of the door and stared at the lock. He was amazed his ploy had worked.

Draper took his place at the door.

"The stairs remain clear. Shall we free the others?"

"Not yet," Landry said.

He pushed open the door, muttering an imprecation at the creak of the iron hinges. He checked the stairway again.

"What now?" Tancrede asked, a roguish grin on his bloodied lips.

"I'm going down that corridor. I want to see what's there."

"Alone?"

"Yes. If Redman and his men return, and all of us are gone, they're bound to find us. We can only expect to have one chance at this. We need to be certain that every detail is worked out."

"He's right," Godfrey said. "Go, brother. Godspeed."

Landry reclaimed his blanket from within his cell,

and hurried out to the common chamber. "I need straw from your pallets. Just a few handfuls from each of you."

The other Templars obliged, handing him bundles of straw through their doors. He gathered the straw in his blanket and carried it back to his cell. There, he arranged the straw and blanket to make it seem that he was bundled on his pallet.

"That won't deceive them for long if they choose to enter the cell."

"I'm going to leave the lock in place, but unlatched," Landry said. "If they choose to enter, the blanket will be the least of our worries."

Draper's eyes widened a bit, but otherwise he merely dipped his chin, acknowledging this. Landry stepped back and considered the pallet with a critical eye. Draper was right. It wasn't very convincing. He hoped darkness and the limited view from outside the door would be enough to keep them from seeing through his artifice.

He slipped out of the cell, closed the door, and set the lock in place, making it appear as though the shackle was still engaged.

"With any luck at all," he said, "I'll be back before Redman returns."

"And if you're not?" Gawain asked.

"Draw his attention away from Draper and my cell. If he notices the lock is open, we're all dead."

Landry started down the shadowed passage, running the fingers of his off hand along the stone wall. After ten steps, no more, he could see nothing in the inky dark. He walked slowly, carefully, favoring his injured leg. He covered what felt like a long distance without sensing the corridor he had noticed last time.

Had he missed it?

He caught sight of the faint orange glow of torches ahead of him. The torture chamber. He thought of retrieving one of the torches from there and carrying it with him down the corridor he sought. As quickly as the idea came to him, he dismissed it. If by some chance Redman and his men came for Brice or Nathaniel with the intent of abusing them as they had the others, he would be discovered.

Landry had just made up his mind to turn back, when the quality of the air changed. The whisper of a breeze from the right. The corridor. He ventured away from the left-hand wall and took a tentative step forward, both arms outstretched.

A second step, and a third. His sword hand skimmed the stone corner of the intersection, making him flinch, sending bolts of pain up to his elbow. Cursing the Monk and Gaspar, he sidled away from the wall and continued down this new corridor.

He stumbled when the stone walkway gave way to dirt. But he kept his feet, and trod on, counting his steps.

At stride forty-three, he sensed another change in the flow of air. Halting, he turned right and slid his feet forward, expecting to bump into a wall. Again, he found a corner, this time with his off hand. He would explore this passage later, after following the one he was on to its end.

"Forty-three," he said, muttering the number, committing it to memory.

He angled back the other way and continued along the path he had been following.

At eighty-eight, he paused, sensing another current of

air. He eased to the right again, reaching across his body with his good hand. A second corridor off this one.

"Eighty-eight. And forty-three."

On he walked. After another fifty paces or so, he thought he saw light ahead. Not light, so much as a break in the absolute darkness. Thirty steps later, the corridor ended in an open chamber. The glow of starlight and torches from a high opening in the wall ahead of him spilled a dim pool of light onto the floor, bringing into relief piles of items he couldn't quite identify.

After the dark of the passages, this light, such as it was, allowed him to explore the chamber. The first of the piles appeared to be old uniforms, some bearing the red cross of the Templars. Others bore the black and white of the Hospitallers. A second pile included more mantles and tabards, but also coats of mail and armored leggings. They were long neglected, the metal rough with dirt and corrosion, but in the absence of the Templars' own armor, these pieces would serve Landry and his friends well enough.

Hope cresting in his heart, Landry hurried to the next pile. More abandoned clothes, and a few more shirts of mail.

He made his way around the chamber, pausing to scrutinize each mound of items. As he dug into the pile just beneath the high window, a shout startled him. He straightened, his heart pounding, his face lifted toward the window, and he listened.

A second cry made him whirl, the blood draining from his face, leaving his cheeks cold. The sound hadn't come from outside, but rather from behind him. The torture chamber. Brice, or Nathaniel. He crept back out of the chamber along the corridor to be sure.

A third scream resounded through the passageways, chilling him. He could sneak up on them, kill the men as they tortured the Templar. He had armor here. Maybe he would find weapons as well.

If he hadn't been wounded, he wouldn't have thought twice. One of the lads was being brutalized. Duty required no less of him. And with his training and experience, he could take on four men and prevail.

Injured as Landry was, though, he knew he could not take on Redman, Gaspar, and the pirates they probably had with them. They would kill him without breaking a sweat, and all would be lost.

The knight bellowed again. Landry closed his eyes and gritted his teeth.

God, by your grace, grant us the strength to endure.

God, by your grace, grant us the will to resist.

God, by your grace, grant us the courage to keep faith.

They had known this might happen. Godfrey had told him he must have faith in his fellow Templars. That meant not only trusting the lad not to reveal what Landry had done, but also understanding that the young knight was prepared to suffer through this torture to give Landry the chance to find them a path out of the prison.

He repeated the litany in a whisper. Calmer now, he walked back into the chamber and to the pile he had left moments before. He halted before it, staring at the mound, hearing another scream from the torture chamber.

Realization crashed through him. These clothes, this armor – it must have come from previous victims of Redman's cruelty. Likely the men to whom the items belonged were long since lost, tortured to death.

He muttered another prayer, this one for the lost souls who had preceded him in this place. Steeling himself, he resumed his search.

Two mounds on, he found what he had been looking for. Beneath still more moth-eaten cloth and rusted armor, he discovered a collection of weapons. Nine swords, three shorter blades, a pair of shields marked with the Templar cross. The swords and daggers had suffered from neglect, just as the mail had. But like the armor, they would serve their function.

Landry hefted one of the swords, gripping it with the hand that was less swollen. Even fighting with his off hand, he could kill. He swung the blade once, and then again. And he glared into the ebon darkness of the corridor, contemplating anew an attack on Redman and his allies. Killing the Monk might not be enough to drag the pirates into chaos. If he could defeat Gaspar as well, then perhaps the other Templars would have a chance, even if he himself was killed. The problem would be fighting through the other pirates to get to their leaders. For a second time, he was forced to concede that he couldn't fight their captors alone. As much as he wanted to, as much as one of his brothers might need him to, it would be a waste of his life.

Deflated, he set the sword back on the pile and resumed his search.

One of the other piles contained additional weapons, and leather sheaths and scabbards for the various blades. Pausing over this mound of weapons, armor, and clothes, Landry had a thought. He dropped to his knees and dug through the sheaths until he found what he sought.

The sheath was designed to be strapped to a belt,

but Landry sorted through one of the previous piles, remembering a leather bracer he had seen earlier. This was made for a forearm, of course, but by loosening the belts all the way, he managed to fit it around his calf. He then attached the sheath to the bracer and slipped a blade into the sheath. He rolled down the leg of his breeches and smoothed the material with his hand. Standing, he walked in a circle, trying to get used to the way the device felt on his leg. He halted, looked down at his calf from different angles. He didn't think the sheath showed.

If they searched him, they were certain to find it. He was willing to take that chance. Now, at least one Templar would be armed.

He found nothing more of value in the chamber. Starting back the way he had come, he heard more cries from the torture chamber. As long as Redman and Gaspar were there, he didn't dare risk the journey back to his cell. Instead, he turned at the nearer of the corridors he had found. Eighty-eight.

The passageway had a dirt floor and no light. As before, he kept his left arm outstretched, his hand trailing along the stone wall. The passageway curved gradually to the right and upward. His wounded leg ached, and he was out of breath, but his need to know what lay at the end of this corridor drove him on. The air within the passage grew warmer with every step Landry took, giving him hope that it led to some means of escape.

A bit farther on, as the air continued to warm, sounds reached him as well. He heard voices and music, much as he had from the cell he shared with Draper. Following a last bend in the corridor, he found himself at an iron gate, barred and locked. It wasn't a solid door with a gap, like the entrances to the cells in which the Templars were held. This was constructed only of bars of iron. Starlight and torch-fire illuminated the end of the passageway.

Landry flattened himself against the wall, sticking to shadows.

He spied no pirates at this gate, no guards of any sort. He eased forward, peering out at the buildings beyond the bars. He didn't recognize any of what he saw. He wasn't sure where in the compound he was. Reaching the gate, he knelt to examine the lock. It was similar in size and design to the one on his cell door. He could open it with the iron spike he still carried. When the time came, this might be their most promising route to freedom.

He listened, marking the direction from which the voices emanated. They were to the right. From the cells in which he and his fellow Templars were being kept, the voices came from the top of the stairway and what he thought of as the front of the building. That gave him at least some vague sense of where he was, and how they could reach the gate of the compound.

He stood, backed away from the opening. After a few steps, he turned and started back the way he had come. Fingertips touching the wall, he strode blindly back down into cooler air, trusting the path. Sooner than he expected, he reached the intersection. He went left, and walked, counting his steps. As he reached forty, he slowed. A few strides later, he came to the other spur. Forty-three.

Landry thought it risky to be away from his cell for too much longer, but curiosity drove him into this dark passage.

The path didn't climb as the other had. The farther he went, the worse the smell. He wished he had thought to bring a sword. The dagger strapped to his calf seemed woefully small.

He walked on, following the contour of the corridor walls, making as little noise as possible. One hundred and sixty-one strides from the intersection, he spotted light ahead of him. Flickering and yellow-orange, it had to come from a flame. A fire, or torches. Eyes fixed on the light, he caught his toe on something a few steps later and fell. His hands scraped on stone. The impact to his knees and hands brought a gasp.

The dirt path had given way once more to stone. Was he back where he had started? Was this merely a different path back to the cells that held the Templars? Or had he lost track of where he was and turned into the original corridor?

Uncertain, he climbed to his feet again and crept forward, watchful now, confused.

He listened for voices as he neared the end of this passageway, thinking he might hear Godfrey or Tancrede. But all was silent within the prison. He had long since lost track of the time; he knew only that it had to be quite late. Had the lad being tortured been brought back to his cell?

On that thought, he halted and half pivoted to look back. He hadn't seen the torches of the torture chamber. This *couldn't* be the corridor back to his cell.

The end of the passageway opened onto a round chamber, much like the one where the Templars were held. Torches burned in sconces. A stairway across from the corridor climbed to... somewhere. Iron doors, complete with barred windows, were fixed in the stone walls around the chamber. This place was, in almost every respect, a twin to the chamber in which Landry and the other knights had been imprisoned.

He stepped to the nearest of the doors and peeked inside.

Two men slept on straw pallets against opposite walls.

"Who the hell are you?"

Landry spun.

CHAPTER 16

A face loomed at the doorway of another cell: dark-eyed, bearded, with long, lank hair. The man glared, brows bunched.

Landry heard footsteps in the other cells. Within moments, men gazed out at him from every doorway. He counted at least twelve of them.

"I asked you a question. Who are you?"

"My name is Landry. I'm a prisoner here. Like you."

The man appeared skeptical. He might have been older than Landry by a few years, but in other ways he reminded Landry of himself. "How did you get here?"

"That corridor," Landry said. "I followed it from… from where I've been held."

"That seems unlikely, doesn't it? If you're a prisoner, how did you get free of your cell?"

Landry didn't answer. He knew nothing about these men, other than that they were being held by Redman and his crew. None of them bore bruises and wounds of the sort inflicted on the Templars. He didn't know what that might mean, but he thought it best not to tell them too much about himself or how he had escaped his cell.

"Caught him lying, didn't you, Kad?" said one of the others. "Look at him. He can't think of a thing to say. Probably sent by the Monk to trick us."

"Yes," Landry said, facing the man. "How clever of you. See how I've beaten myself bloody just to deceive you."

The prisoner's face reddened.

"All right, if you are a prisoner," said Kad, "tell us how you got free."

"I don't think I will. I don't know you, just as you don't know me. Some things are best left unexplained for now. I assure you, Redman and Gaspar have no love for my friends and me. We're eager to escape this place."

Kad laughed. "Good luck with that. We're in a dungeon, in a fortress, in the middle of a deserted island. We're surrounded by two hundred men, we have no weapons, and we're miles from any ship. And you speak of escape? You're mad."

"I've been called worse."

"How many of you are there? You and these friends you talk about."

Landry cringed inwardly. "We are seven."

"Ho! Seven! Well, forgive me, Landry. I thought you were mad, but clearly I've misjudged you."

Landry held up a hand, silencing him. "You've made your point."

Kad eyed him critically. "Yet, here you stand, free of your cell. I would dearly like to know how you did that. And you're clearly strong enough to survive a beating. That counts for something."

"My friends and I are not to be discounted," Landry said. "Redman has beaten nearly all of us in this way, trying to extract information. We've told him nothing."

"What sort of information?"

"You know the man. What do you think?"

"You've got gold somewhere. And he wants it."

"An excellent guess," Landry said. "What does he want with you?"

"Same thing, in a way. We've a rival ship. He doesn't like to be challenged, and when we refused to leave these waters, he hunted us down, destroyed our vessel, and took us prisoner."

"This is all of you?"

Kad nodded, lips thinned. "He killed some, including our captain. Others escaped. I expect he'll sell us to slavers."

"He offered to make some of us members of his crew."

This from a third man in a cell across from Kad's. He had wheaten hair and pale eyes. His skin was browned by the sun, and freckles dotted his cheeks and the bridge of his nose.

"In exchange for the whereabouts of those who got away," Kad said.

"Sure, but he could offer them—"

"We're not talking about this, Henry!"

"You may not be. I am. And just so we're clear, nobody made you captain."

"Captain's dead," said another man in another cell. "Of those of us left, Kad's been part of the crew longest. That makes him captain in my eyes."

The one named Henry scowled and averted his gaze.

"Fine. But that don't mean he makes decisions for me. If it comes to a choice between joining Redman's crew and dying… well, I'll be damned if I'll give my life for Kad's pride."

Kad faced Landry again. "As far as Redman is concerned, we're all that's left. He won't learn of the others."

"Slavers," Landry said. "That's a hard fate."

"There's worse."

Landry raised his brows.

"All right, not many. But what choice do we have?"

"Join with us."

Henry huffed a laugh. "Sure death, that is. Join with you. All seven of you?" He laughed again.

Kad watched Landry, his expression remaining sober.

Landry ignored Henry, keeping his eyes on the leader. "He could be right," he said. "Chances are, when the time comes, we'll get ourselves killed trying to escape this place. We'll take plenty of Redman's men with us, though. Maybe Redman and Gaspar themselves. I'd rather die than be kept here for the rest of my days, or be given over to slavers."

Kad weighed the response of his men, his gaze skipping from door to door.

"You're not really considering this," Henry said.

The man who shared Henry's cell shoved him away from the door. "Shut up, Henry."

"Whatever you did to get free," Kad said, "you can use it on our cells, too?"

"I can."

"Then what?"

"There's a corridor," Landry said, gesturing over his shoulder at the passageway behind him. "A series of them, actually. One of them leads to my friends.

Another leads to an abandoned chamber. There are weapons there, and armor. Rusted to be sure, but serviceable." He paused, eyes scanning the chamber, gauging the reactions of Kad's men. "A third passage leads to an iron gate. It's locked, but it poses no more of an obstacle than our doors, or yours."

Stares met this.

"We'll speak of it," Kad said at last. "If you can find your way back here, we'll have an answer for you. If you can't..." He shrugged. "Then best of luck to you."

"And to you."

"No!" Henry said, forcing himself back to the barred opening in his door. "We won't talk about it! We won't do it! I'm not dying for some madman running loose in Redman's prison!"

"Damnit, Henry!"

Before Kad could say more, the lad bellowed, "Redman!" The echo in that space was deafening. "Redman!" he called again. "A man's got loose! There's a prisoner—"

A blow from his cellmate knocked Henry down and out of sight. A second silenced him.

"Run!" Kad said to Landry. "If they find you, they'll kill us all!"

Cursing the lad with a vehemence that would have shocked Godfrey, Landry wheeled and hobbled back along the dark corridor, moving as fast as his injuries would allow. The pirates would be drawn to Kad and his men first. It might take them some time to learn anything from them, particularly if they managed to keep Henry quiet. He could get back, but only if he spent no more time on exploration. Even so, he would need some good fortune.

He stumbled at the spot where stone gave way to dirt, but he caught himself and continued. The walk back to the other corridor seemed to take a long time. Longer than he had anticipated. In his haste, he had neglected to keep count. There had been no turns off this passageway. He knew he couldn't lose his way, but as he ran on, finding no sign of the next corridor, fear began to intrude on his thoughts.

Reaching the corner at last, and knowing a moment of blessed relief, he turned, counted forty-three paces, and turned again. In the distance, he saw the glow of torches from his familiar chamber.

He heard shouts as well, distant but unmistakable. He hoped Redman and his men were headed for Kad's chamber. If not, they would reach the other Templars before Landry did.

He slowed as he neared the end of the corridor, and used the darkness of the passageway to mask his last few steps. All was quiet in the chamber and the cells of his fellow Templars. He heard voices still, but all from outside. He entered the chamber and stepped to the door of his cell.

The lock remained unlatched, as he had left it. He removed it and opened the door. The instant he did, Draper rolled off his pallet.

"Praise the Lord! We feared you had been discovered."

"Where have you been all this time?" Tancrede asked from his door.

"I have much to tell you, but not now. Redman and his men may be on their way here as we speak. I need to be inside the cell with the door locked."

Landry entered the cell, and started to close the

door. Before it closed all the way, he remembered the knife he had strapped to his calf. He rolled up the leg of his breeches and detached the bracer.

"Where did you get that?" Draper asked.

"I'll tell you everything, brother. I swear it. But not now."

He scanned the chamber, desperate for somewhere to hide the weapon. Each spot he considered struck him as too obvious, or too easily searched. Perhaps if the pirates had left the unoccupied cells open, he could have...

Landry laughed at his own foolishness. Crossing the chamber to one of the unused cells, he slipped the weapon, sheath, and bracer through the gap in the door and allowed it to fall to the floor.

"Why would you do that?" Tancrede asked.

Landry pulled out the sliver of iron and held it up for his friend to see. "Because I can retrieve it whenever I wish."

He entered his cell and closed himself inside. Handing the iron spike to Draper, he said, "Hide this somewhere. I'll lock the door."

The Turcopole took the sliver from him. Landry pushed his arm through the window of the door, lock in hand, and reached down to fasten the door shut once more. Hearing the shackle click in place, he sagged against the door and let out a breath.

"All right, then, Landry," Tancrede called. "What's this all about? Where have you been?"

Landry straightened. The rest of the Templars, except for Brice, had gathered at their doors. He had been free of his cell for only an hour, maybe two. Already, though, it felt odd to be a prisoner again.

"Brice was beaten," he said.

Godfrey nodded. "They came for him soon after you left."

"I heard him. I wondered who it was. How is he?"

"A mess, like the rest of us. But he's alive, and he's sleeping." He gestured. "Go on, brother. Tell us where you've been."

"I followed the corridor that Gawain and I found," Landry said. "And I discovered much along the way." He stared at the stairway, determined that Redman would not surprise him as he recounted his journey through the passageways, and he told them what he had seen and done, sparing no detail. The weapons, armor, and clothes, the other prisoners, the gate to outside – he described it all. As he spoke, he began to piece together a plan of escape.

One of the torches near his door sputtered. At the same time, he thought he heard a boot grate on one of the high steps.

"Enough," he whispered. "They're here."

The other Templars moved away from their doors. He and Draper did the same. Landry's blanket still held bundles of straw in a form that loosely mimicked his own sleeping form. He unbundled his blanket, spread the straw beneath him, and lay down on his pallet just as the pirates' footsteps reached the floor of the chamber.

Seconds later, a fist pounded on an iron door.

"Up, Templars. Now!" Redman said.

Landry took his time responding to the summons.

"I said up!"

He gathered that the others had done the same.

"What do you want with us?" Godfrey asked.

Landry joined Draper at their door.

"I have word from other prisoners that one of you was roaming the tunnels."

Godfrey laughed. "Yes, we all went for a stroll. That's all right, isn't it?"

"Shut your mouth!"

"No, I don't believe I will. How exactly are we supposed to have freed ourselves from these cells and gone on our little jaunt? And while we're asking questions, what prisoners? Who else do you have here, and where are they?"

It was well done. Landry himself would have been convinced.

Redman scrutinized each of their faces, his brow furrowed, as if he believed he could read their intent merely from their expressions. Landry thought he looked like a man with more questions than information. He hoped this meant the other prisoners hadn't told him much.

"You don't need to know about the others. Stand back from your doors. I intend to search each of you, and your cells." He motioned the pirates he had brought with him toward the doors. "Start with them," he said, indicating Landry and Draper's cell.

Redman's men drew their swords. One of them produced a key.

"Take off your clothes," Redman said. "Everything. You'll not hide anything from me."

Landry resisted the impulse to look Draper's way, wondering what the man had done with his iron spike. With the pirates watching them, swords at the ready, they stepped out of their breeches and undergarments, and stood naked before the Monk. Under any other circumstance, it would have been humiliating. But Landry knew much that Redman didn't and he stood before the pirate with his chin lifted, without clothes, but cloaked in his surety that at last he and the Templars had the advantage.

Redman looked them over and turned their clothing inside out. He searched the cell exhaustively, picking through the straw pallets and checking every corner. When he had done all of this he planted himself in front of Landry.

"One of the other prisoners described the man who spoke to them."

"Did they give a name?"

Redman's expression soured. "The one who would tell us anything about him couldn't remember. But apparently, he resembled you. Same hair, same beard, same height."

"He must have been quite handsome," Landry said, schooling his features.

Redman grinned.

Landry wasn't fooled. He braced himself for what he knew would come next.

Redman struck him across the face with the back of his hand and then hammered a punch to Landry's midsection. Landry doubled over. A blow to the back of his neck knocked him to the floor.

"This is not amusing," Redman said.

Landry pushed himself up, grimacing at the pain in his battered hand. "What do you want me to say? We are trapped in these cells, without weapons or tools or any means of escape. And you come here accusing us of wandering the tunnels, when the first thing we would do if we managed to break free is flee this place.

You are making no sense, pirate."

He prepared himself for more abuse, fully aware that he was provoking the man. But after standing over him for another few seconds, Redman turned on his heel and left the cell.

"Come along," he said to his men, sounding furious. "We'll search the others."

The pirates followed him. One man closed and locked the door.

Draper helped Landry to his feet, regarding him with a blend of puzzlement and disapproval. They didn't speak as they dressed.

Redman went to the cell that held Tancrede and Gawain next, and after that to the enclosure Godfrey shared with the young knights. He ordered Godfrey and Nathaniel to rouse Brice and remove his clothing. Godfrey objected and, from what Landry could tell, was beaten for his effort. In the end, Brice was stripped and made to stand as well. Of course, the pirates found nothing that might explain how a Templar had left his cell and ventured to the other side of the prison.

When he had completed his searches, the Monk appeared even more frustrated and confused than he had before.

"You've been made a fool, pirate," Gawain said. "How could one of us have gotten free? Those others – they're having a laugh at your expense."

Landry wanted Gawain to say no more. He didn't wish to bring the pirate's wrath down on Kad and his men. On the other hand, he wouldn't mind so much if Redman blamed only Henry for the alleged deception.

"Not another word, Templar," the Monk warned. "I won't be spoken of in that way. Not by anyone."

Gawain had the good sense to keep silent.

Redman glanced about once again. Then he pivoted and strode to the stairway. He halted there, however, and faced them again.

"My patience with you wears thin. All of you but one have been beaten and tortured, and I am no closer to having the information I want. I believe it is time for me to alter my tactics. If being tortured yourselves is not enough to loosen your tongues, perhaps I ought to make you watch as the last of your brothers is slowly tormented and, if necessary, put to death. Think about it, Templars. Ask yourselves if you are willing to trade your brother's life for a bit of gold."

He spun away again and left the dungeon, his men scrambling after him.

Even after he was gone, Landry and the others held their tongues, lest the Monk or his men were listening.

Landry wanted to ask Draper what he had done with the iron sliver, but he dared not chance that question. Draper limped to his pallet and covered himself. Landry did the same. After this latest encounter with the pirates, he knew they had to attempt their escape as soon as possible. Nathaniel's life depended upon it. Landry also knew, though, that the timing of their effort might well determine whether they succeeded or failed.

"These other prisoners," Draper said, in a whisper. "Do you trust them?"

"Obviously, not the man who called for Redman. I do trust their leader. I believe he can convince the rest of his men to work with us."

"It seems a risk."

"It is," Landry said. "But there are at least a dozen

of them, and none of them have been wounded as we have. I'm not certain that we can get away without them. With them, I believe we have some small chance."

"Landry."

Godfrey's voice. He and Draper stepped to the door. "You have a plan?" the commander asked.

They glanced at the stairway at the same time, their eyes meeting again a moment later. Landry nodded.

"Tell me."

Landry related what he had in mind as succinctly as possible. He noticed as he spoke that he no longer heard voices or music from the compound. Perhaps the pirates had retired for the night. More likely, Redman had put an end to frivolous pursuits and alerted his crew to the possibility that their prisoners had found a means to escape their cells.

As if to confirm his concerns, the torches outside their cells sputtered again, boots scraped on the steps leading to the dungeon, and two men emerged from the stairway: the hulking, bald brothers they had seen before. They said nothing, but took positions at either end of the chamber, one on the near side of Landry's cell, the other on the far side of Godfrey's.

Landry and Draper exchanged looks. Draper shook his head and huffed a silent sigh. There was no way Landry could work on the lock with Redman's men standing beside their cell. If they didn't find some way to distract or overcome the pirates, their escape would be over before it began.

Godfrey watched the Monk's man take his position beside their cell, bile rising in his throat. Redman's threat against Nathaniel frightened him. He had no doubt that the pirate would prove true to his word if they didn't gain their freedom. Landry's plan struck him as perilous to say the least, but no more so than remaining here and waiting to die.

"Commander," Nathaniel said.

Godfrey turned from the door. Nathaniel stood near Brice, who had regained consciousness again.

Nathaniel opened his mouth to say more, but Godfrey held up a hand to stop him and put a finger to his lips, indicating that the knight should remain silent.

He knelt beside Brice, who followed his movements with his eyes, one of them swollen nearly shut. The lad's face was misshapen, darkened by bruises and a crust of blood. The injuries to his hands and legs, though, appeared less severe than those borne by some of the other knights.

"How do you feel?" Godfrey asked, keeping his voice hushed.

"Terrible."

Godfrey's smile was fleeting. "Of course. But I need you to recover sooner than you might prefer. Pay attention to what Nathaniel and I do, remain silent and still until the door to this cell opens, but then be ready to act. Can you do all of that for me?"

"Of course."

"God chose well when he brought you to our Order, brother."

He stood, and approached Nathaniel. "Follow what I say and do," he said, breathing the words.

Nathaniel's green eyes widened fractionally, but he dipped his chin.

"You cannot tell them anything," Godfrey said,

speaking with force. "I don't care what Redman said."

The lad faltered, his mouth opening and closing again. Godfrey watched him, fearing Nathaniel might not be capable of the sort of ruse he had in mind.

The knight surprised him.

"With due respect, Commander," he said, his voice climbing as well, "Redman said nothing about killing you. It's easy for you to demand my silence."

Godfrey grinned for an instant and winked.

"Easy? Are you mad? I've been beaten. We all have, except you. Or had you failed to notice?"

Nathaniel hesitated again. Godfrey made a motion of denial, then pointed to the knight and to the door.

"I don't care about any of that," Nathaniel said. "I'm going to tell him everything I know. I won't die for you."

Godfrey motioned at the door again, put his fist to his open hand. Nathaniel walked to the doorway.

"Hey, you!" he called to the nearer of the two guards. "I want to speak with—"

Godfrey gave him time for no more than that. He grabbed the knight from behind, spun him, and struck him across the jaw. Pain shot through his injured hand, but he didn't care. Nathaniel staggered. Godfrey seized him with both hands and wrestled him to the floor.

They rolled one way and another, grappling, pretending to fight.

"You traitor!" Godfrey roared.

"I'll kill you!" Nathaniel shouted back with such vehemence, Godfrey almost believed him.

"Hey!" he heard from the door. "You two stop that!"

"Ignore him," Godfrey murmured.

"Right," Nathaniel answered. Then, louder, "I will not be tortured to death for you and your gold!"

"Better get in there," the other guard said to the one by their door.

Godfrey and Nathaniel continued their fight, rolling, struggling, and grunting, making a good show of trying to hurt each other. Metal scraped at the door: a key going in the lock.

Godfrey paused long enough to look Brice's way. The young knight already watched him. He gave the slightest of nods before closing his eyes and lying still on the pallet.

With a twist of his shoulder, he indicated to Nathaniel that they should roll toward the wall opposite Brice's pallet.

"Hit me," Godfrey whispered, as they did this.

Nathaniel reared and threw a wild punch, which struck Godfrey high on the temple. This was one spot Redman had neglected to abuse during Godfrey's torture. Though the blow barely hurt, it must have appeared fearsome to the pirate, landing as it did just as he opened the cell door.

"Hey!" the pirate said a second time.

He bent over them and grabbed at Godfrey and Nathaniel both, perhaps trying to separate them. He never had the chance.

Godfrey didn't hear Brice rise or charge them. From the corner of his eye, he saw a form blur into view and crash into the pirate's back. Redman's man tripped over Godfrey and Nathaniel, and slammed face first into the stone wall directly in front of him.

"His sword!" Godfrey said, hissing the words.

Nathaniel grabbed for the hilt of the man's weapon. The pirate, though probably dazed, did the same. Brice kicked the man in the back. Godfrey wrapped his arm around the pirate's neck and pulled. Redman's man grabbed at his arm, allowing Nathaniel to seize the sword.

Even as the knight pulled the weapon free, the other pirate stormed into the cell, his sword in hand.

"What in the Devil's name—"

He got out no more than that. Nathaniel whirled, yellow hair wild with torchlight, and thrust the other pirate's blade through the man's heart. The pirate's eyes and mouth went wide. He swayed, dropped the sword. His legs gave way and he slumped to the floor, blood spreading over his chest.

Godfrey maintained his hold on the first man, and he sensed rather than saw the pirate moving, snaking his arm down to his belt. Godfrey spotted the second weapon just as the pirate's hand reached it. He grabbed for the blade as well.

"Brice!" he said.

The young knight reached for the pirate's blade hand.

Nathaniel rounded, his bloodied weapon poised to strike.

"Don't kill him!" Godfrey said.

A second later, the pirate hollered and released the knife he had claimed.

Liquid warmth flowed over Godfrey's bare arm. Blood, from a wound Nathaniel had inflicted to the pirate's shoulder. Godfrey handed the knife to Brice. Maintaining his grip on the pirate's neck with one arm, he put his other hand over the man's mouth to keep him from crying out again. As it was, they had made too much noise.

Brice held the knife to the corner of the pirate's eye. Nathaniel placed the tip of the sword against his heart.

"I'm going to release you now," Godfrey said, speaking in low tones. "If you scream. If you call for help. If you so much as twitch, you will lose your eye, and perhaps your life. Do you understand?" He moved his hand from the man's mouth.

"Yes," the pirate said, his voice flat, and not too loud.

"Excellent."

Godfrey released him and climbed to his feet. The young knights stood over the pirate, weapons still at the ready.

"Now," Godfrey said. "We're going to free my friends, and then you're going to answer some questions for us."

CHAPTER 17

Landry gripped the bars of his door, his hands aching, his breathing ragged. He wanted to call out to Godfrey, but he didn't know if he should, or if he might distract the commander at the worst possible time.

He hadn't grasped what was happening in Godfrey's cell. Not at first.

"It must be a ruse," Draper had whispered to him as Godfrey and Nathaniel berated each other.

Hearing the words, he knew his friend was right. Godfrey would have understood that, with the pirates outside their cells, they could not hope to escape. The commander had taken it upon himself to overcome this newest obstacle.

When the first guard opened the door and charged inside, and the second man drew his sword and rushed into the cell, Landry feared that Godfrey had miscalculated. For several seconds – an interval that seemed to drag on for hours – he heard nothing from Godfrey and his fellow knights, nothing from Redman's men.

293

At last, someone emerged from the cell. Brice limped as he walked to Landry and Draper's door, his face battered and distorted by the Monk's torture. But he flashed a crooked grin and held up a bruised hand. In it, he held a key.

He unlocked Landry's door, and then the one beside it. In moments, Brice, Landry, Draper, Tancrede, and Gawain stood together in the round chamber.

"Godfrey intends to question him," Brice said, struggling to enunciate. "He wants all of you there."

"Him?" Tancrede asked.

"The pirate. The one who's still alive."

The rest of the knights shared glances. They started to follow the lad, but Landry stopped and requested the key. Brice frowned in confusion, but gave it to him. Landry opened the cell opposite his own and retrieved the knife and bracer he had thrown in there. Once he had strapped the blade to his forearm, he followed Brice and the others to Godfrey's cell.

The pirate sat on the floor. Nathaniel stood behind him, a sword pressed to the back of his neck. Godfrey loomed in front of him, a second sword held loosely in one hand, and a knife in the other. The second pirate lay dead near the first man, his blood staining the stone.

Godfrey acknowledged Landry as he entered, but immediately turned his attention back to the pirate. "I'm going to ask you again, and then I'm going to start slicing away bits of you. Your fingers, your toes, perhaps an eye, perhaps some other appendage to which you're more attached." He pointed the tip of his sword at the man's crotch. "You understand, yes?"

The pirate swallowed and nodded.

"Where are these other prisoners from? Where did you find them?"

"They... they are from a ship," the man said, his words thick with what might have been a Greek accent.

"What ship?"

"I do not remember her name. Another ship of fortune."

"Pirates. Rivals."

The man hesitated. "Yes."

"What will Redman do with them?"

"He has taken their vessel, killed much of their crew. These he will sell to slavers."

"That's what Kad told me," Landry said.

The pirate stared up at him. "It is true, then. You escaped your cell."

Landry tolerated the man's gaze, but said nothing.

"Why would you come back? Why would you lock yourself back in your cell? You might already be far away from here."

"You don't know what it means to be a Templar, or you wouldn't have to ask."

"Where are Redman and his men now?" Godfrey asked, drawing the man's eyes.

The pirate bared his teeth in a fierce smile. "They are everywhere. You cannot avoid them. There is only death for you in this place."

"Tell me where they are quartered, where we are most likely to encounter them."

"I will not." The man faced Landry again. "I understand Templars well enough, Christian. Being in a crew is not so different." To Godfrey he said, "Kill me if you wish. Sever my fingers one by one. I will tell you nothing more."

"I would like to test that," Brice said, flexing his bruised hand.

"One of these corridors ends at an iron gate," Landry said. "How far is that from the main gate of this compound?"

When the man didn't respond, Landry took the sword from Godfrey. "Tie a cloth in his mouth."

"Landry—"

"Do it. I don't want his screams to bring others."

The other Templars watched Godfrey. After a pause that stretched uncomfortably, the commander nodded. Nathaniel tore two strips of cloth from the dead pirate's shirt. One he stuffed in the man's mouth; the other he tied around his head, securing the first cloth and rendering the pirate all but mute.

Redman's man remained still through this, but sweat beaded on his brow and ran down the sides of his face.

"Put out his hand," Landry said. "Hold it steady."

Nathaniel tried to comply, but the pirate fought him. Brice helped him, as did Tancrede. The three knights finally managed to hold the man motionless. He tried to shout through his muzzle. His eyes were wide and wild, like those of a horse caught in a storm.

"Shall I start with your thumb, pirate, or work my way to it?"

The bald man shook his head.

"No? You prefer to lose an eye?" Landry shifted the sword so that it hovered like a bee before the man's face.

He shook his head again, with even more vehemence. The knights continued to restrain him.

"Perhaps, then, you're ready to speak?"

The pirate faltered, glaring at him.

296

"Fine, then. The thumb it is."

He gave a muffled scream. Tears welled in his eyes. Landry grinned. "Remove the gag," he said.

Godfrey untied the strip of cloth, and pulled out the wadded piece.

"Tell me now: where is that gate in relation to the compound's entrance?"

The pirate wouldn't look at him. "It lets out near the center of the fort. You will have to circle this building and follow the path that carried you here. There is no other way out."

"Why should we believe you?" Brice asked.

The pirate glowered at him. "You should not, Templar. You should go the opposite way and die."

"Maybe we should take him with us," Gawain said. "Tie his fate to ours. We'll follow his instructions, and if we die, he dies. If we get away, he gets away."

"No!" the pirate said. "I—I won't go with you."

"If you won't come with us," Landry said, "we'll have no choice but to kill you. It would be too dangerous to leave you behind."

"But Redman—"

"Redman will kill you in the most painful manner possible if he believes, for even a moment, that you intended to help us. Isn't that right?"

The pirate gaped at him, which was all the confirmation Landry needed.

"I thought so. Which means you have all the motive you need to help us."

"We should bind his hands," Nathaniel said.

"No. If we do, we make it clear that we've coerced him. Leave his hands unbound, and Redman might believe we converted him to our cause. As I say, I want to give him every reason to help us escape, even if it means taking him with us off this island."

"Well, if he's coming with us," Godfrey said, "we should leave here now. It's only a matter of time before Redman comes back."

They left the cells and made their way through the shadowed corridor, first to the chamber in which they had been tortured. There, they reclaimed their armor and clothing, taking turns to dress as two Templars kept careful watch on the pirate.

Donning his mail, mantle, and tabard again, Landry felt more himself. His wounds didn't hurt quite so much; the odds against them didn't seem quite so daunting. He saw his own improved spirits mirrored in the faces of his brothers.

He pulled a torch from one of the sconces. Tancrede, Gawain, and Draper took the other three.

"Now where?" Gawain asked.

"It seems to me, brother, that you would be happier with a sword in your hand and a knife on your belt. I know just the place to find such things."

Gawain smiled at this. "Lead on."

They started back along the passageway, turning at the corridor Landry had trod earlier that night. They followed it past the two spurs he had discovered, to its end in the dark chamber that held the piles of old armor and weapons.

He thought once more of the men who had died to leave them this grim bounty. He said nothing about it. He didn't have to.

"All this must have belonged to Redman's victims," Gawain said, scanning the chamber. "Men less fortunate than we've been."

"You'll meet their fate before long," the pirate said, sullen and grim.

Brice gave him a hard shake. "Keep quiet!"

Godfrey surveyed the space as Gawain had done. "You're probably right, brother. The rightful owners of these things likely died in this dungeon. So, we'll take only those weapons and pieces of armor we need. And we'll honor their sacrifice and redeem them by striking back at the Monk and his cutthroats. Agreed?"

"Agreed," the others echoed.

Working by the light of their torches they made a quick search of the mounds. Before long, all of them were armed with blades both short and long. Landry would have preferred his own sword – he was sure his brothers felt the same – but he didn't know where Redman had hidden them, and they hadn't time to search.

"Swords are fine," Tancrede said to Landry and Godfrey, keeping his voice low as they buckled on their weapons. "But we'll need bows before long. If we try to fight through two hundred men in close combat, we'll be dead in no time."

"He has a point," Godfrey said. "I don't suppose you found any in your wanderings?"

"No."

"Well," the commander went on, "we can't delay. If we find bows and quivers we'll take them. If not, so be it. What's our next destination?"

"Kad and his men." He pointed down the corridor. "Back that way and to the left."

They marched out of the chamber, their path lit by their torches, their newly acquired weapons jangling on their belts. For the first time since their ship had been taken, Landry felt like a warrior again. Yet, buoyed though he was to be armed and armored, he was conscious as well of the limp that slowed his progress. Nearly all of them walked with some hitch in their gait. His sword hand remained swollen, forcing him to grip his newly acquired weapon in his off hand. Most of the others had no choice but to do the same. The Templars were known throughout the world for their prowess in battle. Even a wounded knight could overcome most foes. But Landry and the others were grievously hurt, and surely Redman's men knew how to fight as well.

The Templars bypassed the first corridor and took the second, some forty-five paces farther. After walking a short distance down this newest passage, Landry halted, indicating to his fellow knights that they should do the same.

"We should leave the torches here," he said. "Redman put guards outside our cells. I would wager he did the same in the chamber where Kad and his men are held. We need to surprise them."

They set down the torches, leaning them against the stone walls, before forging on in the gathering darkness. They walked without speaking, their footsteps and the ring of their armor and weapons sounding as loud as the clash of armies in the narrow space. After some time, Landry spotted light ahead.

"Watch your step, brothers," he whispered. "The dirt here gives way to stone. I fell my first time through."

They came to the start of the stone a few paces on. None of them tripped, but they slowed here, walking as quietly as possible.

Soon, Landry could make out two figures standing in the chamber. Guards, as he had anticipated. He wasn't the only one who had spotted them.

"Call for Redman!" the captive shouted. "Call for—"

A blow, a grunt, the sound of a body falling to the stone floor. Landry looked back. Godfrey stood over the man, rage contorting his face.

Landry faced forward again. The two guards ran toward them, weapons drawn, torches in hand. They had heard the pirate's cry, but hadn't understood, or hadn't trusted the command.

Landry charged them, Tancrede and Draper a pace behind him.

Seeing the knights, the pirates halted. One of them turned back. The other hesitated, appearing unsure of what he should do.

Landry didn't slow. Reaching the man, he parried a blow, and swung his own blade, hacking into the man's side. Blood poured from the wound and spurted from the guard's mouth. Landry pulled his blade free and the man dropped.

"Down, Landry!"

Landry ducked just as Tancrede's sword flew past, spinning end over end with the whistle of steel cutting through stale air. The sword struck the pirate hilt-first between the shoulder blades. The man lost his balance and pitched forward onto the stone, his own blade clattering ahead of him and Tancrede's weapon falling behind. He scrambled to his feet and tried to reach his lost weapon. Before he could, Draper was on him. The Turcopole struck him across the back of his head with the hilt of his sword. The pirate folded to the ground and moved no more.

Landry and Tancrede caught up with Draper seconds later. Tancrede recovered his weapon; Landry claimed that of the pirate and took from him a second key, which he hoped would work on Kad's cell.

"Is he dead?" Tancrede asked.

"No."

"Shouldn't we kill him?" Nathaniel asked, as he and the others reached them. Godfrey had taken the dead pirate's weapons.

Godfrey shook his head. "We don't kill defenseless men, no matter what they've done. We'll bind and gag him and do whatever we must to keep him from giving away our whereabouts. But we won't kill him."

"What about this one?" Brice asked. He gripped the collar of the pirate they had taken from their chamber. He bore a bloody gash on his face from Godfrey's blow. "He about got us killed."

"He did," Godfrey agreed. "But he's defenseless as well. We'll leave him with this other one, unless Landry still wants him with us."

Landry considered the pirate. "I don't know yet. Let's see how much Kad and his men know about the compound."

With Godfrey's approval, they walked on toward the cells that held Kad and his followers. Brice steered the pirate they'd captured back in their chamber. Tancrede and Landry dragged the unconscious man along the corridor.

Kad and his men stood at their doors, staring out toward the mouth of the passageway.

Seeing Landry and the others emerge from the darkness, Kad muttered, "Who'd have thought it possible?"

"You didn't expect to see me again," Landry said, a statement.

"Not really, no. Especially not after what Henry did."

Only one prisoner stood at the window of the young man's cell. "Where is Henry?"

"Dead, I suspect. Redman came for him a short time ago. Accused him of lying, of making him out to be a fool."

Landry and Gawain shared a look.

"I'm sorry for that. We had to convince him that there was no truth to what Henry said. It was the only way—"

Kad waved off the rest of his apology. "Henry had it coming. He tried to get you killed, and would have doomed us in the process. He got what he deserved." He nodded toward the pirates – the one who was unconscious and the one held by Brice. "What about these two?"

"Their fate is up to you."

"To me?"

"Will you join us? You know the risks, but you also know what you can expect if you remain here."

"If you can open these doors, we'll come with you."

Landry produced the key he had taken from the unconscious pirate. He unlocked Kad's cell first. "Do you know your way around this compound? If we can get out of these tunnels, can you lead us out of the fortress?"

"I can do better than that," Kad said, stepping out of the cell and drawing himself up to his full height. He was taller and broader than he had appeared through the door. He stood half a head taller than Landry. "I can lead you to Redman's ships and pilot you off this rock."

"The rest of your men are with us as well?"

"They are. Better to die free men than be sold as chattel."

Landry proffered a hand, which the other man gripped. Landry then opened the rest of the cells, freeing Kad's men. They numbered fourteen, every one of them unarmed but in better shape than the knights.

Kad's men tore strips of material from the clothes of the unconscious pirate and used them to gag and bind both of Redman's men. They tied their hands as well as their ankles. One of Kad's sailors knocked out the man they had taken from the other chamber, and they laid both pirates in one of the cells. They locked that door, and as an afterthought locked the rest of the doors as well, thinking that perhaps it would slow down Redman's men just a little.

Kad's men took the torches from the sconces outside their cells. Landry and the Templars then led them back to the chamber that held weapons and armor, reclaiming the torches they had left along the way. The sailors picked through the various piles in haste and armed themselves as best they could.

From there, they retraced their steps along the corridor. At the first passageway – eighty-eight – they paused.

"This corridor leads to the gate I mentioned to you before. It was locked earlier, but unguarded. I don't know if it will be now."

"Because of Henry, you mean."

Landry nodded.

"To be honest," Kad said, "a few guards at this gate are about to be the least of our concerns. Redman's men are everywhere. We need a distraction."

"What kind of distraction?"

Kad tipped the torch he held and raised an eyebrow in speculation.

"Will a fire not alert the pirates to our escape?" Draper asked.

"They'll know soon enough anyway," Kad said. "Before long, Redman will decide to torture the last of your knights, or punish more of my men for what he believes Henry did, or simply switch out one set of guards for another. This is not a secret that will keep."

"What would we burn?" Landry asked.

Godfrey smiled. "I know just the thing."

He led them back through the tunnels, past the passages Landry had found, coming at last to the torture chamber. Kad and his men slowed as they entered the space, their cheeks draining of color.

"They brought you here?" Kad asked. He didn't wait for an answer. "Lord have mercy."

Godfrey turned a slow circle in the middle of the room. "By God's grace, we survived. And now, again by His grace, we have the opportunity to ensure that no others will suffer as we did."

He took a torch from one of Kad's men and set it in the gears of the table to which each of them had been bound. Its flame licked at the ancient oak. The knights and sailors placed torches against a wooden pillory, and a second table similar to the first. Within moments, the old wood began to crackle and smoke. They kept the rest of their torches to light their way, and ran from the room as fast as the knights' injuries would allow.

They made their way with stealth to the intersection at stride eighty-eight. There they turned. The sailors and knights followed the corridor as it twisted and climbed, the air warming. Eventually, Landry slowed and signaled for the others to do the same.

"How much—"

Landry raised a hand, silencing Kad. "Quietly," he breathed.

"How much farther?" the man asked in a whisper.

"Not much." Landry gestured for the others to huddle close to him. "The gate is just ahead," he said, keeping his voice low. "Once we're through it, we'll be free of these tunnels. It might be guarded, in which case we will have to approach with stealth."

"If it is guarded," Tancrede asked, "how do we defeat guards on the far side?"

"A fine question, brother. I'm not certain. We'll address that matter when we know if the gate is watched, and by how many. For now, we should leave our torches here and continue in darkness. I want to surprise them."

Once more they placed the torches against the wall before creeping forward. They set their feet with care, and made every effort to keep silent.

Rounding that final curve in the corridor, Landry halted. The gate and the open space beyond glowed with torchlight. Landry counted four guards on the far side of the iron bars, all of them armed with swords and bows.

CHAPTER 18

Landry peered over his shoulder at his companions. Tancrede, Godfrey, and the other knights appeared to share his alarm. He gestured for them to retreat around the corner, and followed when they did.

"Any suggestions?" Godfrey asked when they had gathered in a tight cluster.

"My men are good with knives," Kad said, lank, dark hair framing his face. "Fighting and throwing."

"Through bars?"

"If need be."

"One missed throw," Gawain said, "one blade that bounces off a bar, and we're done. That's a great risk to take."

"What else do we have, Templar?" Kad asked.

The smell of burning wood tinged the air. Landry found Godfrey with his gaze.

"We haven't much time," the commander said.

"The knives, then," Kad said. "At least let us try."

All of them looked to Godfrey.

"Very well. How many knives do we have?"

Four of the knights and seven of the sailors produced blades.

Kad dipped his chin. "That should be enough."

"Wait." Landry slipped the knife from the bracer on his forearm and handed it to the sailor. "An even dozen."

Kad grinned.

"We'll get as close as we can," Godfrey said. "And if we must, we'll shield you from arrows."

"With what?"

"With ourselves, of course."

The sailor blinked. "You're either mad, or the bravest men I've ever known."

"We can't throw," Godfrey said, holding up his mangled sword hand. "The least we can do is protect you while you make the attempt."

"I can throw," Nathaniel said. "I'm pretty good, actually."

Kad handed the young knight the knife Landry had just given him. "Then have at it." He made certain that his men had blades as well. "We'll need to do this quickly, but don't all throw at once," he said. "Two or three at a time until all four men are down."

When all the sailors were armed, Landry and Godfrey led them back toward the gate. As soon as they could see the torch-fire again, they set their backs to the side walls and inched on. Light from outside spilled into the corridor, but only a few yards. The rest of the passage remained in shadow, and with Redman's men in the torch glow Landry thought it possible that they would be unable to discern much beyond the reach of the light.

The pirates lingered in front of the gate, speaking

among themselves. Two of them laughed at something.

Landry and the other prisoners closed the distance between themselves and the cutthroats.

"Do you smell something?" one of Redman's men asked the rest.

"Smell what?"

"I don't know. Smoke?"

"There have been fires burning all night, in every corner of this place." The man who said this laughed, as did the other two.

The first pirate stepped closer to the bars, sniffed, and pointed. "This is coming from in there."

"Now," Kad murmured.

In one fluid motion, Kad stepped away from the wall, cocked his arm, and threw his knife.

A rustle of air, a dull thud, and the first pirate toppled back, Kad's knife buried to the hilt in his chest.

For an instant, the other three pirates stood stock still, mouths agape, wide eyes fixed on their dying comrade.

Three more knives flew. One clanged against a bar. One cleared the gate but hit no one. The third took a second pirate in the neck.

The two survivors unslung their bows, nocked arrows to string, and fired. Kad's sailors ducked. As the pirates reached for their quivers again, three more men threw their knives. One of the pirates spun and fell, a blade in his shoulder. He cried out in pain.

The last man standing loosed another arrow. It soared past, clattering against the curved wall behind the knights and sailors.

Two more of Kad's men threw their knives. One glanced off a bar and missed the pirate. The other embedded itself in the man's thigh. He dropped to one knee, but launched another arrow.

A scream from Brice reverberated off the tunnel walls. The knight fell, clutching his leg.

The last two men – Nathaniel and a sailor – hurled their weapons. Both struck true and the pirate fell onto his side, knives jutting from his chest.

The wounded pirate continued to cry for help.

"Get that gate open!" Godfrey said.

Landry raced to the bars, flung himself to his knees, and reached through the bars for the lock. He dug out the key he had used to free Kad and the sailors. It didn't fit in the keyhole.

"Damn!"

He remembered the second key, the one that had opened his own cell and those of the other Templars. This one didn't fit either. Shouts echoed from elsewhere in the compound; he couldn't tell from which direction they came, but he had no doubt that the pirate's screams would draw men from everywhere.

"Draper! The sliver of iron I gave you! Tell me you still have it!"

Draper hobbled to him and pulled the sliver from within the gathering of his hair, which, as always, he wore tied back.

Landry took it from him with a huffed laugh. "Serves me right for not wearing my hair longer."

He worked the spike into the keyhole, and twisted it much as he had when trying to free himself from the cell. Holding the lock in his hand, being able to see what he was doing, made this a far simpler task. In seconds he defeated the mechanism, unlatched the shackle, and pushed open the door.

Tancrede strode through the door and to the pirate,

who shied away from him. Tancrede set his blade to the base of the man's neck. The pirate ceased his screams. Draper joined Tancrede, and the two of them hoisted the man to his feet and pulled him back inside. In short order, they bound and gagged him.

"Take him deeper into the tunnel," Godfrey said. "Bring back our torches; leave him there. Alive."

"Awake?" Tancrede asked.

Godfrey eyed the man, shrugged. "I'll leave that to you."

Tancrede and Draper started away with the man.

"We haven't much time," Godfrey called after them. To Kad, he said, "Which way?"

"Left out the gate, then left again toward the main entrance to the fortress. As far as I know, that's the only way out."

"That would also be where we're likely to encounter the bulk of Redman's crew."

Kad's expression darkened. "Yes."

Tancrede and Draper returned, bearing the torches. "The tunnel is filling with smoke. We have to go now."

"There has to be another way out of here," Godfrey said, taking a torch from Draper. "No fortress has only one egress; that would be folly."

• Kad took a torch as well. "We don't have time to find another."

"Don't we?" Godfrey asked. "If it's hidden – a sally port of some kind – Redman will assume we can't find it. He'll mass his men at the one gate we've seen, thinking that's our only choice. All we need to do is find the other way out, and we can avoid his army."

"And if they hunt us down first?"

"We fight, as we've planned all along. But do you

honestly believe twenty-one of us can battle our way through two hundred?"

Kad's silence was answer enough.

"Think, brothers," Godfrey said, "where would we find a second gate?"

"Not so close to the main gate that soldiers can be seen leaving," Gawain said. "But not so far that they can't make a quick sortie against those laying siege."

"East or west?"

Landry lifted a shoulder. "Who's to say there couldn't be both? One for use when the sun is low in the east, the other for use at dusk."

"All of this is beyond me," Kad said.

Godfrey started toward the gate, motioning for the others to follow him. "Just as talk of ships and sails is beyond me," he said over his shoulder. "Stay close. Make as little noise as possible. We turn right out of the gate, and make our way to the fortress wall. Friend, will you lead the way?"

"Of course." Kad took his place at the fore and led them out into the night.

The sailors and knights didn't worry about stealth as much as they had done in the tunnels. They made their way toward the fortress wall. If not for the Templars' wounds, Kad and his men would have run. As it was, they walked at a brisk pace. Landry gripped his sword, gaze flicking from building to building, shadow to shadow. His swollen hand itched to grasp a weapon, but he didn't think it strong enough to endure the force of blade-to-blade combat. Glancing behind them, he saw smoke rising from the barred windows of the dungeon building. He also saw men pursuing them.

"Godfrey!"

The others whirled.

At least twenty pirates advanced on them.

"They're here!" one of them shouted.

Kad muttered a curse.

"Let us take the center," Godfrey said, already positioning himself to do just that.

Kad matched him stride for stride. "You're hurt."

"We're knights," the commander said in a tone that put an end to their discussion.

Landry, Tancrede, and the other knights gathered with the commander, the sailors at their backs. Redman's pirates reached them seconds later, with cries of battle and the clangor of steel on steel.

Landry found himself facing a brawny man, bald, about his height, with dark eyes and a sword stroke as heavy as a smith's sledge. The man's first blow nearly ripped the sword out of his hand. The second sent rays of pain through his arm and into his shoulder.

The third told Landry all he needed to know about the man's tendencies. He tipped his head each time he drew back his blade, and though his attacks were powerful, they were slow.

Landry parried this latest stroke, and flicked out his blade, slicing the man's forearm. The pirate hissed a curse. He raised his arm to hammer at Landry again. Landry stepped to the side, pivoted, drove his blade into the man's gut. He pulled his sword free, and spun away, not bothering to watch the man fall.

He struck out at the next pirate. This one was leaner, quicker, with a longer reach. He lacked the first man's strength, however. Landry parried and shifted, drawing on his own quickness. With his sword hand he might have battered the man into submission, but he didn't have that luxury. They traded strikes, swords sparking in the darkness. Landry swung his torch at the man, forcing him to duck and then parry a sword strike. But for every attack Landry launched, the man countered with one of his own. Landry's muscles, still sore from the torment Redman had inflicted on him, weakened by days of inaction and deprivation, soon tired. His reactions slowed.

This man should have been no match for him. He saw openings, opportunities for a swift and decisive victory. By the time he struck, though, the pirate had recovered enough to defend himself. Sweat dripped into his eyes. He brushed his brow with a swipe of his wounded hand.

The pirate attacked again, driving Landry back a step. This was intolerable. He bellowed his frustration and leapt at the man, sword descending, torch sweeping within inches of the man's face. The pirate blocked the sword blow, but fell back in turn. Landry hacked at him again, and a third time. The pirate went down on one knee. Landry feinted another chopping attack. When the pirate raised his sword again, Landry altered his strike, sweeping his blade at the man from the side. The sword bit into the pirate's shoulder. He cried out, his arm dropping. Landry finished him with a second sweep across his neck.

He turned again, expecting another assault. None came. Pirates lay dead at their feet. Godfrey's chest heaved with each breath, and he bled from a cut on his brow. Tancrede dispatched a pirate with a thrust to the heart. Gawain struggled with a man as broad in the chest and shoulders as Landry's first foe.

Landry and Tancrede rushed to his aid at the same time. The pirate backed away, regarding them both with panic in his eyes. He didn't see Gawain hew at his neck until it was too late.

"Thank you, brothers," Gawain said.

They paused to survey the carnage. All the pirates were dead. One of Kad's men had been killed as well, and another had sustained a vicious wound to his arm. Draper attended to the man, but when Landry caught his eye, the Turcopole gave a subtle shake of his head. Landry didn't know if his friend thought the sailor would lose his arm or his life. Either way, they had no time to do more for the man here.

"Come on," Kad said, taking the lead once more. "There'll be more of them before long."

They ran on, bloodied swords held ready.

Tancrede fell in beside Landry. "You're hurt."

"I am?"

The lean knight actually laughed. "Your cheek and your shoulder."

Landry glanced at his shoulder. It bled from a wound he hadn't felt. He touched his cheek; his fingers came away bloody.

"They're nothing." Landry looked Tancrede over. "You're all right?"

"For now. I'm weary already, and I shouldn't be."

"Yes," Landry said, biting off the word. "So am I."

They snuck around the back of a large stone building. As they cleared the far corner, another band of pirates set upon them: ten, this time. Too small a force to do much damage, but they caught the sailors and knights off guard. Kad ducked under a sword stroke that would have severed his head. He stumbled, and the pirate pounced.

The sailor parried desperately. Redman's man gave him no chance to rest. He lashed at Kad again. His blade glanced off the sailor's sword and sliced into Kad's forearm.

Godfrey and Gawain stepped in front of the sailor to take up his fight. The pirate retreated, but Godfrey kept after him.

The other Templars and sailors engaged the remaining pirates. They had the advantage of numbers, though one of them had fallen and another was too weakened to fight. Landry battled a man on his own, hacking at him with his blade. First high, then low, then high again. The man blocked each strike, but he struggled with the third. Landry brought his sword down as if to strike low a second time. When the man lowered his guard, he spun toward the man's off hand and aimed his attack high, at the pirate's head. The pirate wrenched himself to the side, trying to parry. He wasn't quick enough.

Landry tugged his blade out of the man's skull and let him fall.

Gawain and Godfrey had killed Kad's attacker. Gawain tied a strip of cloth around the sailor's wounded arm.

Seven of the remaining pirates were dead or wounded. The last one fled. Two of Kad's men threw knives at the retreating figure. One embedded itself in the man's back just below his shoulder. He staggered, grabbed at the knife but couldn't reach it. Still he stumbled on.

"Can you keep going?" Godfrey asked Kad.

"Do I have a choice?"

"Not really, no."

They ran on. After only a few steps, however, Draper slowed and stopped.

"Do you smell that?" he asked.

Landry smelled nothing, and said so.

Godfrey returned to where the Turcopole stood. "What is it, Draper?"

"Oil. I smell lamp oil."

As soon as he said this, Landry smelled it too. It was strong enough that he didn't know how he could have missed it.

Draper turned slowly in place, stopping at last and pointing at a small wooden building a few yards away.

"In there."

They approached the structure, which had no windows and a single wooden door.

It was secured, but Landry defeated the lock in no time. Opening the door, they gazed inside. One of the sailors thrust his torch into the space, no doubt to see better. Draper pushed his arm back.

While the stink of lamp oil was enough to make Landry's eyes water, the vats of oil were not what drew his gaze. Rather, his eyes alighted on a haphazard pile of weapons and shields. Their weapons, their shields. He took a tentative step forward, picked up his sword, and sliced the heavy air with a satisfying *whoosh*.

"Yours?" Kad asked.

"Yes."

"Take them," Godfrey said. "And whatever else you think we might need. Then we burn this place to the ground."

The Templars reclaimed their swords and shields. Landry hooked the rusted blade he had been using in his belt, glad to have his own weapon once more.

The knights left the building, except for Draper, who remained behind, his sword sheathed, a torch in his hand. He appeared nervous.

Seconds later, he emerged from the building limping at speed, a container of oil cradled in each arm.

"Move!" he said.

Landry and the others rushed to keep up with him. They hadn't taken ten steps when the building exploded with a great ball of yellow fire. Flaming fragments of wood flew in every direction, and a cloud of black smoke rose into the night sky. Pieces of the structure rained down on adjacent buildings, setting at least one of them ablaze.

The knights and sailors stared for a moment.

"Well, now they all know where we are," Kad said.

They broke into a run again. Voices echoed through the compound from every direction – Redman's men, converging on the fires and on them.

"You have something in mind for those?" Landry asked Draper as they fled.

"I thought it unwise to use all the oil on a single building. I could not abide the waste."

Landry smiled, as did Draper.

They came to another building, similar to the one they had destroyed: wooden, windowless.

"Open this one," Draper said.

Landry mastered the lock and pulled the door open. There was no oil in this structure, but there was grain, rounds of cheese, and what appeared to be half a dozen barrels of rum. Draper set one of the vats of oil aside. He pulled the stopper from the other and tore cloth from his own shirt.

This he wadded down into the neck of the container,

leaving a short tail of cloth hanging out. He set the vat in the middle of the building and lit the cloth with his torch. Then he reclaimed the other container of oil and hurried from the building, pulling the door shut behind him.

"I suggest we move along," he said.

Kad led them around the back of a larger stone building, still angling them toward the outer wall. They managed to cover a short distance without being discovered, but as they emerged from a narrow passage between two buildings, they encountered a large contingent of pirates. Two dozen, perhaps more. Landry considered a tactical retreat, but already Redman's men had blocked off the entrance to the byway they had followed. They would have to fight their way through.

"Keep close to each other," Godfrey said, speaking to Kad and his men. "Again, we'll take the center."

Kad cast a quick look at the men blocking their escape, who had begun to advance through the passage. "What about those behind us?"

"Draper?" the commander said.

"Of course."

The Turcopole pulled the stopper from the second vat of oil. He heaved it back between the two buildings. It struck one of the stone walls and shattered, dousing the passage with oil. Draper took Landry's torch and threw it into the byway as well. Flames erupted, climbing the soaked stone wall and creating an impassible barrier. It would burn out eventually, but for the time being the pirates behind them could not join the fight.

Those in front of them presented enough challenges. They charged, with a battle cry that resounded off the surrounding buildings. Landry slung his shield over his shoulder and drew his second sword, gripping it as well as he could with the swollen, pained fingers of his right hand. The other Templars fought with both their weapons as well. Godfrey whipped his blades around him with controlled fury, his wheaten hair and the silver of his weapons blurring amid the torch-fire.

Two men bore down on Landry. He had time to register their size – both were tall and muscular. Both favored their right hands. Then they were on him. He met their initial assaults with his swords raised. The blows shocked both arms, sent tremors through his chest, tore a grunt from his throat. He held on to both weapons, though. A small victory.

A cry from behind him distracted him for an instant. The two pirates attacked again, pounding at him in unison. He barely parried one blow with his own sword. He took the second poorly with the rusted weapon in his wounded hand. The pirate's blade careened along the length of his own, and skipped over the hand guard and across his wrist. The bracer he wore offered some protection, but he hissed a breath at the pain. A wash of blood warmed his hand and dripped to the ground.

The pirates pressed their advantage, slashing at him again.

Landry parried a third time, with more success. But he couldn't keep this up indefinitely. Standing in tight formation with the other Templars had seemed a good idea at the start. Now, though, he needed room to move. As the pirates readied their next assault, Landry struck at them, swiping at each with his blades. They had to defend themselves. As they did, he slipped between them, spun, and attacked again, whipping both swords at only one of them. He raised the rusted blade, leveling a blow at the man's head. A blow he knew the pirate would attempt to block.

By the time the man realized his mistake, Landry had used his off hand to slice the man open from armpit to navel. The pirate went down, blood gurgling in his throat.

Landry whirled again to meet the other pirate's attack. It didn't come immediately. Wary now, the pirate circled, looking for an opening. Landry gave him none. He bounded at the man, lashing with both weapons, high on the left, low on the right. The pirate evaded the blows, but tripped, fell onto his back. Landry swooped over him and delivered a killing blow to his chest.

He yanked the weapon free, turned, and ran to Gawain's aid. Three pirates had him trapped against the nearest building. He bled from wounds to his arm, shoulder, and brow.

Landry plunged his blade between the shoulder blades of the middle pirate. The man's back arched and he dropped his weapon. Landry shoved the man's body off his sword and rounded on a second man. This cutthroat backed away. Landry advanced on him, feinted with one sword, and stabbed him through the throat with the other.

By the time he spun again, Gawain had killed his remaining foe. The Templar nodded to him, grim and breathless. They took in the destruction around them, both searching for their next opponents.

Several of Kad's men had been killed. Landry had no time to make a careful count. The lead sailor himself fended off two attackers and looked to be overmatched. Blood soaked his shirt and covered one side of his face.

As he parried a blow from one man, the other appeared poised to deliver a killing strike to his back. Landry shouted at warning and sprinted to Kad's aid. He knew, though, that he wouldn't reach the sailor in time. Still running, he heaved his rusted sword at the second pirate. The flat of the blade struck the man in the face, knocking him off balance. Landry collided with the pirate a heartbeat later. Both sprawled to the ground. The pirate's sword flew from his hand; Landry held on to his. He pounded the hilt into the man's face, then drew back and pierced his heart.

Kad still fought the remaining pirate. He held his off arm tucked to his side, and grimaced with every parry.

Landry scrabbled to his feet, and jumped to the sailor's side, taking the next strike on his sword. The pirate lashed at him, then spun – a move Landry had used countless times before. He countered with a pivot of his own. When the pirate completed his turn, his sword poised to strike, Landry was ready. He hacked at the man's sword arm, nearly severing it just below the elbow. The pirate screamed. Landry finished him with another thrust to the heart.

As the pirate fell, Landry searched for another opponent. Seeing none left alive, he straightened, let his sword hand fall to his side.

"I believe this is yours." Kad handed him the rusted sword he had thrown.

"My thanks." Landry lifted his chin in the direction of the sailor's injured arm. "How bad is it?"

"I'm all right. Let's just get to the wall and find that sally port." He paused to survey the scene, his gaze lingering on the men he had lost.

Landry counted four dead. All the Templars lived still, though every one of them had sustained fresh wounds. Godfrey and Tancrede leaned on their swords. Gawain clutched at the leg he wounded in Acre.

Landry didn't know how many more encounters of this sort they could endure.

"This way," Godfrey said, motioning toward the fortress wall.

"Godfrey."

All of them turned at the sound of Draper's voice. Another band of pirates, at least thirty strong, drew near. They were armed with swords and cudgels. At the fore walked a man in chain mail and a tattered, stained tabard bearing a Templar cross.

Redman.

CHAPTER 19

"I put this on just for you, Templars." The Monk gestured at the tabard, a smug grin on his angular face. "I'd wondered if I would have occasion to wear it again."

Gaspar stood a pace behind him. He appeared to be enjoying himself as well.

"Surrender," Redman said, mirth fading.

"So you can execute us?" Godfrey answered. "I think not."

"I've an idea," Landry said softly. "But we need to retreat."

"Funny," Tancrede said. "Retreat was my idea, too."

"You will die no matter the choice you make, Templar," Redman said, still addressing Godfrey. "But think of the sailors fighting with you. They need not perish as well."

"We've been through this before," Landry said, remembering the men lost aboard the *Melitta*. "We need to go back, now."

Godfrey took a moment to consider the force arrayed before them. "Yes, all right. Lead the way."

Landry turned and ran, waving the others after him. "Follow me, brothers!"

The Templars and Kad's remaining men ran with him. Landry explained what he had in mind as they ran. Redman and the other pirates pursued.

He couldn't lead them far. Hobbled as they were, the Templars were unable to remain ahead of their captors for long. Fortunately, for his plan to work, he didn't need to cover much distance. He just needed to do so in time.

The first pirates caught up with them as the Templars and sailors reached the building they had left burning. Much of it was engulfed in flame, but to Landry's relief it stood largely intact. He and the others backed away from the burning structure, keeping it in front of them.

The pirates stalked them, perhaps sensing that the prisoners could not survive many more battles. Redman and Gaspar trailed behind, appearing content to watch their men finish off Landry and his friends.

This fight began much as the last one had. Landry, Godfrey, Tancrede, and the rest of the Templars stood shoulder to shoulder, each wielding two blades. As the pirates descended on them, they spread, giving themselves room to maneuver. Kad and his men guarded their flanks.

Redman's men battered them with blow after blow. Landry faced three men this time. It was all he could do to parry their attacks and prevent any of them from getting behind him. His brothers struggled as he did. They were biding their time, waiting for what they knew would come, what *had* to come eventually.

Still, the punishment meted out by the pirates forced him to consider that he might have erred in leading them back this way. Another of Kad's sailors fell, a cry torn from his heart and then cut short.

"How long can this take?" Landry hollered.

The pirate directly in front of him frowned at his cry, no doubt wondering what he could possibly mean.

And in that moment, the first of the rum casks exploded, as the knights and sailors had known they would. The pirates, who had their backs to the building, flinched at the explosion, losing their balance and lowering their guards.

The Templars struck at them, cutting down several men before the pirates recovered enough to raise their blades again. The second and third casks erupted, blowing the roof off the building and driving several of the pirates to the ground. Burning planks of wood pelted down on the combatants. The Templars and Kad's sailors fought through the onslaught, like men caught in a flaming rainstorm.

Two more explosions made the ground tremble and scattered burning debris in every direction. In the confusion, Landry and his comrades managed to kill and wound nearly a score of pirates.

By now, though, the fire had destroyed the structure. There were no rum barrels left to explode.

At the first explosion, Redman and Gaspar had raced forward to help their men. They reached them now, and threw themselves into the battle. Landry tried to get to Gaspar, but a burly pirate stood in his way, wielding a cudgel that must have weighed two stone at least.

Tancrede engaged Gaspar. Brice pitted himself against Redman.

The pirate swung his hammer. Landry dodged rather than parried. Tancrede fell back under Gaspar's assault. Brice parried desperately.

The pirate swiped at Landry with the cudgel again. The iron head passed so close to Landry's face that he felt the rush of air, smelled the tang of metal. The swing left the pirate off balance. Landry hewed at him with both blades, carving open the man's back and shoulder. The pirate howled. Landry dropped the rusted blade and, gripping his sword with both hands, hacked off the man's head.

He spun.

In time to see Redman drive his blade into Brice's chest.

The young knight went rigid, mouth open. He dropped his sword, clawed at the blade of Redman's weapon. The Monk, eyes alight with reflected fire, twisted his sword and ripped it out of the lad. Brice fell.

Landry roared. He reclaimed his second sword and bounded toward the Monk.

"Good!" Redman shouted, seeing his charge, a fearsome smile distorting his features. "I hoped to kill you myself. You are the cause of all this." He waved his blade as he spoke, a shimmer of steel that encompassed all the damage the Templars and sailors had inflicted on his compound.

Landry said nothing. Reaching the man, he struck at the Monk with both blades. Redman parried one blow with his sword, the other with his shield, which also bore the red cross of the Temple.

He countered with a flick of his own sword. Landry swiped at the man's blade, but he was too late. He felt a stinging high on his cheek, a trickle of warmth running down into his beard.

"First blood is mine," Redman said. "I hope the rest of this won't be so easy as that. I expected more of you, Templar."

Even as he spoke, the tip of his sword whipped out again. It nicked Landry's neck, drawing more blood.

"He was a friend of yours, the boy I killed." He gestured with his shield toward Brice's body. "Ah, but of course. He was your brother. You are all 'brothers.'" He laughed.

Landry sprang at him, swords whirring. Redman parried one, twisted away from the other, and landed a blow of his own to Landry's side. The edge of Redman's blade didn't penetrate his mail, but it sent Landry tumbling and stole his breath.

He bounced to his feet again and circled the Monk, adjusting his grip on his swords. He had sparred with his fellow Templars in training. He knew what it was to fight men as skilled as he. But he was wounded, weary. Redman was neither.

Landry feigned an attack with his right hand, stepped closer to the Monk, pivoted and pounded at him with both swords. That, at least, was what he intended.

His weapons, though, carved through nothing but air. Redman stabbed at him from the side. This time, the point of his sword pierced Landry's armor, slicing into him just above his waist.

Landry gasped, flung himself down and away. The blade tore his flesh. Blood soaked his side. White-hot pain paralyzed him for the span of a heartbeat.

Redman prowled toward him, mockery gone, murder in his gaze.

Landry forced himself up, raised both swords.

After a moment's consideration, he tossed away the rusted blade and unslung his shield.

"A good choice, I think," Redman said. "Not that it will matter in the end."

Landry rushed him, shield raised, sword sweeping out toward Redman's neck. The pirate blocked the sword strike, and pounded the hilt of his sword into the side of Landry's head. Landry stumbled, fell again.

He dragged himself up, sucking at the air. The gash in his side screamed agony. Blood loss made his hand tremble. His legs were uncertain beneath him.

He stared at Redman, watching the pirate saunter toward him. The Monk made no attempt to shield himself. He didn't seem to think Landry was much of a threat.

In truth, he wasn't. Exhausted as he was, his weapon might as well have been forged of lead. He could stand, but he wasn't sure he could take another step, or even move his shield to counter a killing stroke.

He had come to believe that they would find their way out of this fortress, that they would cross the Mediterranean to France and, eventually, reach Paris. Yes, there had been a time when he doubted, but Godfrey had challenged his faith, and he had come to see in that challenge a chance to redeem himself before the Lord. If he believed, if he reclaimed his faith in God, God, in turn, would deliver him and his brothers. That was what he had told himself again and again in this last day.

Now, it seemed, he had been wrong. About so many things. They would not all be going home. Brice lay dead only a few feet from where he stood. The young knight would not see Paris again.

Neither would Landry. He would die on this cruel rock in the middle of the sea, his blood spilled by a fallen Templar.

Redman loomed before him, smiling again. His sword raised to deliver this final blow.

Do I deserve this fate, Lord? Landry wanted to ask.

But he didn't. He feared the answer. And as it happened, he didn't get the chance.

So many things he had gotten wrong.

Including, it seemed, the number of barrels of rum that had exploded.

One last explosion from the scorched building shook the ground. Landry, facing the fire, raised his injured hand to shield his face.

Redman had his back to the structure when the barrel exploded. He half turned to see what had happened, even as the force of the explosion staggered him, sent him reeling toward Landry.

Landry had some strength left after all. He stepped to the side, brought back his sword, and swung with all his might. Redman appeared to remember at the last moment where he was, what he was doing. His gaze snapped back to Landry. His eyes widened. He tried to flinch away, to raise his blade in defense.

He did manage to raise his off hand, as if warding a blow. Landry's sword sliced through the Monk's fingers and then cleaved his face in half. Redman swayed, Landry's sword holding him upright. A shower of blood stained the pirate's old tabard, the red Templar cross seeming to vanish as the cloth was soaked crimson.

Landry pulled the blade free, allowing Redman's body to sag to the ground.

He turned. Gaspar stood perhaps twenty paces away, staring at the Monk's bloody corpse. Four pirates stood with him. Not enough to fight the six surviving Templars and the eight men Kad had left. The pirates backed away. At last they wheeled and ran. Landry took two steps, intending to pursue them, but Godfrey called his name.

"They're going to find more men," the commander said. "We can't defeat them this way. This is our chance to get away."

Landry knew he was right. "What about Brice?"

"We have no choice but to leave him."

"Godfrey—"

The commander cut him off with a raised hand. "I know what you would say. We left dead men in Acre as well. Do you doubt that the Lord saw to the preservation of their souls? He will do the same for Brice. We will pray for him. But we must get away from here."

Landry eyed the lad's corpse, breathed a quick prayer, and crossed himself. His brothers did the same. Kad and his men waited in silence. When the Templars finished their devotions, all of them, knights and sailors, made their way at speed back toward the nearest expanse of wall.

Fires burned in several buildings, including the prison that had held them. A cloud of dark smoke hung over the fortress, its underside stained a shifting, baleful orange by the flames. Landry heard shouts from every direction, but Redman's pirates seemed to be in chaos. The knights and sailors encountered a few individuals along the way. Most fled when they saw the escapees. The few who dared try to stop them died in the attempt.

Upon reaching the stone wall, they turned and followed it in the direction of the main gate. Before long, they found what they had sought: an unadorned stone door, all but indiscernible along the façade of the defenses.

Kad pushed the door open and waved his men and the knights inside. A few still carried torches. Landry did not. He stepped through the doorway, into a narrow space that smelled of must. An iron gate bolted into the opposite wall guarded a second doorway. Landry mastered the lock, opened the gate, and pushed on the second door. It opened as easily as the first. Beyond it loomed the jungle through which they had been led so many days before.

They walked around the fortress, keeping close to the wall, shrouded in shadow, out of sight of the guards atop the ramparts. In little time, they came within sight of the main gate, and the road leading away from it. Redman's men stood watch there. The Templars and sailors halted, and after a bit of discussion, cut away from the wall and entered the tangle of trees and brush. They moved with stealth, even after they were hidden within the jungle.

Redman's men patrolled the stone road as well. Landry and the others crept through the shadows parallel to the thoroughfare, monitoring the guards, remaining out of sight. They knew that eventually they would reach the dirt path they had followed from the ship, on the day Redman and Gaspar brought them to this place.

When they did reach it, they veered onto the path and quickened their pace, no longer concerned with making noise. The journey back to the water proved longer than Landry recalled, but also easier. Rather than climbing, the path descended over much of the distance. He and the other Templars could not run, but they maintained a brisk gait, navigating the rough trail by the light of the moon.

The wound to Landry's side ached, and fresh blood still soaked his shirt and breeches. He was weakened, light-headed. Walking such a distance couldn't be good for him, but since the other choice was death, he swallowed his complaints.

Tancrede walked just ahead of him and glanced back his way at intervals, concern etched in his gaunt face. He said not a word, perhaps understanding that nothing he could say or do would help. They needed to leave the isle. Then, Draper could tend to Landry's injury.

Landry had no doubt that Gaspar pursued them. After watching his leader die, he would not simply allow the knights and sailors to escape. More, he had to know that they would head to the cove where the pirates' ships were anchored.

The others knew this as well. No one celebrated their liberation from the fortress. No one sheathed his weapon. A tense silence hung over them as they wound among the trees.

He heard the surf before he saw it. His heart lifted at the gentle brush of waves across the sand, at the scents of brine and fish and seaweed that seasoned the air. Minutes later, a last dip of the path deposited them onto the strand's moon-whitened sand.

Upon reaching the shore, Landry dropped to his knees, and took several long, deep breaths.

A shadow loomed before him. He looked up into Godfrey's lined face. The commander extended a hand, pulled him up, and led him across the expanse to one of the skiffs resting on the wet sand by the water.

Kad's men had already taken up the oars.

Godfrey and Tancrede helped Landry into one of the vessels and shoved it into the water. They then hopped into a second skiff that already bobbed in the shallows. A third skiff they lit on fire. The sailors began to row them away from shore, to one of the large ships anchored some distance out on the water.

"Our ship was the *Petrel*," Kad said. "She was fast, and well-equipped to fight off most adversaries. I'd dearly love to have her back. But we've no choice but to take one of Redman's ships."

Landry noticed that they were headed to the smallest of the vessels.

"This one ahead looks to be the swiftest," Kad went on. "I hope I'm right."

"We'll defer to your judgment, Captain," Godfrey said.

Despite the darkness, Landry saw the man's face color. "I'm no captain."

"I believe you are. You'll have to be. Your men look to you for leadership. And none of us, not even Tancrede, knows as much about sea-craft as you do."

Kad bore many injuries. Blood darkened half his face and he held his wounded arm tucked to his side. But he pulled himself up to his full height, in that moment appearing every bit the captain he needed to be.

The sailors rowed them alongside the vessel, and tied the skiffs to the ship. One by one, they climbed the lines onto the deck. Landry barely made it up. He collapsed onto the wood as soon as he cleared the rails. Draper helped him up and out of the way to a corner near the stern.

Tancrede and Kad hoisted the ship's anchor. Two men climbed back down the lines bearing torches, cut the skiffs loose from the ship, and lit those on fire as well. When Gaspar and the pirates reached the shore to give chase, they would need to swim out to the remaining vessels.

"Shouldn't we burn those other ships as well?" Landry asked.

Kad turned. "I fear taking the time to do so. Better we should get away."

Kad's sailors rowed their vessel away from the strand toward the open sea. Tancrede, Nathaniel, and Godfrey prepared the sails so that they could be raised as soon as they were out of the cove.

Draper helped Landry strip off his tabard, mantle, and mail. The Turcopole sucked in his breath when he saw Landry's injury.

"This does not look good, my friend."

"Do what you can," Landry said. "I will not allow this wound to be the death of me. I won't let Redman win."

Draper grinned. "No, of course you will not. You are a stubborn man, Landry."

Noise and light from the strand drew their gazes.

Gaspar and his men streamed onto the sand. Several men carried bows. They ran to the water's edge and loosed their arrows. Already, though, Kad and the other sailors had oared them beyond the archers' reach.

Gaspar shouted orders to the pirates. Then all of them waded into the water and began swimming toward the two ships still anchored in the cove.

"We'll be able to put some distance between us and them," Kad called. "That's something at least."

Something, but perhaps not enough. If it came to a battle at sea, the sailors and Templars would be overmatched. Again.

The Templars' ship emerged from the cove a short time later. They had too few men to make much headway on sweeps, and even after they reached open water, the wind remained light. Tancrede and the others raised the sails while the sailors shipped the oars. Wind filled the cloth of the sails, all of which were marked with black crosses. Still, the ship's speed did not increase by much.

Landry continued to watch the pirates while Draper dressed his wound. Despite the loss of the skiffs, Gaspar and his men were soon aboard the two vessels. Due to their own progress beyond the cove, Landry lost sight of the pirates before they went to sweeps, but he had little doubt that they would give chase before long. Whatever advantage the knights and sailors had gained would not amount to much.

Kad piloted them eastward away from the cove – a decision that seemed to be based solely on the direction of the wind. He steered them parallel to the shoreline, keeping them close enough that if they had to flee to land, they could.

Landry stared back from the ship's stern, watching the mouth of the cove, waiting for the pursuing vessels to appear. As the minutes passed, and the distance between their ship and the cove increased, his hopes rose. Perhaps their lead on the pirates was greater than he had credited.

The pirate ships surged out of the cove moments later, still on sweeps. They turned to the east, and hugged the coastline as they carved through the water after the Templars' ship. At first, they appeared to be gaining, but this didn't last long. Maybe Gaspar's men were weary, or perhaps there were too few of them left alive to row the ships at the speed required to close the distance. Whatever the reason, they chased, but they did not draw nearer.

The sky ahead of them brightened with dawn's approach. Silver-gray at first, then tinged with gold as the sun neared the horizon.

Landry hoped that daylight might bring a stronger wind, but it didn't. He peered back again. In the light, the pirate ships appeared closer than they had at night, and the Templars' advantage far more tenuous.

"Damnit!"

Landry faced forward again to follow the line of Kad's gaze. His heart sank.

Another ship had appeared ahead of them, angling in from farther out to sea. It was also on sweeps, and it would cut them off before long. They were trapped between Gaspar's pirates and this newest threat.

CHAPTER 20

"Do we make for the shore?" Godfrey called from along the rails.

Kad shook his head and spat a curse. "We're too far, and the ships behind have gained too much on us. If we steer to the coast we'll lose the wind and have to tack in or go to sweeps. Either way, they'll be on us before we make land." He glanced Landry's way. "Perhaps you were right. Forgive me."

"Never mind that," Godfrey said. "What can we do?"

"I'd suggest you pray, Templar. Pray that ship is not filled with Redman's pirates."

The third vessel bristled with oars and moved at speed, cutting across the swells as if propelled by Poseidon himself. As far as Landry could tell, it was headed directly at their ship. It might have intended to ram them with its high, curving prow.

He looked back again. Gaspar's vessels remained close. The few men on the ships' decks had turned their gazes on this strange ship. Gaspar had a spyglass raised to his eye. Whoever was aboard the third vessel, they did not appear to be known to the pirates. Landry was heartened by this.

Still, the ship's pilot appeared to pay little heed to the pirate vessels. It adjusted its course repeatedly to bear down on the Templars' ship.

Landry gazed up at their sail again, at the black cross, which he recalled from the day Redman captured them. He turned and studied the furled sails of the pursuing vessels. He couldn't make out much, but they did appear to bear some sort of black marking as well. Crosses? Did those aboard this unknown vessel believe the Templars' ship and Gaspar's ships were together, rather than at odds?

If so, attacking the lead vessel made a great deal of sense, particularly if they believed they could incapacitate the ship before being engaged by the trailing vessels.

Landry had put his shirt back on when Draper finished bandaging him. But his mail, mantle, and tabard remained in a pile on the deck.

He strode to them now, grabbed his tabard, and crossed to the main mast.

"Landry," Tancrede called. "What are you doing?"

He and Kad intercepted Landry before he reached the mast.

"What if they think we're with Redman?" Landry said. "Or that Redman himself is aboard this ship? That may be why they seem intent on ramming us." He held up the tabard. "I want to fly this from the mast. Let them see that we're Templars."

Tancrede and Kad eyed the approaching vessel,

before peering up at the top of the mast.

"That's not a bad idea," the captain said.

"I know—"

"But you're in no condition to climb. Give it to me."

Landry recognized the wisdom in this. He handed the tabard to Kad, who gripped it between his teeth and began to climb.

Even wounded, the captain climbed like a desert cat and was soon at the top. There, he tied the tabard to the mast and allowed the wind to take it. It snapped in the breeze, the red cross clearly visible to any who might look for it.

But Landry wasn't convinced that those on the unknown ship would notice.

He marked the vessel's progress: every dip of every oar into the azure waters, its unwavering track toward the Templar vessel. Soon it would be too late. Even if someone aboard did notice the tabard, they might not be able to alter the course of such a grand vessel in time. And Gaspar's ships continued to hunt them. They had escaped the prison for nothing. He and his fellow knights were in much the same predicament they'd been in the day Redman took them prisoner.

"They're turning."

He fixed his attention on the unknown vessel once more. It took him a moment to see that Tancrede was right. The ship had changed its course. Not by much, but enough. Now, rather than being on course to collide with the Templars' ship, they would soon set themselves between the Templars and the pirate ships.

A form appeared on the deck of the new ship. Slight, dark-haired, a glass raised to eye level and trained on their ship. Landry raised a hand, as in greeting.

Could it be?

"We have bows, arrows as well!"

Nathaniel had emerged from the hold bearing at least a dozen bows and several quivers filled with arrows.

"Excellent," Godfrey said. "Every man who can should take up a bow."

"This newest ship may have turned, but we can't simply trust—"

"I think the ship is piloted by Melitta," Landry said, still watching the vessel.

"*What?*"

Seconds later both Godfrey and Tancrede were at his side.

"The one on the deck with the glass?" Godfrey asked.

"Yes."

"But how would she have gotten away? I thought Redman had killed the *Melitta*'s crew, or at the very least sold the survivors to slavers."

"That looks like a slaver's ship," Tancrede said. When Landry and Godfrey both stared at him, he added, "I'm just offering an observation."

As the large vessel drew nearer, a familiar voice – a woman's voice – shouted from its deck. "Ahoy, Templars! Glad to see you're alive!"

"And you!" Godfrey called in reply. "What would you have us do?"

"Come about. Help us fight off the trailing ships."

Before Godfrey could relay the instructions to Kad, the captain said, "I heard! Coming about!"

Kad and his men succeeded in turning the ship in a tight arc. Nathaniel distributed the bows and quivers. Landry had to refuse. With the wound dealt him by

Redman, he hadn't the strength to draw a bow.

Melitta's ship bore down on Gaspar's lead vessel. Too late, the pirate captain appeared to understand his peril. He tried to change direction, but that proved an error as well.

By this time, archers on both Gaspar's ship and Melitta's vessel had taken to the decks and were exchanging volleys of arrows. But as the pirate's vessel altered course, it exposed the side of its hull to Melitta's ship.

Melitta cried out to the oarsmen below deck. Landry couldn't make out what she said, but the effect of her words was unmistakable. Those in the hold quickened the rhythm of their strokes. The ship sped up, and crashed through the side of Gaspar's ship.

The rending of wood was like a thunderclap. Men screamed.

The oarsmen on Melitta's ship rowed on, so that their vessel drove itself through the pirate ship, splitting it in two. Dozens of men spilled into the sea, some flailing as they fell, others dropping like stones. The ruined halves of the pirate ship began to take on water and sink.

Kad tacked their ship in Melitta's wake, so that the two vessels closed in on the second pirate vessel.

This ship had commenced its turn at the same time as Gaspar's ship. When Melitta's vessel cleared the wreckage of the first ship, the second had already completed its turn. Whoever was captaining the vessel seemed unwilling to engage Melitta's ship and the Templars. They were content, it appeared, to flee and live another day.

Pirates swam in the waters around Melitta's ship and that of the Templars. Landry wanted to urge his fellow knights to use their arrows on the men, to exact some measure of revenge for their ordeal at the hands of these cutthroats. He knew, though, that there was little difference between killing a defenseless man with his sword, and slaughtering these men in the water.

"Should we rescue them?" Gawain asked, joining Landry and the others at the rails. "Do we let them drown, or be eaten by sharks?"

Tancrede stared down at the men. "They would have killed us had they caught the ship. I feel no need to save their lives." He faced Godfrey. "But if you order us to do so, I will, of course."

The commander considered the pirates below as well. "I know that. I'm torn."

"What about him?" Tancrede asked, pointing.

Landry looked in the direction indicated. Gaspar clung to the side of Melitta's ship, a sword still on his belt. He was climbing stealthily toward the deck.

Three bows thrummed, almost in unison. Arrows loosed by Godfrey, Gawain, and Tancrede arced into the clear sky and carved downward toward the pirate.

They struck in quick succession. One pierced Gaspar's neck. The other two buried themselves in his back, close to his heart. He fell away from the ship, his body slapping the surface of the water and floating there. Blood stained the sea. He didn't move again.

"That was well done," Tancrede said. "It's a shame the two of you couldn't find his neck as I did, but still, well done."

"As you did?" Gawain rounded on him. "It was my arrow that took him in the neck."

"Actually, I'm reasonably certain it was mine," Godfrey said.

Tancrede shook his head in the manner of a disappointed parent. "You're both wrong. I understand how hard it must be for you. In truth, it wasn't that difficult a shot."

"Landry," Godfrey said. "Would you settle this please? Tell them it was my arrow that killed the man."

Landry raised both hands. "I don't think I want any part of this conversation. All I know is, if I could have drawn a bowstring, I would have taken out his eye."

He regarded the pirates again. Most of those who remained had grabbed hold of scraps of wood from their ship. He didn't believe any of them would drown. As for sharks, especially with Gaspar's blood in the surf... well, if they started for shore now, they might make it there in time.

Kad steered their ship clear of the wreckage and the survivors, angling it toward Melitta's vessel, which had turned again and was easing in their direction. The second pirate ship continued its retreat, showing no inclination to double back and offer aid to the men from Gaspar's vessel.

Landry and the other Templars checked their ship's hull to make certain no pirate was trying to gain access to their deck. Seeing no one, they moved forward to the prow to greet Melitta and the crew of her ship.

In short order, the two ships had lashed themselves together far enough from the ruined ship and its unfortunate crew to know they would not be boarded.

The Templars were welcomed aboard Melitta's vessel. Some of the men they saw there Landry recognized from the crew of Killias's vessel. Others he had never seen before. Melitta herself appeared none the worse for whatever had befallen her since their last encounter.

She asked them how they had escaped Redman and they related their tale, one knight picking up the account where the last left off. When they were done, Godfrey asked for her story.

Melitta lifted a shoulder, her gaze wandering over the open sea. "There is not much to it, really. After Redman killed my father, he took the rest of us as hostages, as he did you. Us he sold to slavers. It seems that by myself I brought him a lot of gold. The man who was captain of this vessel thought to make me a personal prize, and he had me brought to his chamber – to his bed – that first night." She flashed a quick, mischievous smile, her eyes finding Landry. "Your vows of celibacy might not be such a bad idea after all, Templar."

She reached into her bodice, and pulled from between her breasts a small, wickedly sharp blade. She produced a second, similar knife from a hidden sheath at the small of her back.

"The captain didn't survive the night. When I was certain that most of his crew had taken to their pallets, I snuck from his chamber and freed the men who had been part of my father's crew. Together we took the ship. The slavers we didn't kill, we threw overboard. The men they had intended to sell were more than willing to join us as free sailors. We've been searching for Redman and his ships ever since.

"To be honest, I never thought to see any of you alive again, or else we would have been looking for you. My father…" She steadied herself with a breath. "He counted you as allies. I would as well." She smiled again. "If you'll deign to ally yourselves with a pirate, and a woman at that."

"We would be honored," Godfrey said, speaking for all of them.

Melitta's smile faded, leaving her looking grave, and lovely, and very young. "Have you had any word from Simon and Adelina?"

Godfrey shook his head, sympathy in his pale eyes. "We have not. I'm sorry. If it is any consolation to you, I believe them to be safe. I expect they're on their way to Paris, even as we speak."

"That's good," she said. The words seemed to come at some cost. "That's... I'm glad."

Melitta's ship carried food, healing herbs, and clean cloth for bandages. For much of the day, men from her crew tended to the wounds of the Templars, Kad, and his sailors, which were numerous and, in some cases, severe. Landry's injury demanded a good deal of attention. Even after the poultices and bandages had been set in place, the pain in his side deepened.

Every movement hurt; every muscle in his body felt as though it had been abused.

Still, a decent meal of fish stew and well-watered liquor did much to raise his spirits. He slept that night on a comfortable pallet, beneath a blanket that was both whole and free of vermin. After all he had been through, he could ask for little more.

The following morning, Melitta joined the Templars on their ship.

"Where do you intend to go from here?" she asked.

Godfrey didn't bother to consult with the others. "Home," he said. "Paris."

She faced Kad. "And you?"

He shrugged. "I hadn't given the matter much thought. I've been sailing these waters for years. I'm not in any rush to leave. Especially with Redman gone."

Melitta nodded at this, thoughtful. "I would see you to the French coast," she said after a time, turning back to Godfrey and the other Templars. "I believe my father would expect no less of me. After that, I plan to return here, and continue as he would have." She cast another sly look at Kad. "I'll need men to crew my ships. I might even need a captain or two, if you're interested."

"I would answer to you?"

She raised an eyebrow. "Is that a problem?"

"Not necessarily. I've just never taken orders from a woman before."

Melitta nodded, her expression unchanged. "I see. I take it, then, that you've never been wed."

Once their laughter subsided, Kad agreed to her offer. So, too, did Godfrey. The Templars were too few, and too weakened by their captivity, to sail themselves back to France. All of them knew it. Landry welcomed their escort with a profound sense of gratitude; to Melitta, to her crew, to the Lord.

They ate a small breakfast, and passed much of the morning enjoying the sun, the wind, and the mere fact of their freedom. Sea eagles circled above the sea, halfway between the ship and the shoreline. Occasionally they plunged into the water, some emerging with fish clutched in their talons, others laboring into the sky once more, their efforts unrewarded.

Another meal at midday was more than Landry could stomach. It wasn't that he felt ill. But he had gone so long without proper nourishment that his appetite had yet to return. He knew it would, but for now he sipped his watered spirit and contented himself with a small morsel of fruit. He noticed that the other Templars did much the same.

Late in the afternoon, with the sun low in the west, its golden glow gilding the ships and deepening the blue of sea and sky, the Templars gathered near the prow of their ship. All of them bore cuts and bruises. Gawain and Godfrey both walked with pronounced limps. The men who had been subjected to Redman's torture still had not gained full use of both hands. Landry's side ached.

Yet all of them wore smiles. It seemed to Landry that years had been lifted from Godfrey's shoulders. Draper, Nathaniel, and Tancrede laughed at a joke Landry hadn't heard. Even Gawain, usually so somber, appeared at ease.

Their conversation, though, soon shifted to matters of weight.

"I do not know what awaits us in Paris," Godfrey said. "But whatever we find there we will face together, as always."

"We have unfinished business in the Holy Land," Gawain said.

Landry nodded. "Indeed."

Godfrey opened his hands. "That is not for me to say." Gawain started to argue, but the commander continued over him. "If I thought we could recover the Grail, I would turn this ship myself and sail us back to Acre. For all we know, the Grail was destroyed. As for our return to the Holy Land, that is for men far wiser and more influential to decide. We will go back to Paris, and we will do whatever the Master of the Temple asks of us."

DAVID B. COE

"Do you think he'll send us this way again?" Landry asked. "Do you think the Pope intends a new Crusade?"

Godfrey shook his head. "I don't know. Such questions are beyond us. We are Templars. We serve the Temple and the Catholic Church, by the grace of God."

"By the grace of God," the others echoed.

"In the meantime, we will rest, and recover, and regain our strength. Because I promise you, whether in France, or in the Holy Land, or somewhere we can scarcely imagine, we will have need of all our skills before long. Such is the world we live in."

None of them dared argue, hearing the truth in Godfrey's words.

The commander lowered himself to one knee. "Pray with me, brothers."

Landry and the others knelt as well. And as the sun dipped to the horizon, and the sky darkened, they thanked God for their deliverance and asked His protection for whatever awaited them on the morrow.

ACKNOWLEDGMENTS

Deepest thanks to the good people at the Jessie Ball duPont Library of the University of the South, in Sewanee, Tennessee. I'm grateful as well to HISTORY® and A+E Networks® for trusting me with this project and allowing me access to series scripts and all the first season episodes well before they aired.

I'm grateful as ever to my wonderful agent, Lucienne Diver, and to Gary Budden, Miranda Jewess, Laura Price, and all the great people at Titan Books.

Finally, and always, my deepest gratitude is reserved for Nancy, Alex, and Erin. They make everything else possible, and infinitely more fun.

ABOUT THE AUTHOR

David B. Coe is the award-winning author of more than twenty books and as many short stories, spanning historical fiction, epic fantasy, contemporary fantasy, and the occasional media tie-in. His novels have been translated into more than a dozen languages. He has a Master's degree and Ph.D. in U.S. history, and briefly considered a career in academia. He wisely thought better of it. He and his family live in the mountains of Appalachia.

Visit him at http://www.davidbcoe.com.